The Secret Letters

By Taryn Leigh

KINGSLEY
PUBLISHERS

For my beloved family. Shane and Luke, who bring joy into my life, and for Alshandra who's own story inspired this story, and her kindness brought restoration to my own.

Table of Contents

Prologue

She clawed her skin as her nails dug deep, drawing the blood that lay beneath the surface. The pounding of her heart rising within her ears, running at the speed of her racing thoughts.

She peered between the leaves, holding her breath in fear of being heard, hoping, praying he wouldn't find her cowering here in the bushes.

Slowly she moved out from behind the shrubs looking for her father's car. She felt the tattered remains of her dress hook itself onto one of the branches and the cold breeze lick against her bare skin. This was meant to be the happiest night of her life. Her graduation from high school. The start of a new chapter. Yet here she stood, shivering in the cool night air, as the stench of him still clung to her skin.

He had come out of nowhere, it felt. Grabbing her and thrusting her into the toilet, trying to tear her clothes as he assaulted her. She'd known him for the past six years and never had she thought he'd be capable of this. He had always been charismatic, the popular one whom everyone loved, always attentive, fully engaged. She shuddered. If it hadn't been for the stranger who rescued her, she wouldn't have managed to get away.

She squinted, moving back behind the bushes, trying to recall the strangers face. His silhouette seemed vaguely familiar, yet all she could recall was the sound of his fists pounding hard at her tormentor's face, his voice gruff with burning anger, screamed at her to run.

Her sweaty palms tried to smooth the dress her mother had chosen for her. After months of excitement to find the perfect one, they'd settled on a floor length coral satin dress embellished with silver sequins to define her tiny waist.

Her waist. Right now, she detested it. The same waist he ran his filthy paws up and down as she tried to fight him off with all her might. The pounding in her head grew worse, as her fingers wiped away the blood pouring from the cut on the side of her face. He'd seemed determined to ruin her. Determined to defile her. A chill sprinted up the ridges of her spine as it dawned on her what would have become of her had she not been rescued. She had no way of even thanking the person who rescued her now, no way of telling him how she appreciated him saving her life. If only she had seen who he was. She was eternally in his debt.

The bright headlights jarred her thoughts as her father's car pulled up. Breathing deeply, she rose like a phoenix from the ashes, with a determination not to let this consume her.

The flaps of torn satin betrayed her confidence as she ran, barefoot, to her father. His eyes met hers as he flung open the car door and ran towards her, tearing off his jacket to cover her. His strong arms wrapped themselves gently around her as he lifted her and carried her to the car. Tears pricked his eyelids, as the realisation of what had happened dawned on him.

Slowly and gently, as only a father could, he lay her on the backseat of their SUV, kissing her cheeks as tears from his eyes washed over her bloodstained face.

'We will get through this, my baby, if only I was there to protect you.'

'It's okay, Dad, someone did come and help me. I just don't know who he was,' she said, as he tucked his jacket around her. Hope sparked in his eyes that the worst hadn't happened.

Slowly, he got into the driver's seat, and let the car move forwards, to a new future. A future that would forever be tainted.

She lay motionless, *his* final words ringing in her ears,

'This isn't over, this isn't the last you'll see of me!'

Chapter One

'You have got to be kidding me,' Amelia said, giving Rachel a pretentious scowl through slated eyes. 'I thought I was only meeting you for lunch, not the two of them.'

Rachel laughed, knowing all too well Amelia loved Max and Snuggles as much she did. 'What would lunch be without some slobber around your ankles?' Rachel giggled, giving Amelia a kiss on the cheek before giving her two golden cocker spaniels space to go and lick Amelia hello.

'Aargh, you two are lucky you're so cute,' she said rubbing them merrily behind the ears. Max and Snuggles enjoyed the attention before settling in a shaded spot underneath the table.

'So, how's the new office in the looney bin?' Amelia asked, referring to her friend's new post at St Theresa's Psychiatric Hospital in Pretoria East.

'It's going well. The new hospital looks more like a hotel. You should come past and have a look.'

'I think I'll pass thanks. You can send me pics. I still don't understand how you choose to go to a psych ward every day as a job. I prefer clothing.'

Rachel laughed as she signalled for the waitress to place their usual order of peppermint tea and pistachio and chocolate cheesecake. They'd become regulars here at Jane's Tea Garden, a quaint restaurant flanking a massive public park.

The afternoon breeze whispered against their skin, reminding them that Spring had sprung a few weeks earlier. The telling sign of the purple jacaranda trees marked October off on their calendar, as the warm South African sun began to make its way back into their lives, leaving behind the cold winter days.

Jane's Tea Garden had a long entrance path leading up from the park, lined with the infamous Jacaranda trees. Who choreographed their spectacular show each Spring by blossoming their purple flowers in perfect splendour during the eight weeks of October and November. It was said that there were almost seventy thousand jacaranda trees planted in Pretoria, imported from South America. The city became so alive with its purple hue that the locals called it Jacaranda City.

It was their perfect weekly meeting spot, and Rachel had to admit it was the calm she needed from her life as a psychologist. Amelia had never understood how she could choose to listen to people's problems all day, but for Rachel, it was so much more than that. The ability to see someone transform week after week gave her joy.

Amelia would argue that she got the same joy from seeing people wearing the clothes she sold in her boutique, but Rachel knew that the two jobs could never be compared. They had their rewards, each in very different spheres of humanity.

The tea and cake arrived drawing Max and Snuggles's attention, Rachel reached in her bag to give them both some dog treats.

'So, how's Will?' Amelia enquired between sips of tea.

'He seems okay, I guess. We just seem to be missing seeing each other. With me moving offices and him juggling his teaching and music careers, there just aren't enough hours in the day.'

'You both need to figure it out. Life gets busy but you've been dating for what? Ten years now? Either get married or move on.'

Rachel knew Amelia was right. She and Will had been together for eleven years, actually. And with them both a year away from turning thirty, she knew it was about time they tied the knot. Will hadn't yet proposed, and she wondered whether he had the same reservations about marriage as she did. The only problem was, she could never figure out whether her reservations were about marriage or about him.

They'd started dating in university. Although they'd attended the same high school for six years, somehow their paths hadn't crossed. Then, during her first year of university, he'd caught her eye as he sang in one of the student bars. Maybe it was the dark musty club, or maybe his silky voice, she never knew. But that night, she'd stopped in her tracks as his voice floated through the speakers and into her heart.

He told her later that night that he'd been watching her the whole time and was waiting for the moment she'd turn to see him. She found his quirky confidence somewhat charming, and he worked endlessly to make sure she couldn't refuse him when he asked her out on a date.

'So, how's Amelia Designs going?' Rachel asked, in an attempt to change the topic from Will.

'Amazing actually. I've decided to start a range of home décor to add to the clothing collection. For now, mostly throws and blankets made from wool. I've also sourced some wooden tables and décor from a place in the Western Cape.'

'Oh fabulous. So, you're expanding. When do I get to view this new collection? My apartment needs a pick-me-up.'

'I should get some samples in the next week, then you can give me your feedback. I've kept to neutral tones. So, the entire range with the raw wood and wool have a very natural feel. Hopefully, the décor range can bring me some extra money in time for our holiday to Rio de Janeiro next March.'

The thought stirred Rachel's excitement. They'd been saving for this holiday for the past three years. It had taken ages for the four of them to decide on a place to go to.

They came up with a fun way to make a decision. Each couple chose a country and taught the other about that country before they all made the final call.

Rachel and Will chose Spain, while Amelia and Carlos – Amelia's boyfriend of four years – chose Rio. They found different ways to share information about their respective country from dinners in their countries theme, to putting up PowerPoint presentations of which country was the ultimate holiday destination. And in the end, they all agreed that Rio was the destination for the party of a lifetime.

'I can't wait for the holiday. It's all I've been thinking about. We need new clothes for the trip. You need to start thinking *Rio* when you bring in your next collection for the store,' Rachel said.

'Do you even know me? What do you think I've been planning all these months? I've got sexy bikinis coming in floral prints of canary yellow, blue, and green. I even have some mini beach dresses with feathers on the trim inspired by the Rio Carnival. And not to forget a range of dance shoes so we can get our groove on,' Amelia said, jiggling her shoulders from side to side in a mock samba.

Rachel laughed, reminding herself to book those samba lessons for Will and herself. Samba was definitely on the agenda, she just needed to learn how. They were arriving at the end of February just in time for the Rio Carnival and staying for the following two weeks in March. Rachel had to admit that the biggest selling point was the videos of the carnival. The city seemed to come alive like nothing she'd ever seen.

'So, our clothes are sorted. The boys can figure out their own wardrobe,' Rachel said excitedly, wondering what crazy coloured shorts Will would wear. In the Rio heat, she doubted he'd hide his muscular frame behind a T-shirt.

'Carlos has already mapped out a ton of places to visit, so prepare yourself. We need to pack some comfortable shoes for the trip.'

Rachel giggled, imagining the scrapbook Carlos had probably already made filled with Internet clippings of all the places he wanted them to visit. It was good having an organised member in the team.

She was quite chilled in her personal life, willingly going along with the wind. It was in her professional life that she was more structured, but then again, it was needed more there.

Carlos's grandfather was originally from Brazil, before moving to Mozambique and eventually landing in South Africa. Carlos and his family had never gone back there, so Rachel had a sneaky suspicion this was why he wanted to go to Rio so badly.

Rachel looked around at the people chatting and eating, she loved it here, in this quaint tea garden, where they could sit and chat undisturbed, watching the dogs chase after birds, or children creating make-shift fishing rods, trying to catch fish in the river flowing through the park.

Their weekly ritual of meeting had begun five years earlier. Rachel recalled how she'd come to the tea garden after a long stressful day, wanting some solitude. Amelia, who had just moved up to Pretoria from Durban, was sitting alone at a table and decided to ask her if they should sit together instead of alone. It caught Rachel off-guard but thinking back, it was the best decision she'd ever made. They had so much in common. Both growing up with brothers, and having the same love of reading, which is what spurred the friendship on. Soon they began meeting weekly to discuss their latest read, but as time went on, it progressed into deeper conversations about life, and their bond grew.

'Hey, you seem miles away,' Amelia said seeing a weird smile on Rachel's lips.

'Was just thinking of when we first met. I was horrified by your request to sit together, and even more horrified by that crazy elf hat you were wearing,' Rachel said remembering the green, white, and red hat that adorned Amelia's head that day, announcing her arrival with a ringing bell on top.

'Hey, you said you loved my Christmas hat?' Amelia pouted.

'Yes, now perhaps, but then I was horrified! I'd never met someone who wore a crazy Christmas hat throughout the month of December. Who does that?'

'Me,' Amelia said laughing as she realised how odd it might seem to a stranger. She'd always worn different hats to mark down the Christmas calendar. The rule was it needed to have something to do with Christmas. So, over the years she'd sew different things together, from elf to Santa Clause or reindeer inspired hats. The more it felt like

Christmas, the better. 'That's actually where my love for fashion started.'

'Really? You didn't tell me that,' Rachel said, trying to see the link.

'Well, after my parents' divorce I started the tradition. It was practically the only stable thing over Christmas, because my brother and I were shipped from one house to another. So, my hat was the one constant item that stayed with me whether I was in my mother's house one week or my father's house the next. Soon, I started dreaming up different designs and I would make them myself out of anything I could find. An old dress or odd socks. Anything served a purpose.'

'Makes sense now. You should create a collection for the store. No one else really does it. People always have the same boring red and white Santa hat. You, however, have some wacky and unique designs.'

'Good idea. I knew I became friends with you for a reason,' Amelia said winking at Max as if he understood her joke. Max looked up sleepily at her, giving off a whimper, his best attempt to show her some support.

'Hey, don't get my dogs on your side now, their loyalty lies with me.'

Amelia laughed as she reached down and rubbed Max. 'You had to take me with my hats, and I had to take you with your dogs.'

'True story,' Rachel said thinking back to how Amelia hadn't initially been a dog lover, but they'd grown on her the same way her hats had grown on Rachel. 'Where's Snuggles by the way?' Rachel looked around, trying to see her other dog.

'Aargh, you know Snuggles, she isn't loyal. She's probably curled up under someone else's table.'

'Let me go find her,' Rachel said, rising from the table.

Snuggles was a strange dog. Rachel chuckled to herself. When she'd first brought her home, she decided to send her to Doggy Day Care during the day while she was at work. After two weeks there, Snuggles decided she preferred the home of the owner rather than Rachel's and she'd growl when she came to fetch her.

Rachel devised a plan to sort Snuggles out. She went and bought another puppy, Max. Little did she realise that Max was such a soft-hearted little spaniel that instead of lording over Snuggles, he allowed her to bully him. The plan seemed to work as Snuggles tried harder to get Rachel's love and attention, and so the growling at Doggy

Day Care stopped. Her loyalty, however, never improved, and to this day, Snuggles still tries to go wherever she thought the grass was greener.

Rachel meandered through the charming restaurant, looking for where Snuggles might be. She rarely came inside as she and Amelia always opted for an outside table. The restaurant was decorated as if it could have been her mother's home. There were wooden tables with chairs that had tapestry backs. All the displays with the cakes, and scones, and puddings were on mismatched plates and saucers. All in bold geometric patterns mimicking the South African landscape. On the tables were enamel coated mugs, that were being used as pot plants, filled with different varieties of succulent plants. She could see the owner loved the Sempervivum 'Othello' Succulent most, as there seemed to be more of those than any other variety.

The restaurant seemed to follow the Othello theme in plant, as well as hues of deep red, blue, and green. It also seemed to follow the theme in Shakespeare's *Othello*.

All around on cushions or in frames were quotes from the book. Her eye caught one of the quotes engraved onto one of the wooden beams against the back wall *"But I will wear my heart upon my sleeve"* she'd worn her own heart on her sleeve for so many years when she was younger… until that night when she felt her innocence leave.

That night seemed to shadow all her memories of school, it marred them with the desperate determination of one person bent on destroying another. She'd felt it in him that night, his desire to ruin her. She'd spent so many days crying and wondering why he hated her so much. Why had he chosen her? She'd kept her heart closely guarded since then, even from Will. She never knew if anyone would be able to help her let her walls down.

She looked around the restaurant and wondered for the first time why the owner had chosen the *Othello* theme. It seemed like such an odd fit, considering *Othello* was a story of tragedy. Perhaps that was the real reason she came here; she could identify with tragedy.

Finally, after winding through the tables, she spotted Snuggles curled up on one of the couches next to an old man who was lovingly petting her. As Rachel approached, Snuggles made no attempt to move in her direction. *Typical*! Rachel thought, amused.

'Snuggles, it's time to go home,' she said smiling politely at the elderly gentleman.

'Oh, forgive me, my dear, I didn't know she belonged to a fellow customer. I presumed that she belonged to the restaurant.' He smiled gently, his voice husky from years of speech.

'How she'd love such a life,' Rachel replied, seeing the reluctance Snuggles had to move. 'Thanks for showing her some attention. She acts like a love starved puppy, when in fact it's quite the contrary,' Rachel said, feeling the need to explain.

'I didn't mind at all; I rather enjoyed the companionship, I must say. We old folk don't find many people to just sit and pass the time with.' His face smiled, as the creases bunched up into valleys and mountains, showing a landscape of history.

'Well, I walk her and Max every second Saturday at the Irene Market if you'd like to join us?' Rachel asked, realising she'd just asked this old man out on a date, almost.

'I would love that. Meet you at the entrance at nine in the morning?'

'Sounds perfect. Would you like to give me your mobile number?' she asked, grabbing hers out of her jeans pocket.

' I don't have a mobile my dear. The best I can give you is my word that I'll be there. Would that suffice?'

Somehow, the assurance of his word gave her comfort. Very seldom did she come across people these days who made their word their bond.

'Yes, sure. I'll see you on Saturday,' she said, suddenly counting down that it would be five more sleeps to move her from Monday to Saturday. The thought of her date with this gentleman was exciting. She tapped Snuggles lightly on the behind, jarring her to the reality that she had to go home with her.

Amelia had already settled the bill as she found her way back outside to their table. Filling Amelia in on her newfound friend, they made their way through the purple jacaranda pathway to their cars. A new sense of purpose filling Rachel as she prepared for her weekend with… oh no, she didn't even get his name. She made a mental note to make sure to ask him on Saturday. She giggled as she drove home. What had got into her she didn't know, but it made life a little more exciting.

Chapter Two

Rachel wrapped her hands around the honey and nut flavoured cappuccino in the hospital restaurant. Sitting here each morning seemed to have become a ritual in the two weeks since she'd started work here.

Initially, her psychology practice had been in a medical centre in Johannesburg, but when they built St Theresa's hospital she opted to move her practice into the medical suite adjoining the mental healthcare facility as it was closer for her to travel from home.

Gone were the days of old-fashioned psychiatric hospitals where the patients were treated like prisoners rather than patients. Instead. this facility has been designed and decorated to foster a sense of peace and tranquillity to assist patients in their recovery.

The hospital practiced a holistic approach to mental healthcare and had an array of medical professionals on-site for the patients' wellbeing. There are dieticians, physiotherapists, occupational therapists, nurses, psychologists, and psychiatrists. They even had beauticians and hair stylists on call should a patient want to spoil themselves with a treatment.

Despite there being a restaurant in the medical suite, she preferred coming into the hospital for her meals. It was generally empty in the mornings and mid-afternoons as the patients were in their group therapy classes and she grew to enjoy the quiet solitude on her own. Occasionally, Dr Ruari Harris, aka Will's older brother, would also be there, but he never sat with her. He always seemed to opt for the corner table, reading some medical journal or some other medical related book.

Ruari was a psychiatrist, and he was four years older than her. The age gap had seemed like an insane number when they were in high school. He was in grade twelve when she was in grade eight at Woodlands College. But now, as adults, the gap seemed irrelevant. At least it seemed irrelevant with anyone other than Ruari.

Despite her knowing him most of her adult life, due to her dating his younger brother, the chasm between them only seemed to grow like a huge sinkhole.

To date, Rachel couldn't understand what she'd done to deserve Ruari's aloof behaviour, it was as though he detested her from the day they met.

She could still recall their first encounter. She'd known of him in grade eight. He was the head boy of their school, but they'd never interacted. After she'd been dating Will for a while, he took her to meet his parents and left her in the family lounge while he went to let them know she'd arrived. Ruari walked in, shocked to find her there. At first, he seemed kind and gentle, greeting her, and asking her how she was. But the conversation didn't have time to mature, as Will walked in.

When the realisation dawned on Ruari that she was Will's new girlfriend, a darkness descended over his face, and that was the last she saw any sign of humanity in him. From then on, he'd grunt hello and goodbye, and when they bumped into each other on campus, he'd act as if they were strangers. Yet strangely, it always felt as if he was watching her in the shadows somewhere.

She wondered now, briefly, whether her hunch that he was watching, was why he'd started working in the hospital and why he came and sat in the same restaurant as her almost every day. The thought made her skin crawl.

Rachel shuddered and forced her mind to focus on something else. It was no way to think of her future brother-in-law. She checked her phone. No messages. Gauging the time, she made her way back to her office for her next appointment. As she walked, she couldn't help looking back every time she saw a shadow, wondering if it was him lurking in the darkness.

****

Kailee seemed happier than normal, Rachel noted, taking in the speed at which she spoke. She'd been her patient for the past three months and had always come across as a quiet, respectful woman. Her main reason for seeking Rachel's help was work stress. She'd come to her looking for coping mechanisms on how to deal with an ever-growing fear that someone was trying to work her out of her position. Her paranoia was that her corporate company was intentionally trying to sabotage her job and create an environment to force her to leave. Rachel discovered, after some investigation, that it was common practice in big corporates these days, and Kailee's fears might not be unfounded.

Kailee spoke about the last month since their last session. She seemed to have a sudden love for shopping. Rachel scanned her appearance, taking notes as she spoke. Her hair was tied up in a ponytail but was not in its usual neat style. There were pieces of hair straggling her neck like frayed fabric. Her jacket was a bright neon floral pattern, and she wore tights with *Alice in Wonderland* Cheshire Cats on. The only thing that seemed close to her usual self was the black T-shirt she wore beneath the jacket.

Rachel eyed her more closely. Noting her purple nail polish, and the way she continually seemed to ring her hands as if she was extremely restless.

'How have you been sleeping?' she asked, as Kailee was telling her of the new friends she'd made at the office.

'Not much. But it's been awesome. It's spurred on this great business venture I've planned. My best thinking is done at night while I'm wide awake,' Kailee babbled.

'What business venture is this?' Rachel pushed, alarm bells starting to ring.

'I have this amazing idea to start my own cat walking business. I don't know why no one has thought of it before now. It's brilliant. It's an open market. I'll have absolutely no competition. I can do it every day after work, and soon, I can leave that terrible place once and for all.'

Rachel smiled, nodding as she took notes. She could tell that Kailee wasn't in her best frame of mind. She didn't have enough depth of knowledge about cats to trial such an unconventional business idea. If she gave it more thought, she might question the real reason no one had such a business.

'How long have you been feeling like this?' Rachel asked, trying to see how long she'd been in what she now suspected was a hypomanic state.

'About two weeks or so. I really feel great. Things are turning around for me. I actually wasn't going to come for our appointment today, there was no need. I think I can cope on my own now.' Rachel watched as Kailee kept ringing her hands and swinging her feet as she spoke.

She'd always made certain to sit directly opposite her patients with no desk between them. She found it easier to build a rapport with them if there wasn't a huge wooden structure blocking her view. As a psychologist, assessing someone's behaviour was vitally important. It was a telling sign of their state of mind.

Kailee was usually soft spoken. She wore muted coloured matching clothing. Her nails, if painted, were neutral shades of pink or off-white, and she was always impeccably neat, not a strand of hair out of place. She was a thoughtful speaker. Not one to rush and offer information, and most often, she was reserved. Her hands always sat still, clasped on her lap, and only moved to brush off a tear should one form as they chatted. Yet today she was on a high. If Rachel didn't know better, she might think she were on drugs. Her speech was racing, her judgement seemed impaired.

Kailee was definitely not a risk taker, so her desire to start such an uncertain business and leave her job went against her cautious nature. Rachel suspected she might be witnessing a hypomanic episode, and that Kailee could have Bipolar II disorder. She knew that meant referring her to a psychiatrist who would need to confirm the diagnosis and give her medicinal treatment.

It was common for woman to start exhibiting signs of Bipolar in their early twenties, so Kailee fit the profile. She'd also suspected in their previous sessions that Kailee had exhibited signs of depression, but it hadn't seemed to affect her enough for her to suggest medication.

'I would like you to go and see Dr Harris for an assessment. He's a psychiatrist here in the hospital.'

'Why? I feel fabulous,' Kailee said, flinging her hands in the air like peacock feathers to accentuate her point.

'I know, but I would just like him to make sure you're okay.' Rachel knew she was being ambiguous, but she wasn't sure if Kailee was in the right frame of mind to hear she might have Bipolar disorder. She was afraid it might prevent her from making the appointment. 'I trust him, so I know you'll be in good hands.'

I trust him? Did those words just leave my mouth? She pondered on her words as she went to look for his contact details on her laptop. Writing them down, she wrestled with herself about referring her to him.

She had to be honest, when it came to his ability as a psychiatrist, she did trust him. He had an impeccable reputation with his peers, and not only that, the nurses had nothing but praise for him. A measure to successfully determine how good a doctor is, is by listening to the nurses' opinion. They were the ones who spent most of their time with patients on the wards, and they were witness to which doctors seemed to have patients relapse, and which seemed to find the right formula to keep their patients leading normal lives in their own homes.

Kailee would be the first patient she referred to him, however. Normally, she sent her patients to Dr Francis, but he was in Johannesburg at her old practice. It would be a good hour's drive for Kailee, so Ruari was her best option, despite her personal feelings about him.

Rachel handed Kailee a piece of paper with his details on it. 'Please call and make an appointment with his receptionist. If you could get there at their earliest booking, that would be great.'

Kailee eyed the paper before looking up and smiling. 'I will, but like I said, I'm fabulous. I'll go just to put your mind at ease. I guess that means our time's up?' Springing up, and grabbing her handbag, she bounced out the door.

Rachel cringed. TV really had made it seem like mental healthcare professionals were clock watchers. In essence, they were but only because it was a therapeutic tool used to model time management for patients and to encourage consideration for others by arriving on time. It also helped to teach the patient self-worth as time is valuable. TV, however, implied that they clock watched because they were uncaring, and trying to squeeze in as much money in a day as possible, which Rachel knew wasn't true. At least not in her case, or any of her colleagues'. She couldn't imagine anyone choosing this career if they only did it for the money. It would become soul destroying.

She sat down behind her desk. Kailee had left ten minutes before the end of her session. That was enough time for her to send Ruari an email telling him about Kailee and her suspicions regarding the diagnosis. She also gave him a brief history about her, and the changes she'd witnessed.

She looked at the time. Twelve o'clock. She could hear the rumbles of starvation in her tummy. She picked up the phone and asked her office manager, Chloe, to order her some lunch. Opening her drawer, she grabbed a handful of nuts and shoved them in her mouth to try to fill the gap, just as her next patient walked in. Her diary was fully booked until six o'clock that evening. She looked up, smiling as Matthew entered, she ushered him to the chairs.

Rising from her desk her eye caught the pop-up message giving her a sneak peek of an incoming email. She clicked to open it.

Dear Rachel Johnson,

I've told my receptionist to prioritise Kailee's appointment.

I'll make sure to see her at her earliest convenience.

She's in good hands.

Many thanks,

Dr R. Harris

Rachel frowned. *Dear Rachel Johnson*? Did he have to be so formal and use her full name? When she emailed, she'd addressed him as Ruari, and not Dr R. Harris or Ruari Harris. It was common practice to talk to each other on a first name basis in their line of work. What the hell was wrong with his guy? She felt her nails dig into her flesh as she made a fist. Even if she married Will, she would never see Ruari as family if he carried on like this.

She scanned the email again and saw how he'd mentioned *she's in good hands* as if he knew she had her doubts about him. Rachel closed her eyes briefly to shut out her frustration, before standing up to go sit next to Matthew and give him her undivided attention.

Chapter Three

Max and Snuggles' ears perked, watching from their side of the back seat. Their doggie breath making mist marks against the car windows. They knew exactly where they were. This was one of their favourite outings.

She parked the car feeling fortunate to have these two beautiful dogs as her companions. Their golden colour was unique here, as most people seemed to have chocolate brown spaniels. As a result, Max and Snuggles sauntered around the market on their bi-weekly visits like celebrities. Everyone wanted to touch them, and kids wanted to take pics with them. Snuggles loved the attention, of course. She'd perfected the loving puppy-dog look with every admirer, consequently gaining their sympathy and affection.

It was Saturday, and it was nine o'clock. It was time for her date with the elderly gentleman.

Max and Snuggles bounced out of the car, each trying to be the first to touch the dirt.

Making their way through the car park, towards to the entrance, it didn't take Rachel long to spot him. Standing tall with his beige Fedora hat, dressed in a matching suit, wiping his brow with a red tartan handkerchief. What was he thinking dressing so warm on this hot spring day?

'Hi,' Rachel said.

'Hello. I'm glad you didn't stand me up.' He teased, with a twinkle in his aging misty blue eyes.

'Not a chance.' she said.

'Now for some proper introductions, because in my mind, you're Snuggles, after your dog,' he said, reaching down steadily to pat both Max and Snuggles on their heads.

Rachel laughed, not wanting to tell him, she'd been referring to him as *the old man* on her phone calls to Will and Amelia.

'Well, I'm Rachel,' she said extending her hand towards him.

'You can call me Mr Lemon.'

Rachel shook his hand, as Max and Snuggles pulled on their leashes, signalling it was time to start walking.

'So, tell me a little about yourself, Mr Lemon,' Rachel began, eager to find out about her new friend.

'I'm a single, eighty-year-young man. Never married. But I was quiet the Casanova in my day.' He winked mischievously at her. She believed him; he had a way of making you feel instantly connected to him. 'Needless to say, that resulted in me having a son out of wedlock. He lives in Australia now. We've never been close, unfortunately. Life's circumstances were never in our favour.'

Rachel nodded politely. Putting together the unsaid words that perhaps the soured relationship with his son's mother must have influenced that lack of closeness. 'Well, there is still time to change that,' she tried, ever the romantic that all relationships can have a happily ever after.

'I do hope so, my dear.' He paused to look at one of the hand carved wooden frames at the first stall.

'Although it seems highly unlikely. I don't even have his address to write to him, and even if I did, I'm not sure he would want to hear from me. I've been told he's married now with two children, who I've unfortunately never met.'

Rachel frowned. 'Is he not on Facebook?'

'Face what?' he asked, looking at her bewildered, as they moved along to the next stall.

Rachel laughed, realising if Mr Lemon didn't own a mobile, there was no chance he had a laptop, and even less likely he was on Facebook.

'Well, Facebook is a digital platform that allows you to connect with people you know through your computer or smartphone. You can post pictures of yourself and share them with your friends.'

Rachel noted the dazed expression on his face, so she pulled out her phone. Opening the camera, she set it to take a selfie. Standing beside him, she held up her phone, and told him to smile. She laughed as she tapped the side of her phone, making it snap the pic.

'So that type of pic is called a *selfie*,' she said, showing him their smiling picture and then opening the Facebook app to post the pic to Facebook.

Tapping lightly on the screen she demonstrated how to post the picture and tag their location.

Chilling with my new friend Mr Lemon at Irene Market she wrote as the caption to her picture.

Mr Lemon watched intently as she showed him her family on Facebook, their timelines and photo albums.

'See, it's a great way to keep in touch with people,' she said brightly. Leading him to a stack of hay for them to sit for a moment. 'What's your son's name? Perhaps I can look him up?'

'Travis Lemon.' She noted the nerves in his voice.

Slowly she typed in his name in the search bar, realising that this was a big moment for Mr Lemon who had never seen his grandchildren.

His profile wasn't difficult to find as there weren't any other Travis Lemons living in Australia. She looked up at Mr Lemon reassuringly, as she opened up Travis's profile.

There was a head shot of Travis as his profile picture, and a family photo of him, his wife, and their two daughters playing in a field as his cover photo. The picture looked like it was part of a professional photoshoot, so Rachel scrolled down to his albums and opened up that one. Mr Lemon pulled out his handkerchief and wiped the tears from his eyes as he connected for the first time with his family. Rachel didn't speak in fear of ruining his moment.

Sensing his vulnerability, Max and Snuggles lay down and relaxed themselves curled up at his feet.

'They're beautiful,' Mr Lemon whispered between tears. 'From what I know, the older one is Mandy, and the younger is Jessica,'

She sat beside him as he scrolled through the pictures. Slowly. Taking in each shot, as if trying to imagine he were a part of the moment.

'Do you think I could do this FacePhoto thing?'

'Facebook,' Rachel corrected. 'First, you need to get yourself a smartphone. Then I'll create a profile for you.'

'Okay, thanks. I'll try to get a phone during the week. Could you come over and help to set it up for me?'

'Sure. Only problem is how to give you my phone number. You don't have a mobile to save it on and I don't have pen and paper to write it down.'

'Oh, how technology seems to hamper you from the simplest tasks,' he teased, reaching into his jacket pocket and pulling out a Parker pen and leather-bound mini notepad. 'Are you implying my old memory can't remember your phone number?'

'Perhaps when phone numbers were only six digits long, that would have been possible, but now they're ten digits long and your memory is ten decades old,' she teased back writing her number down and giving the notepad and pen back to him.

He placed it neatly back in his pocket and shot her a mock shocked expression. Laughing, they stood up and began walking to the next stall.

Rachel enjoyed his company. There was something calm and serene about him, as if life had weathered down the rough shards that usually poke out from so many people's personalities. He was content just being in her company, and the conversation seemed to flow easily as they walked around aimlessly.

She stopped at one of the artisan soap stalls to buy handmade soap. They stood and listened to the lady explain how she cured the soap for six weeks and makes it with one hundred per cent natural ingredients. Rachel watched Mr Lemon show intense interest in the soap making process and pushed the lady for more information.

It was a stark contrast to most people she knew, who never spent time indulging in a moment.

The soap maker, wrapped up the soaps Rachel picked out as a memento of their first date. She chose a mint and eucalyptus glycerine soap for herself, and for Mr Lemon she bought a kalahari melon and lemongrass soap, despite his insistence to pay for it himself.

They walked from stall to stall and soon Rachel heard the familiar sounds of Will and his band warming up for their live session starting at eleven.

'So, I forgot to mention that my boyfriend Will is in a band called Heartbeat. They perform here every second week. That's one of the reasons I come, to support him.'

'Oh, that's lovely, dear. I presume the sound coming through the speakers is his band setting up?' he asked, pointing his index finger into the air.

'Yes,' Rachel said. 'They're mostly an AfroPop band. If it's okay with you, perhaps we can grab something to eat and make our way to where they're performing and watch?'

'Couldn't think of anything better. Lead the way,' he said, making room for her to start walking in the right direction.

They moved on to the food section of the market. There was an array of food to choose from. Greek dishes, like moussaka or lamb souvlaki. Traditional South African dishes like pap and boerewors or biltong salad, as well as Italian dishes like lasagne or pizza. But in the end, she settled for a biltong quiche with a cappuccino while Mr Lemon ordered a spinach and pomegranate salad with a pressed carrot, ginger and apple juice.

Finding a table under a wild pear tree, (which Mr Lemon informed her was actually called a Dombeya rotundifolia tree), they sat to eat their brunch. Rachel filled one of the market's doggie bowls with water and put it beside Max and Snuggles, giving them both their favourite yogurt covered dog biscuit.

Will winked at her from the stage, as he prepared to start.

'So, I'm guessing that's Will?' Mr Lemon said, seeing the wink.

'Yip, that's him all right.' Rachel giggled, suddenly feeling like a giddied fan getting noticed by the lead singer of a band.

'Well, I hope you've found the one you want to spend your life with, my dear. It's something I longed for, but for some reason the women who were available never felt like Mrs Right, and the one woman who did feel like my soul mate, I let get away.'

Rachel noticed the regret in his eyes. 'Where is she now? Your soul mate, that is?'

'Aah, she lives not too far from me actually,'

'And?'

'She's a widow now. We are close again, but sixty years are between then and now. We can't get sixty years back. Take some advice from me, seize each glorious moment that presents itself. Don't waste time on people who add no value. Make memories that count.'

Rachel pondered his words watching Will. Eleven years they'd spent building their relationship. It seemed they made fewer glorious moments together. What would their lives be like at eighty years old, if they carried on with their busy lives avoiding meaningful time together?

Will began to sing, and Rachel's heart leapt. His voice was raspy with contrasting soft, gentle tones. She watched as it managed to hush the crowd and draw everyone's eyes to only him. His thick, pitch-black hair matched his dark eyes. It was untidy and long, just missing his shoulders where it curled at the ends. When he sang, he seemed more romantic and in tune with her. His eyes were mostly on her, and it felt like her own private concert. Yet in reality, he seemed more self-consumed. It had worked perfectly for her in the beginning, when she was focussed on her studies. She enjoyed having her own identity apart from him.

But sitting here next to Mr Lemon, his presence somehow seemed to capture the perspective of how an all-consuming love seemed more meaningful. The kind of love where you felt as if your partner was the end to your beginning. The type where you were so in tune that as you aged, you wanted nothing more than quiet days with your best and longest friend. How awesome it would be for that friend to be the man you married?

Rachel watched as a little girl holding an opened glass bottle move through the crowd. She looked as if she were trying to catch something as she swung it merrily from side to side in the air. Smiling sweetly, she came past Rachel, reaching to pet Snuggles and Max who were taking their nap at her feet.

'Are you collecting something?' Rachel asked.

'Yes,' the little girl answered. 'My brother is in hospital, and my mother said I can catch the sound of the market in my magical glass jar and take it to him.' Her two ponytails shaking as she spoke.

Her mother, seeing her talking to Rachel, came over and apologised for the interruption sending her on her way back to her father who sat not far off.

'Sorry again,' she said quickly turning to walk away.

'She said her brother was in hospital?' Rachel asked, before she could leave.

'Yes,' she said warily. 'He has a drug addiction. They're really close, and it's affected her not being with him. She doesn't want to go anywhere and have fun without him. So, I made up this story that she can capture all the happy sounds of the market in her magical glass jar and take it to him. It's working, and he goes along, acting like he can hear it when we visit.'

Rachel nodded, seeing the strain on her face as she walked away. A strain she'd seen too often in parents of drug addicts. She watched as the little girl continued to fill her glass jar with all the joy she could muster up for her brother.

Will's band took a break, and they sat waiting for his next set to begin.

'Is he coming to say hi?' Mr Lemon asked, in a sort of fatherly way.

'No, he only says hi after he performs. He doesn't like me to be a distraction,' Rachel knew how stupid it sounded. She still couldn't understand Will's logic. She thought she heard a scoffing sound come from the back of Mr Lemon's throat, but he seemed to recover and smile back at her.

'So, what work do you do?'

'I'm a psychologist.'

'Perfect job for you,' he stated ardently, as if he knew her better than she knew herself.

She laughed at his assurance. 'Thanks. What work did you do?'

'Me? I was a private chef.'

'Wow, really? That's a way more fabulous job than mine.' She could imagine all the creative things he must have made. 'Who did you work for? Someone famous?'

'No, not famous, as in celebrity status. He was a business tycoon. Not much time to cook. He was a health freak. I think the modern term would be to call him a nutritarian. So, I travelled mostly with him. Taking over hotel kitchens in order to feed him the types of meals he needed.'

'What's a nutritarian?' Rachel asked, unfamiliar with the phrase.

'I'll explain when you come over to teach me about FaceCall,' he said, nodding towards the stage as Will came back up to sing.

They sat again in silence, watching as Will and the band performed their second set. The sun intensified as afternoon peaked, and soon they'd to move to a more shaded spot.

It surprised her to see Mr Lemon enjoyed the contemporary style of music, knowing full well this was not what he grew up accustomed to. Her own parents still struggled to come to terms with the generational divide in songs. Their comments always centred around the fact that older music had more meaning. They were potentially correct, as older music seemed to be more descriptive. But modern music seemed more poetic, allowing the listener to be the sole interpreter of what the song meant.

Will's set ended and he bounced off the stage towards her, kissing her hard on the lips.

'Mr Lemon,' he turned, facing him as he extended his hand out. 'I'm glad Rachel finally knows your name. Nice to meet you.'

Mr Lemon shook Will's hand while giving Rachel a confused look. 'I messaged him from my mobile and told him your name,' she explained, in answer to his silent query of how Will suddenly had this info.

'The mobile. I need to get up to date with technology.' He smiled warmly back at Will.

'Did you enjoy the music?'

'Yes, not what I'm used to, but I must say in this setting, it really adds to the atmosphere.'

'Glad to hear it,' Will said, turning to Rachel, 'I must be off. I've got some papers to mark this weekend. Thanks for the support, you're my muse.' He winked kissing her on the cheek.

'Hope to see you again soon,' Mr Lemon said as Will smiled and headed off.

'He's a high school teacher,' Rachel said, explaining his reference to marking papers.

'I see,' Mr Lemon said politely, watching as Will high fived his band members before checking his phone and heading for the market's exit. 'I think I best be off as well. It's been a lovely day, and very kind of you to spend time with an old man like me.'

'The pleasure was all mine,' Rachel said, as she tapped Snuggles and Max lightly on their bottoms to wake them from their slumber. They both grunted at her for the disturbance, but stirred in time to lick Mr Lemon goodbye, as the four of them made their way to the car park.

Rachel beamed on her way home. It had been a lovely afternoon. Mr Lemon brought the same sort of comfort her father always gave her. She had to introduce them when her parents arrived next week on holiday. She could imagine them hitting it off despite her father being fifteen years younger than him. They seemed the same age at heart.

Chapter Four

Rachel curled into a ball as the heavily weighted feather down duvet covered her weary body. For some reason, the day spent with Mr Lemon had exhausted her, and she'd come home and had an early night.

She peered out from the duvet as the Sunday morning sun shone brightly into her room. Covering her head again she closed her eyes, trying to recall if there was anything she needed to get up for. Nothing. She smiled. Wriggling herself deeper under the covers, she prepared to sleep in.

Suddenly she heard what sounded like a glass shattering on the floor downstairs. She threw the duvet off and looked around the room. Snuggles and Max were laying at the foot of her bed, so it definitely wasn't them.

'Oh shit,' she heard someone shout as her feet found the stairs. Her blood running cold as she wondered what she'd do when she reached the bottom of the staircase.

'Who's there?' she screamed, hoping it would scare the intruder off. Silence. At the bottom, her legs give way as she was thrown to the ground.

'Baby, baby, I'm so sorry.' She heard Will's voice speak into her neck. 'Flip!' he said, trying to help her off the floor. 'This was supposed to be a surprise. If only I didn't drop that damn glass which woke you up, then body slammed you into the ground.'

'What the hell are you doing here, Will?' Rachel asked, confused and dazed. So much for her sleep in.

'I'm sorry, I came to surprise you,' he said spinning her around in the direction of the dining room table.

The table was laid with all her favourite breakfast items: croissants, custard Danishes, scones, muffins, and a bouquet of flowers that had obviously come from the petrol station.

'Will, what's all this?' she asked, surprised by the breakfast and flowers.

'I realised how I've missed you and I wanted to do something to show you how I appreciate you,' he said, leading her to sit at the table.

'Orange or strawberry juice?'

'Strawberry thanks.'

Rachel watched as he poured her strawberry juice and put some pastries on a plate. She didn't know what to make of this sudden affection. She couldn't recall another time that Will had ever done something like this for her.

'Good thing I have the spare key, so I could surprise you.'

'More like give me a heart attack.'

She watched him hand her a plate and sit down beside her. He behaved like the guy she'd fallen in love with years before.

'So, what happened to you needing to mark papers?'

'I managed to do it all last night.' He shrugged, stuffing a Danish in his mouth.

Rachel heard Max come down the stairs and make his way to where the food was.

'Hey, buddy,' Will said, as he pat Max on the head.

'Can you believe these dogs of mine? An intruder is in the house and they don't even flinch. Sometimes I wonder why I have them.'

'Since when did I become an intruder?'

'You know what I mean. These dogs haven't seen you in a month, yet they don't even go to investigate the noise downstairs?'

'Hey, they love me, just the way you do,' Will said, stroking the back of Max's neck.

Rachel grinned up at him, although he didn't seem to notice the moment that should have followed his statement. Instead he reached for his phone which was vibrating in his pants pocket. Rachel saw a cloud of anger cover his face, as he clicked to reject the call.

'Who's that?'

'Just someone looking for payment.'

'On a Sunday? Which debtor calls for payment on a Sunday?'

'They know you don't expect it then,' he said, but she had a strange suspicion he wasn't being honest.

'So how about a movie?' he said suddenly jarring from his anger and reaching for his bag. 'I brought our favourite: *Transformers*.'

Rachel winced as he pulled out the box set of DVDs. That wasn't her favourite. It never had been. No matter how many times she tried to tell him that, he just never heard her. Today though, she wouldn't point it out. Today he was trying to reconnect with her, and she'd give it her all. That's what love was about wasn't it? Sacrifice for each other? Putting the other first?

Will grabbed her around the waist and kissed her passionately, forcing her to remember how she hadn't yet brushed her teeth. He didn't notice though. For once he appeared to be present, as if he really wanted to be with her. It was the first time in a long time, so she kissed him back.

Will went to put the DVD in the DVD player. 'An entire day of *Transformers* with my baby. What could be better?'

Smiling, she went to throw a bag of popcorn in the microwave.

'We can't have *Transformers* without popcorn and Coke,' she called, over the buzz of the microwave.

'You know me so well,' he yelled back.

Rachel allowed the popping of the corn to drown out the little voice in her head that wanted to call back and tell him that he definitely didn't know her. Instead she replaced it with the therapeutic pop that came as the corn succumbed to the heat and burst forth in magnificence.

This relationship had been magnificent at one stage, but somehow it seemed to lose its fizzle. She questioned whether it was something she did or whether the sneaky suspicion she had inside, that Will just wasn't so into her anymore, was true. She felt now as if she needed to protect herself in case he broke her heart.

Pulling the popcorn out of the microwave she shook her head. What was she thinking? He was here, wasn't he? He came to surprise her. So clearly, he still loved her. Maybe she was just insecure because they barely spent time together anymore.

Will came up behind her, interrupting her thoughts. 'So how was your date with Mr Lemon yesterday?'

'It was really lovely. I'm going to see him again soon to help him set up his Facebook account. Hopefully, he can find a way to bridge the gap between him and his son.'

'Well, I'm glad you've found yourself a new project,' Will said sarcastically.

'A new project?'

'Well, yes, you know how you love finding people who need you.'

'Will, I wouldn't call helping someone reunite with their son a *project*. Also, Mr Lemon doesn't need me. I'm just being kind to a stranger. Why does that seem so foreign to you?'

'I just don't see the need, that's all. I have my own life to deal with. I don't have time to worry about other people's issues.'

'That's a sad way to live. Imagine if everyone in the world thought like that, then no one would care about anyone else.'

Rachel heard no reply. She knew she'd stepped too far implying he was self-obsessed. She stopped pouring the Coke and swung around to apologise. To her surprise, Will didn't even notice her, instead he was engrossed in a message he was reading on his phone. She watched as his face lit up into a smile, happy with the contents of the message.

'Um, *Rach*, listen, somethings come up. I have to leave. Sorry,' he stuttered, not offering much of an explanation.

'Huh? Was it something I said? Will, I'm sorry, can we just forget what we were talking about and just have a nice day together.'

'Sorry, babe—' he kissed her cheek '—chat later.'

Rachel stood holding the glass of Coke in her hand, confused. Either he was hiding his anger towards her, or there was something else going on that had something to do with the message he received.

Sliding down onto the kitchen floor, she heard the front door slam shut as he left. If it wasn't for the fact that her parents were arriving this week, she'd probably obsess over Will's behaviour. For now, though, she'd just park these feelings away until things made more sense.

Chapter Five

Rachel drove to Irene Dairy Farm, the sun warming the back of her neck as she found herself thinking of Will again for the hundredth time, even though she'd sworn not to.

He'd messaged late last night apologising again for leaving so suddenly, saying there was a problem with one of the band members, and confirming if they were still on for salsa that night. She'd completely forgotten she even booked the classes. He had a funny way of remembering everything she didn't expect him to.

She parked the car in the parking lot at the dairy farm, feeling no urge to move. Sitting back in her seat she watched the cows graze in the field. Something about Will just didn't feel right, and she didn't know how to fix it, or whether she wanted to fix it.

Her relationship with him had almost been a welcomed distraction in university. His adoration of her made her feel pretty again at a time when she'd started hating herself after the assault. He seemed so easy going and chilled that he completely disarmed her enough to date him. He gave her enough space to hide away the pain she felt, but in that she'd never allowed him to fully know her, and now she felt she needed more of him, and he gave the impression of being further away.

Could she really expect more from him now eleven years later, when all along she had walked through life so independently, not needing him emotionally?

Still despite her unanswered questions, she didn't know how to move forward from here. She felt as if she were losing him.

Opening the car door, she checked her watch, it was twelve o'clock on the dot. Time to meet Mr Lemon.

Rachel spotted him seated on the balcony of the restaurant. She loved the dairy farm, but the smell and flies she just couldn't get used to. The restaurant tried to keep them both at bay, but it wasn't always possible, and today seemed to be that day.

'Mr Lemon, good to see you again,' Rachel said, hugging him when he stood up to greet her. He came around and pulled out the chair for her as she sat down.

'Thanks for coming at such short notice, my dear.' He slid a menu in her direction. 'Let's order and then you can get going on showing me how to use this phone. I don't want to take up too much of your time.'

'Lucky for you, my diary was empty this afternoon. I usually meet my friend Amelia on Mondays, but she cancelled, so I'm all yours.'

'Good thing she cancelled then.' He smiled 'Do you know what you want to eat?'

'I think I'll just have the burger and chips,'

'Me too,' he said, signalling to the waitress and giving her their order.

Rachel reached for the phone and began to show him how to use it. She taught him the basics, how to make a call, send a message, and open the Facebook app. After signing him up to Facebook and taking a photo of him to add as his profile pic, she added herself as his very first friend.

'I doubt there are many people I know on this thing,' he mused, as they tried to think of anyone else to add. After managing to find a few of his friends' children, and sending them invites, Rachel typed in Travis's name.

With bated breath she watched as she let Mr Lemon shakily tap the *add friend* button.

'Let's send him a message,' Rachel suggested, 'and when he's online, he can read it.'

Mr Lemon nodded as Rachel opened the Messenger app. She typed as he narrated what he wanted to say.

Dear Travis,

How are you? I hope you're well.

I have a lovely friend helping me to reach out to you. I know I haven't been a good father to you, and I was never good to your mother.

For that I must apologise.

I would love to get to know you, and from there, you can decide if you want to allow me into your life. If you do not wish to see me, I fully understand.

Love, your father

Rachel pressed send and showed Mr Lemon that Travis wasn't online at the moment to see the message.

'Let's hope when he is, he'll reply,' she said patting him reassuringly on the shoulder. 'So, what happened between you and his mother? If you don't mind me asking?'

'I was stupid to be honest. To me she was just a fling at the time, much younger than me too, I was about forty years old and she was only twenty nine, and when she told me she was pregnant I completely denied that the child could be mine. I hurt her terribly, never supported her financially or emotionally, and abandoned them both.'

'Where is she now?'

'She passed away about eleven years ago. I'd tried to reach out to her when Travis was ten, but she wouldn't allow me to see him. I would go and sit outside his school and watch him. He looked just like me, I couldn't deny he was mine any longer. One day, she caught me sitting there watching him on the playground and she slapped me across the face. I, like the fool I was, pushed her to the ground, and she got a restraining order against me.'

Rachel reached out for his hand as the waitress put down their drinks.

'When she died, I tried to reach out to him. I went to the funeral, and tried to tell him how sorry I was, and what a fool I'd been. He was in his late twenties then. I don't think it was the time or place to approach him, to be honest, and he completely ignored me, as if he were looking through glass. After that I never had the courage again to see him. Soon afterwards, he moved to Australia, and it was the end of a chapter, I guess. Until you came along, that is.'

Rachel's heart felt his pain, and also the pain Travis and his mother must have felt, she hoped somehow, they could both find healing and restoration.

'I'm sorry you've been through this,'

'Oh, I'm the one who's sorry. I'm sorry it took me so long to come to my senses. I hurt many people, my dear. I wasn't a good man when I was young, and for that I've paid a high price, but what hurts the most is I dragged other people along into my messed up world, and they've paid a price as well. I know I can't change the past, but I sure hope I can do something good before my time on earth is done.'

'When you know better, you do better,' Rachel said, quoting Maya Angelou.

Mr Lemon nodded tears filling his eyes. 'Yes, if only I'd known better earlier. Don't waste time like I have, my dear, live the best possible life you can live, as soon as you can live it.'

The waitress brought over their food as they sat in comfortable silence eating, each in their own thoughts. Occasionally, Rachel would check his phone hoping Travis would reply to his message while they were still together. She knew it was night time in Australia, but that didn't stop her hoping.

'Remember I told you about *the one that got away*?' Mr Lemon began, winking at Rachel.

'Yes, I remember,'

'Well I asked her to meet us down by the lake,' he said checking his watch. 'She should be there now, if you don't mind us going to see her together? I would love you both to meet.'

'I would love to,' Rachel said, excited to meet the one woman who had captured his heart. 'Why didn't you ask her to join us for lunch?'

'She had some errands to run before she could come through, I told her we'll meet her for dessert. So, let's grab some ice creams from the deli there, and take one down to the lake for her as well.'

Rachel nodded excitedly.

They walked to the lake with two ice cream cups in hand, and a sugar free iced latte for Mr Lemon. Rachel spotted the lady from a mile away. She was exactly as she'd imagined. Her hair white as snow, short, and styled to perfection. Smartly dressed in a gold shirt with khaki pants, sitting on the bench feeding the ducks some breadcrumbs.

'Joanne Crawford, I would like you to meet Rachel,' Mr Lemon said, as they approached the bench.

'Rachel, dear, how lovely to meet you, I must say you have swept him right off his feet,' she said, winking playfully as she gave her a tight hug.

'From what I hear, you're the only one who's ever swept him off his feet,' Rachel replied playfully.

'Oh, Albert, have you been telling people our soppy stories again?'

'Not entirely, but I did tell her you were the one who got away.'

'No fault of mine,' Joanne said.

Rachel handed her an ice cream and they began walking through the farm. She watched as Mr Lemon took a hold of her handbag and carried it for her.

'So, about that soppy story,' Rachel asked eagerly, 'any chance I can hear it?'

'You're hearing too many stories from me today, so perhaps Joanne should tell you this one.'

'Mrs Crawford, I would love to hear your version,' Rachel said.

'Please call me Joanne, dear, I'm not as formal or as old as Albert. Now, where to begin,' she said thoughtfully.

'How about when you first met?' Rachel prodded.

Joanne took a deep breath as she paused and reached out to one of the cows to lick her hand.

'We met in school, way back in what now feels like another lifetime. Albert was a senior, and I was a junior. He was the talk of the school. Every girl wanted to date him, he was popular and handsome, and he knew it too. Very arrogant.'

'She's right, but she knew how to bring me down to earth,' Mr Lemon interjected.

Rachel chuckled watching as he reached out and rubbed her back.

'I was probably the only girl there completely not smitten by him.'

'Really?' Rachel questioned, 'Not even a little?'

'Not even a little. I was too absorbed in my schoolwork. That didn't stop him from trying though. My parents had brought me up to focus on my studies and only start dating after school.'

'So, she gave me the let's be friends speech,' Mr Lemon said, sarcasm dripping from his lips.

'I wanted to see if he'd be willing to be my friend, get to know me first, and wait for me before we started dating.'

'This must sound very old fashioned to you Rachel,' Mr Lemon said, 'because it sounded very old-fashioned even to me at the time.'

Rachel laughed. 'Actually, I think it's the sweetest thing I've ever heard.'

Mr Lemon rolled his eyes playfully as Joanne continued.

'Well he didn't think it was that sweet, because he agreed to it, but still dated other girls.'

'I was young and stupid. Living for the moment, not seeing myself at this old age,' Mr Lemon explained.

'After school though, he still pursued me, and eventually I gave in and dated him, but he never made time for me. It felt like everything else was more important than me, so I told him I needed sometime apart.'

'I was stupid enough to agree to it, not realising that time apart would be a lifetime.'

'Yes, it was in that time apart that I met John, who I eventually married. He was a good solid man; he took care of me. In a way, perhaps I settled for him out of a need to matter to someone, but I have no regrets.'

'I'm the one with regrets. I begged her not to marry him, to marry me instead, but it was too late then. I swore I would never marry after that, I just couldn't deal with the pain and loss I felt of losing the one person I truly loved, but I was too stupid to treasure that love at the time. I put my friends and job and anything else before her. Looking back now, none of those things I thought were so important then matter anymore. What matters is love, and companionship, and even though we have that today, I've missed out on decades of memories that we could have made together.'

Joanne reached for his hand, and they all made their way to the nearest bench. Rachel watched as Mr Lemon helped her to sit, then took their ice cream cups and threw them in the bin. She could feel the love they had for each other, even if it was a love built on heartache and missed opportunities. She didn't want to live with the kind of regrets that they had, she wanted to make the most of her relationship and time on earth, but she still wasn't sure if Will felt the same, and if he truly loved her. One thing she knew is that she didn't want to be sitting here forty years later telling someone the exact same story she'd just been told, but she needed to know how Will really felt about her. If this was just a phase they were going through, she would ride the wave with him, but if it wasn't, and he didn't love her, then she knew she didn't want to waste another moment on someone like him when she could be finding everlasting love with someone else.

'Did you know just how much Mr Lemon loved you when you were dating?'

'Oh, my dear, I never doubted his love for me. When I was with him, I knew beyond a shadow of a doubt that I had his heart. I just didn't want to feel second best to other priorities he had at the time. You know us woman, always looking at the biological clock, and giving into peer pressure to marry. If I'm honest, I chose marriage over true love, and I knew it when I made the choice. I wasn't patient enough to wait for him to figure things out. But as for knowing if I was loved. His love consumed me. It still does because every day even in our separation it just increased.'

Rachel smiled; she wasn't sure if Will loved her that way.

Chapter Six

The robust, rhythmic beat of samba vibrated up the dance floor as Rachel entered the studio, scanning the crowd for Will. The room was dimly lit, and a smoke machine bellowed in the corner. Rachel felt her body respond to the infectious rhythm as she moved to where she spotted him standing, his eyes glued to his phone.

'Hey, Rach,' he said as he kissed her lips, 'thought you were going to stand me up?'

'Sorry I'm late, I took an afternoon nap after my day with Mr Lemon and woke up late,' she said over the sound of the thumping music.

'No worries, seems you weren't the only one late, so you didn't miss anything.'

The instructor called the class to order, and they all found a spot on the dance floor.

'I'm Galvin and today we will learn basic samba figure and the bounce exercise,' he said, as Will squeezed Rachel's hand excitedly.

'First things first, everyone face me. We will start with the bounce exercise. So, bend your knees slightly forward, and then come up and straighten your core. At the same time as you bend your knees, move your pelvis forwards and backwards.'

Rachel and Will giggled along with the rest of the class, as they watched each other move stiffly trying their best to look sexy.

'Keep your stomach in and neutral, and a one and a two and a one and a two,' he said sounding out the beat, 'now face your partner and bounce with each other.'

Will turned to face Rachel, and they tried not to laugh. She knew he might be a great singer, but he definitely had no rhythm.

They spent the next hour trying not to tramp on each other's toes as they eventually found the beat and moved harmoniously. Rachel knew samba wasn't the easiest dance form, but she had no idea how hard or how tiring it was. Her abdominals felt as if she should already have a six pack from all the squeezing.

She was grateful when the class ended, and they headed outside into the cool night air.

'Wanna go grab some coffee?' she asked, hoping they could have some quality time together.

He wrapped his arms around her waist. 'I need to get my beauty sleep, babe, been having a lot of late nights the past few days.'

'Oh?'

'Yeah, you know work and stuff.'

'Well, listen my parents arrive tomorrow, do you want to come with to get them at the airport, or meet us on the weekend?'

'I'm working, so I can't, sorry, babe. And the weekend Ruari and I are going away camping.'

'Oh,' Rachel said, feeling suddenly deflated after the pumped-up salsa class.

'Please tell them I'll make it up to them when I'm back from the camping trip. I promise. It's just that Ruari's going through some stuff, and I didn't want to turn him down you know? He barely asks me for anything.'

Rachel nodded stiffly. She knew she couldn't come between him and his brother no matter what her thoughts of him were.

'So where are you going?'

'Bushwillow Tented Camp,'

'That's not camping.' Rachel laughed, punching him in the arm. 'That's glamping, way too glamorous to be a real camp site. You have hot water, and a kitchen and everything there.' She found it amusing that these men were too scared to rough it out properly.

'You say it's glamorous, but would you go there?'

'No. But I don't do camping, with all the snakes and spiders. No thanks.'

Will laughed. 'Exactly. So, if you won't go there, then it's rough enough to be considered real camping.'

'So, who is going? Those tents sleep about six people, don't they? They're huge.'

'Just the two of us.'

'Are you sure? Is there anything I should be worried about? You guys have never been camping alone before.'

'Geez, Rach, don't give me the Spanish inquisition okay. My brother wants to spend time with me, and I said yes. Why is that suddenly a problem?'

'It's not, I'm sorry. I'm just going to miss you that's all.'

'Well, say that then,' he said, grabbing her and holding her tight. 'I'll miss you too. Absence makes the heart grow fonder, remember?' He bent down and kissed her before walking off to his car.

Rachel watched him leave, wondering when did time apart become a way to make you love someone more.

Chapter Seven

The doors burst forth with swarms of passengers flooding the terminal. The buzzing grew louder as people were united with their loved ones. Elation erupting after the long wait of an eighteen-hour flight finally coming to an end.

Rachel scanned the crowd searching for her parents' familiar faces. She smoothed back the few stray strands of hair that threatened to expose her nerves and excitement. It had been a long time since she'd last seen them. Two years to be exact. Two very long years.

She watched as a diverse range of people entered the terminal. Some businessmen, others holiday makers, all with their own reason for being here. She noticed a young man watching the doors with eager anticipation. Soon his face burst into ripples of joy as an elderly woman walked slowly towards him. He ran to her and picked her frail body up. Rachel overheard her thanking him for bringing her to see him. It was the first time she'd ever flown. She smiled as she imagined the joy her son must feel being able to give his mother such an opportunity.

The people seemed to come in like a flood and trickle off like a stream and still her parents had not appeared. She began to feel the prickle of panic as she checked her phone to see if they'd sent her any messages.

She felt his protective touch on her shoulder and Rachel swung around to see the wrinkles that surrounded her father's striking blue eyes.

'Rachel, sweetheart,' Peter said, engulfing her in his arms. The wisps of his greying facial stubble brushed against her skin as she smelt the familiar scent of Hugo Boss aftershave.

'Daddy!' she exclaimed, allowing his arms to take her back to her place of safety. 'I missed you,' she whispered into his neck feeling her eyes prick with tears. He kissed her cheek and hugged her tighter in response, before moving aside for her mom to see her.

'My baby,' Rachel's mother cried out, kissing her daughter and brushing back the golden-brown threads of hair Rachel had failed to tame earlier. 'You look more beautiful every day,' she stated, scanning her daughter's face as only a mother could.

She observed how Rachel seemed more mature each time she set eyes on her. The childish playfulness in her clear blue eyes had long gone, and her skin was still the same pale biscuit colour, remaining unchanged since birth. Mary noted how she seemed to have lost more weight, making her high cheek bones peak up like mountains on her face, meeting the rise of her dainty nose. Mary sighed happily. Her baby girl was okay. Perhaps a little too thin, her clothes hanging on her frame much too loosely, but that was easily corrected. The main thing was that the peace on her face and the joy in her eyes were there. Her eyes were alive. That's what Mary had been waiting to see again for two years. 'You look as beautiful as ever.' She smiled, tracing her daughters' face, before squeezing in one more hug.

'So are you.' Rachel mused amazed at how her sixty-three-year-old mother still managed to keep a killer figure and look so young without the use of Botox or plastic surgery. She silently thanked God for giving her those good youthful genes because she knew that if her mom looked this good at her age, then she had nothing to fear.

'So how was the flight?' Rachel said, taking the handles of the trolley to push their bags in the direction of her car.

'Not too bad actually,' Mary said, 'We slept for most of it.'

'You mean you slept, and I was your pillow,' Peter teased smiling at his wife of forty years.

'Ignore your father. He was snoring the entire trip, so I don't know how he knew he was my pillow.'

Rachel laughed. This has been her life. Her parent's constant loving banter with each other. If Rachel allowed them, they would go on all day.

'So, what's the plans for today?' Peter asked, eager not to waste any time of their three-week holiday.

'I thought you'd want to rest?' Rachel said watching her dad's eyes light up mischievously.

'Not a chance.'

'Okay, great. I have an idea. How about we make tourists out of you?' She saw the confused expressions on her parents' faces. 'You both come here all the time, but you never visit any typical tourist destinations,' she continued as she met with their perplexed glances. 'Urgh, you know what I mean. Have you ever been on a safari, or to the Mandela house, or the Apartheid Museum?'

'Well no, but we never thought to do any of those things since we lived here before.'

'Exactly. That's exactly why you should. We assume because you lived here there is no need to visit places that people plan holidays around. So today we'll be venturing off to Vilakazi Street for lunch.'

'Sounds perfect,' Mary said, excited to be a tourist in her home country.

Rachel was chuffed that she'd convinced her parents to do something besides the usual shopping malls they loved to visit. They loaded the car with their bags and headed for their destination. They chatted to her about work and Spain and the political affairs in South Africa, before finally falling asleep twenty minutes later.

Rachel enjoyed the comfortable silence and her father's soft snores, as her GPS guided her closer to Vilakazi Street.

This renowned street was in the district of Soweto and was the only place in the world that housed two Nobel

Peace Prize winners, Nelson Mandela and Desmond Tutu, who had at one stage had their permanent residences here.

Rachel loved the vibe she felt as she entered the street and slowed down to look at the vendors selling colourful items for tourists to take home. There were shirts and scarves with Nelson Mandela's smiling face, wire made cars and even wooden carved miniatures of South Africa's big five animals.

'Wakey wakey,' Rachel said, as she parked the car.

'Oh, sorry, darling, we didn't mean to fall asleep,' Mary said drowsily.

'It's okay, I knew you were tired. So, what do you want to do first? A tour of Nelson Mandela's house or lunch?'

'How about the tour? Not too hungry yet,' Peter said dragging himself out of the car.

They made their way along the pulsating crowded street towards what used to be the home of Nelson Mandela and now stood as a museum. They all marvelled at how the house was kept in the same condition it had been since he lived there.

'You feel greatness when you enter,' Peter said as he walked up the red *stoep* and through the front door.

The house was tiny, and they all felt cramped standing inside of it. They tried to imagine Madiba cooking and eating here with his family all those years before. Peter took photos of every nook and cranny as they listened to the tour guide tell them the history of the home. He explained how Nelson Mandela initially lived there with his first wife Evelyn in 1946, and then later brought to this home his second wife, Winnie Madikizela-Mandela. They saw the bullet holes still visible in the walls, as the family's lives were threatened by the Apartheid regime.

Rachel felt her heart swell with pride as she realised the price Nelson Mandela had paid. Being imprisoned for twenty-seven years so that her generation could be free to live where they chose, marry who they wanted, and be free from control. He sacrificed his freedom so that an entire nation could have it for generations to come.

Rachel could hear his rich voice give the infamous speech that he gave at his trial in 1964.

'During my lifetime I've dedicated myself to this struggle of the African people. I've fought against white domination, and I've fought against black domination. I've cherished the ideal of a democratic and free society in which all persons live together in harmony and with equal

opportunities. It's an ideal which I hope to live for and to achieve. But if needs be, it's an ideal for which I am prepared to die.'

Rachel turned around to see the tourists come in with different accents indicating the ends of the earth they'd been drawn from. People from different countries coming together to experience a part of history.

She glanced through the room, appreciating each person who was here because they loved Madiba.

Suddenly she felt it like a bullet piercing her heart. Fear. Shocking and violent wrestling her peace until it overcame her. Her breath caught in the back of her throat as his silhouette came into her view. She tried lifting her hand to grab her father, but the tremor betrayed her, and she dropped her arm in a cold sweat.

She was rooted. In one spot. He was there.

For what felt like an eternity the world stopped. In slow motion his silhouette came into full view as their gaze met. His eyes flashed in waves, first recognition, then lust, torment, and mockery.

She saw the faint curl of his lips as he let her know he saw her. He scanned her up and down to tell her he owned her. She found her voice as her fear turned into anger, then hatred. 'Daddy… it's… it's…' she stuttered. 'It's him!'

Peter's eyes flew to where his daughter's strained expression was affixed. He didn't need her to explain who the stranger was because the haunted look on her face told him all. He lunged forwards with all his might as twelve years of vengeance surged within him for his daughter's pain. Twelve years of him living with the guilt that he wasn't there that night when this monster tried to rape her. Twelve years of feeling hopeless because the police threw out the case due to a lack of evidence.

Jack ran, and Peter chased him. His sixty-five-year-old body no match for this twenty-nine-year-old coward. No matter how hard he tried the gap between them grew larger until finally he'd lost him in the crowd.

Defeated, Peter headed back in search of Rachel. He found her seated in her car, her eyes staring into nothing, Mary sat holding her as tears wet her cheeks.

'Baby girl, you're okay. He can't hurt you ever again. You do know that, right?' Peter said, as Mary moved aside for him to sit with her.

'Did you see the smirk on his face?' Rachel asked her words slow. 'I thought by now he'd be a decent human being, but he seems more twisted than ever.'

'He can't hurt you. Let's go to the police station and get a restraining order against him.'

'On what basis, Dad? The police couldn't help me twelve years ago. How will they help me now? We were in a public space. He didn't even touch me.'

Peter slumped down into the car seat, crushed. She was right. The feeling of guilt flooded him as he realised there was nothing substantial he could do to protect her.

They sat in silence. Mary recalled the years gone by as she'd nursed her teenage daughter back to life. She remembered how a piece of Rachel's innocence had evaporated in that moment and had never returned.

Rachel turned to face her parents. They were her strength. If it hadn't been for them and the person who rescued her, she couldn't have recovered from that night. She opened her car door and shut the memory of Jack out of her mind. She'd done it twelve years before; she could do it again.

She nestled in her father's arms as she recalled her trip to the Mandela Museum and reminded herself that true freedom was the freedom of your mind, not just the freedom of your body. His words comforted her.

'As I walked out the door toward the gate that would lead to my freedom, I knew if I didn't leave my bitterness and hatred behind, I'd still be in prison.'

They made their way through the crowd towards Sakhumzi restaurant. Peter watched as Rachel chatted to her mother, and he feared that her ability to shut this off so quickly would come back to haunt them.

'We're here,' Rachel said as they stood on the sidewalk outside the restaurant. 'This is the home of traditional *Kasi* food, otherwise known as township food for you tourists.' She winked at her parents. 'This is considered the home of authentic home-cooked South African traditional food.'

Mary and Peter exchanged glances, not knowing quite what to expect. They'd heard about this infamous restaurant at the heart of Vilakazi Street, but they were not used to the idea of eating traditional township food.

'We better just go with it, she needs the distraction,' Peter whispered to Mary and squeezed her hand as they walked into the restaurant.

'Hi, my name is Lungi and I will be your waitress today.'

'Hi, Lungi,' they all echoed in unison. Lungi led them to a table outside under the tree just in front of the house.

'Can I give you a few moments to decide what to eat?'

'Thanks, that will be good,' Rachel said, as she opened the menu handed to her.

'I'll be back in a few minutes to take your orders,' Lungi said, as she turned to attend to another customer.

'So, what shall we have?' Peter asked scanning the menu and taking in the traditional items like tripe or steamed chicken with chakalaka and pap.

Deciding to go with what was most familiar he chose grilled lamb chops with rice.

'I think I'm going to have the Soweto steak with mashed potatoes. What you having, Mom? Perhaps some ubuntu ox liver and onions with dumplings,' Rachel said winking at her dad. She knew her mom was out of her comfort zone.

'I think I'll have the Klipspruit hake with chips.'

Peter and Rachel laughed. 'Hey, you two weren't any better. Neither of you chose anything traditional.'

'I know, but it was fun to watch you squirm,' Rachel said.

Lungi came back to take their orders, the sounds of Afro Jazz wafted in the breeze as the band played and Rachel filled her parents in on her move to the new hospital and her time spent with Mr Lemon.

'How's Will and Amelia?' Mary asked, noting how Rachel hadn't once mentioned Will.

'They're fine. Will has been busy with work and the band. Amelia's business is growing from strength to strength, she's really doing well.'

'I thought you'd have brought Will to meet us for lunch today?' Peter asked, concerned at the lack of sparkle in his daughter's eyes as she spoke of Will.

'I asked him, but he has class today and couldn't get time off. He said he'll try to see us next week when he is back from his camping trip with his brother.'

Peter nodded apprehensively. A man who loved a woman would move heaven and earth to be with her. Will's sudden crazy schedule told him a different story.

Chapter Eight

Rachel dipped the silver spoon in and out deliberately. She never usually asked for whipped cream in her coffee, but her mom always used to give her strawberries and cream when she was sick – and today she felt sick. Seeing Jack was a nightmare come true, and she hadn't slept all night as a result. Every feeling that taunted her twelve years before came rushing back like a flood.

She touched her face unconsciously, seeing his eyes on her again made her feel filthy and ugly.

For years after the attack she'd wondered what she'd done to entice him. Wondered if it was how she dressed, or how she looked. She'd grappled with low self-esteem that took years of therapy to undo, and here she sat feeling it all again. She knew better now than to believe the lie that something was wrong with her, or that she'd done something to encourage him, but it didn't stop the thoughts from swirling in her mind like a storm.

'Hi.' She heard somewhere in the far distance. 'Rachel, are you okay?'

She looked up to where the sound came from. His eyes gentle and concerned. She could swear she saw his arm almost twitch in a strained effort not to reach out and tap her from her thoughts.

'Umm, hi, Doctor Harris,' she said, seeing the words cause the wall between them to return. Any concern he might have had seemed to vanish as she spoke in the same formal tone of his email.

He stepped back. Almost pained by her brashness.

'Rachel, do you mind coming to chat in my office?'

'What for?' she asked, annoyed that he felt the need to order her around.

'Kailee,' he said, looking around the hospital restaurant to indicate he couldn't talk here.

She followed his eyes, shocked at how full it suddenly was. She could have sworn she was here just for a moment, and it was empty when she'd arrived. Pulling her wristwatch in view she noticed that her perception of a moment had actually been two hours. Two hours? Had she really been sitting here for two hours playing with the same cup of coffee?

She shook her head to regain her composure and got up to follow Ruari to his office, making sure to keep a few steps behind him. The beat of his shoes as they hit the floor became almost hypnotic. Each step like a drum to the pounding of her heart. She needed to not allow her encounter with Jack to put her in the same state of mind it had done years before. She'd come too far.

Ruari's office was pristine. Strangely enough, she'd imagined him in a more traditionally styled office with a large oversized dark wood table and gaudy gold framed pictures on the wall. However, it was the complete opposite.

To the right was a massive window overlooking the garden area of the hospital. The blinds were drawn to allow full sunlight into the space. Beneath the window were couches in different shades of patterned green fabric, mimicking the garden outside. In the centre of the couches was a stark white shabby chick rug that sat on newly laid light French oak wooden flooring.

His desk sat across from the entrance and stood immaculate in white melamine with rounded ends. Behind his desk was a large grey bookcase that ran from one end of the wall to the other. Books filled the shelves with plants in clear glass jars serving as book ends.

Rachel walked around the room looking with interest at how calming and serene it felt. There were glass and steel side tables next to the couches and large lamps whose stands matched the floor and shades matched the cushions. Her eye caught sight of a canvas on the back wall that had an oil painting of a chameleon transforming into spectacular colours of green, blue and yellow against a stark white backdrop.

'Why the chameleon?' she asked, as she walked towards him.

'It reminds me that people can change, for good or for bad. Also, that no one is truly as they seem at face value.'

She looked at him her eyes meeting his. 'I guess that's good to remember in our line of work.' He nodded as he took a seat behind his desk.

Pulling out a file from the drawer, he motioned for her to take a seat in front of him.

'So, about Kailee…'

'You could have sent me an email,' she said, suddenly remembering whose office she was in.

'Yes,' he said patiently, aware of her apprehension towards him. 'The reason I thought we should discuss the case in person is because I've decided to admit her into the ward.'

'Oh,' Rachel said, feeling suddenly annoyed that he's only telling her this now.

'It just happened,' he said quickly, sensing her anger. 'I just saw her this morning. You were right, she's exhibiting signs of Bipolar disorder. I'll need to start her on medication. However, I prefer to have my patients close to me in the ward. That way I can monitor their reaction to the drugs. I think it's important that you continue your psychotherapy with her while she's admitted, to deal with her anxiety and fears over her job. Would that be okay?'

'Thanks.' She could see Kailee was indeed in good hands.

'I think these issues could go deeper than just her job. I get a feeling she hasn't been forthcoming about her life. So, keep digging a little deeper to get to the root cause.'

Rachel nodded.

'Also, could you perhaps share your notes with me after each session? You will be spending more time with her; I don't want to miss any signs that could help me find the correct drug dosages for her.'

'Yes, of course,' Rachel said feeling suddenly disarmed. This was a side to Ruari she'd never seen before. 'I'll make sure to see her today. I usually have a full session with my patients in the wards in the mornings and a five-minute check in before I leave, just to get a feel for where they're at.'

'Perfect. So, I'll leave the psychotherapy to you, and I'll just stick to drug administration. If anything does come up when I see her that I think will help your therapy, I'll make sure to tell you.'

'Thanks.' Rachel pushed back her chair, sensing that the meeting was now over. 'I guess we'll be in touch.'

'Yeah sure,' he said, putting the file back into his drawer. She noted how he was so opposite to his younger brother. Will was laid back and all over the place, whereas Ruari was so composed and neat.

'Enjoy your weekend away,' she said reaching for the door handle.

'Excuse me?' he looked up surprised.

'Your weekend away,' she echoed, facing him. Seeing his confused look, she added, 'You and Will, on your camping trip this weekend? Will told me you're going away to Bushwillow this weekend?'

'Yes, sorry, I forgot' he answered, but she could see his jaw clench from across the room.

'Sorry for getting personal' she said quickly and exited the room, leaving no chance for him to reply.

Walking back towards her office, she felt annoyed with herself for even thinking for one moment she could relate to him as Will's brother. From his reaction she could tell that he was annoyed that she'd gotten personal when he was being so noticeably professional. Her steps grew more and more rigid with each stride and she started to wonder what she was so infuriated about. Was it the fact that Ruari was so annoyed by her reference to the weekend, or was it that Will thought it was okay to plan a weekend away with his ridiculous brother, when she'd wanted him to spend it with her and her parents?

She reached for her phone in her pocket.

I need to see you. Can you meet me at our spot in an hour?

She waited for a reply noting the online notification on WhatsApp.

Sure. What's up? Amelia replied.

Tell you when I see you, Rachel responded tapping hard on her screen.

She reached her office and grabbed her bag and car keys; she needed her friend's listening ear.

Chapter Nine

The tablet hissed in the glass of water as it bounced up and down before bubbling into effervescence and fizzing away. Rachel straightened her posture as she gulped down the flu effervescent. She felt sick, right now though, she was convincing herself it was a state of body and not a state of mind.

The waiter nodded in her direction to see whether she was ready to order. She scanned her phone again for messages but nothing. Amelia was late, it was already an hour and a half after her message to say they would meet in an hour. She lifted her hand to signal the waiter to come over.

'Can we try something different? What new teas do you have?' she asked, deciding to change it up from their usual peppermint tea.

'How about hibiscus tea?' the waiter offered. 'It's a herbal tea made from the roselle flower, with a tart cranberry-like flavour. We serve it hot or as an iced tea.'

'Okay, can I have it as an iced tea, and my friend will have it hot.'

The waiter nodded as she made notes on her notepad, before turning on her heels to process their order.

'You're late,' Rachel said as she saw Amelia walking towards her.

'Sorry, I had to wrap up a few things before I could leave. What's so urgent?' she asked seeing the empty glass on the table with the residue of the effervescent tablet still in it. 'Are you sick?'

'Feel a little fluey.'

'So, what's up?'

Rachel filled Amelia in on her morning and her frustrations with Will and Ruari. She was tempted to tell her about Jack, but somehow couldn't bring herself to say it. That was something she'd never told anyone, and she feared Amelia might think less of her if she knew.

She could acknowledge it was an important part of her life, and her boyfriend and best friend should at least be the two people in the world who knew, but it was something she'd kept hidden deep within her for so many years. She felt if they knew it would unearth the pain that she'd managed to mask all this time. She also never wanted them to look at her sympathetically like a victim.

'I'm starting to wonder if you really should be with Will. I know I keep harping on about this, but you need to make a decision. Do you think you're going to marry him, or should you just move on? And as for Ruari, who cares about him anyway?'

Rachel sighed as the tea arrived. 'I ordered us something different. Must be my mood.'

'Maybe it's time for change?' Amelia said lifting the lid of the tea pot to smell the tea. Rachel had a sneaky suspicion she wasn't only referring to the tea.

Amelia abruptly closed the lid and looked as if she could throw up. 'Umm, I don't think this is for me,' she said through clenched teeth.

'The hibiscus tea?' Rachel asked, reaching for the pot to smell it herself. 'The aroma is beautiful. I'll drink it,' she said pulling the tea and cup towards herself.

She signalled to the waiter to get the usual peppermint tea for Amelia.

'Sorry, I think I must be coming down with something. Feeling a bit nauseous. So, what are you going to do?'

'About what?' Rachel asked still perplexed by Amelia's reaction to the sweet-smelling tea.

'You and Will?'

'I don't know. I think maybe we're just going through a phase you know? Maybe I just need to give him the space he obviously wants and see where it takes us.'

Amelia nodded slowly as a pot of peppermint tea was lowered down in front of her. 'Well, the choice is yours, friend,' she said, pouring the tea. Rachel watched as she slowly pushed it away from her choosing not to take a sip.

'Maybe you should go see a doctor. How long have you been feeling sick?'

'Just the last two days or so. If I'm not well by tomorrow, I'll go.'

Rachel shot Amelia a sceptical glance.

'I promise okay?' She laughed, knowing Rachel knew full well she hated the doctor.

'So, how is our latest book of the month read? We forgot to chat about it last week.'

'I'm still on chapter three,' Amelia laughed. 'You?'

'I haven't even opened it,' Rachel confessed. 'It's been a crazy month so far. Or maybe it's spring fever,'

Their chatter moved from their latest read, *The Address* by Fiona Davis, to Rachel's plans to take her parents on the Red Bus Tour that coming weekend.

'How's Carlos?'

'We've been fighting a lot lately.'

'Why haven't you mentioned this?' Rachel probed.

'Because it's been over such silly things that it wasn't worth mentioning. We'll be fine though. Maybe we should plan a group date? Just to change things up a bit.'

'Done,' Rachel said. Realising that perhaps Will was also tired of them just hanging out at her place and doing the same thing all the time. Perhaps that's why he appeared to lose interest in her. She also knew she was wrong for never wanting to go to his place, even though he had given her a key. She just enjoyed being in her own space more.

'Any ideas where to go?'

'Perhaps bowling or laser shooting? Something fun that will spur on conversation afterwards,' Amelia suggested.

'Okay, I'll check with Will and see when he's free.' Rachel sighed knowing that in itself was a mission. She couldn't imagine throwing away eleven years so easily, so either she fought for this relationship or walked away. Today she chose to fight.

Chapter Ten

Her palms grew sweaty as she picked up the pale pink eye shadow and applied it stroke by stroke. It had been two years since she'd last seen him, the brother she once adored.

Daniel was three years older than her, they shared an inseparable bond. He was once her hero, the one she looked up to.

Their childhood had been filled with happy memories, they believed they should have been twins. Her favourite memory was of them sneaking into the kitchen at midnight to steal an extra scoop of ice cream when their mother was asleep.

They had an inseparable bond. Until *she* arrived… Claire. They met during his first year at university. Slowly she seemed to wangle her claws into him. Deep enough to take him away from them all.

At first, Rachel noticed the subtle changes. He stayed away at Claire's place on weekends, putting an end to their Friday ritual of sharing their secrets under the stars. He kept making excuses, kept pushing her away.

Their moments together became distant memories. Soon she stopped going to the fridge for one more scoop of ice cream, hope disintegrated that he'd wake up and join her. He was gone. The brother she knew and loved had turned into someone else.

When she was attacked, she never got to tell him, he never returned her calls.

Rachel put down the eye shadow. Her hands trembled with anger. She'd needed him all those years ago. She'd needed to share that secret with him. She'd needed him to make her laugh, to be her strength, but instead he left. His rejection created the biggest scar on her heart, and he didn't care.

If it weren't for her parents, she'd choose never to see him again. To afford him the same courtesy he afforded her: complete coldness. But she knew they loved him regardless. He was their son. So, whenever they visited

South Africa, they were granted the privilege of being invited to meet them one night only for dinner in a restaurant.

Rachel felt it again, the anger, the bitterness, the resentment for this woman who stole her brother. This woman who thought it was okay to break their bond and end her memories. This woman who'd turned them into virtual strangers.

'Ready to go, baby girl?' Peter asked stepping into the room.

'Why do you even bother, Dad?' Rachel felt the tears prickle her eyes.

'One day, when you have children of your own, you'll know what the meaning of unconditional love is.' He reached down and wrapped her in his arms.

Rachel allowed herself to melt in his embrace, finding the strength she needed to face her brother who she bore no connection with any longer other than her DNA.

They arrived at Kream Restaurant early. They knew better than to be late. If they were, Claire would use that as an excuse to cancel the dinner. They gave the hostess their names, and she escorted them to the table Claire had reserved for them. They were already there, seated, in silence.

'Mom, Dad,' Daniel said, standing to hug them. He briefly made eye contact with Rachel before patting her on the back.

Claire remained seated and smiled stiffly, her botoxed face incapable of making any natural human expression.

'How are you doing, son?' Peter asked, making no attempt to look at Claire. He had given up trying to include her in the family when they decided to get married and chose not to invite them.

'Well thanks. We just moved into a new house in Sandton,' Daniel said, trying to make small talk. 'How has your trip been?'

Mary found her voice and proceeded to tell them all about their experience on the Red Bus Tour with Rachel. She rambled on nervously trying to colour in the awkwardness like a painter fills a blank canvas. She described in great length the stops the bus made at Gold Reef City, and the Apartheid Museum. She waffled on about their trip into the city, and their beer tasting at the SA Brewery Company.

'That must have brought back good memories, Dad, of when you worked at the Brewery?'

'Yes, it did.' Peter nodded warmly.

Daniel turned to Rachel, looking at her properly for the first time. 'You've lost a lot of weight, squirt,' he said, calling her by the nickname he'd given her as a child. She squirmed as she remembered them running around in their swimming costumes squirting each other with water pistols, laughing until their tummies hurt. Somehow, he just started calling her squirt from then. This was the first time he'd called her that since he'd left home.

'Yeah,'

'Where's Will? I thought you'd bring him along again?'

Again? He said that as if these meetings were a regular occurrence. She'd only brought Will along the last time because she wanted her brother to finally meet him. But she'd realised her mistake the minute Will sat down and Daniel made no effort to get to know him.

'He had another engagement,' Rachel lied, not wanting to let him know why she hadn't invited him again. Pushing her chair out, she excused herself and headed for the bathroom. Her heart felt as if it were going to explode.

'Rachel, wait.' She felt Daniel's hand on her wrist. They were behind a wall hidden from the view of the table. 'I'm sorry, okay? I know I'm no brother to you anymore, and I don't blame you for hating me. This is my life now. I can't change it. I'm concerned about you. Something's changed since I last saw you. What's wrong?'

'Don't act as if you care now, Daniel. Go back to your wife, your life, where I play no part in it. If something were wrong, you'd be the last person I'd confide in.'

'You're my sister, squirt, no one knows you better than I do. If something's wrong, you need to tell me,' Daniel pleaded.

'You knew me as a child. I'm a stranger to you now. Don't think for one moment that you know me. I'm not the person I was then. You broke the bond we shared. You did that. It was your choice.'

Daniel looked away, defeated. 'I know, and I don't know how to explain it to you. Just know I still love you,' he said, squeezing her arm. 'I have to go back before Claire wonders where I am.'

Rachel burnt with anger. After everything she just told him, he still cared more about what Claire thought.

She went to the bathroom and washed off the make-up she'd applied earlier. A part of her felt sorry for him. He was miserable, she could see it. Even if he thought that what he shared with Claire was love, she knew it wasn't. It was a twisted relationship of control. Over time, Daniel had adopted Claire's way of seeing the world and began accepting her ways as normal. He could easily justify ignoring his family now. She wished they both could realise how much more valuable their lives could be if they allowed people to be a part of it. Surely, they could see that people weren't meant to just live in isolation once they married. If that were true, then what was the point?

Rachel breathed deeply, she felt like the past few weeks had been a lesson on what different types of love looked like, and she knew she never wanted the type of love Daniel had with Claire. She didn't bring out the best in him, instead, she magnified the worst until the best seemed to disappear.

Despite her feelings towards them both, she knew her brother was in there somewhere, he proved that to her now by running after her. So, she decided to take whatever she could get, and enjoy the time she had with him.

She returned to the table as the waitress came to take their orders. Claire ordered for both herself and Daniel. Daniel opened his mouth to protest, but defeated, he looked away. Rachel decided to have the exact same thing Claire ordered for Daniel. He looked up at her, and she allowed her eyes to make the connection with his. For the first time in years she really looked at him and saw just how strained his face looked.

'So, how have you been, Claire?' she said in her sweetest most sisterly voice. She could feel the shocked expressions from her parents as their eyes zoomed in on her.

Claire cleared her throat, not expecting Rachel to speak to her. Why would she, they'd never really spoken.

'Fine thanks, Rachel,' she replied tartly.

'Where is it you're working these days?' Rachel asked, watching Daniel out of her corner of her eye as he shuffled in his seat.

'Oh, I don't work. Daniel brings home enough money for the both of us,' she drawled, her lips moving like a puffer fish.

'Oh, I see. So, what do you do all day?' Rachel asked.

Ignoring Rachel, Claire turned to Daniel. 'I'm going to the ladies,' she said more as an instruction than a statement. On cue, Daniel stood up and pulled the chair out for her.

Rachel turned to him as Claire sauntered away. 'I know we aren't that close anymore, Daniel, but you're right, you're still my brother and I love you too.'

'Thanks, squirt. I know it's hard for you to understand things, but I chose this life and I have to make the most of it. Me not seeing you or talking to you doesn't change the place you have in my heart, okay? I want to be there for you, you don't seem okay?'

Rachel kept quiet and looked out the window. She so wanted to tell him all about Jack, but she knew it would be pointless. He couldn't help her, no one could. He wouldn't be there for her, so what would be the sense in spilling her guts only for him to walk away and see her in two years' time again.

'I'm fine. Promise,' she replied, seeing Claire making her way back.

Rachel did everything she could to make the most of the time she had with her brother. She found ways to include Claire in the conversation and kept things as light as possible for her parent's sake.

The evening seemed to wind down amicably, and by the time they said their goodbyes, Rachel had settled her relationship with her brother in her heart. She would choose to love him, even if it were from a distance.

Chapter Eleven

Rachel poured orange juice for her father who sat playing with the dogs outside on the stoep. She was excited that today they would finally meet Mr Lemon.

'We really need to get you satellite TV,' Peter commented while they waited for Mary to get her handbag. 'You live here alone, and there are only so many DVDs you can hire. This house must be really quiet.'

'It's how I like it, Dad. If I paid for a subscription, it would be a waste of money,' Rachel protested. She'd never found the need to get satellite TV. Whenever she wanted to watch anything, she'd just pop into her local video store and hire a new DVD.

'Well, I'll be the one paying for it. That way, at least I know you can turn on the TV and fill in the silence. Also,

DVDs will soon be a thing of the past. I'm amazed you can still hire them.' Rachel sighed. It was pointless arguing with him. She watched him look up the phone number for the Digital Satellite Television company and called them to organise installation. After giving them his credit card details for a debit order, he ended the call satisfied that his daughter would have TV as her new companion.

'You really shouldn't have,' she said in defeated protest.

'The engineers will be here next Saturday. It's the earliest date they can come.'

'But you're leaving on Friday, so what's the point?'

'It isn't for me,' he chuckled, 'I have my own to enjoy back home. Just say thanks.' He winked, getting up to kiss her on the cheek.

'Thanks,' she mumbled sarcastically rolling her eyes.

Mary came in, bag in hand, ready for them to go and see Mr Lemon. He had invited them over for lunch, a chance to school her on nutritarianism he'd quipped.

Mr Lemon's home was just as Rachel had imagined it. Cluttered. There were recipe books in every corner, pot plants in the hallway, and furniture that probably dated back to the eighteen hundreds. Rachel watched as her mother settled herself into the chair opposite her.

'Could I get you some Rooibos tea, perhaps?' Mr Lemon offered. 'If you take milk, it will have to be soy unfortunately, I don't consume dairy.'

'Milk free Rooibos is fine for us,' Peter and Mary echoed.

Mr Lemon signalled for Rachel to help him in the kitchen.

'Is something the matter, dear?' he questioned Rachel when they were out of ear shot.

'You have good intuition,' she said. She knew that was probably her opportunity to tell him about Jack, but instead she told him all about her brother and his strained relationship with her and their parents. Mr Lemon listened intently while he boiled the kettle for the tea. He pulled out a silver tray and put the pot of tea neatly on top, placing the teacups and saucers adjacent to them, and adding a glass jar filled with honey instead of sugar as a sweetener.

'So, your parents and I have something in common,' he said after Rachel had finished filling him in. 'We both know the pain of an estranged son. Perhaps our meeting now was no mistake after all. Hopefully, soon we'll be able to compare stories of our once lost sons coming back to us.'

Rachel smiled at him fondly. He had a way of finding the good in every situation.

They carried the tea back to the lounge and Mr Lemon ducked out again, returning with some nuts and fruit for them to snack on. 'I guess you can see I'm not a biscuits and tea kind of person.' He laughed, seeing the strange look passing between the room. 'I explained to Rachel previously that I follow a nutritarian way of life.'

'I've heard of that, but I don't fully know what it entails,' Peter said.

'Well, nutritarian is the modern terminology for something I've been practicing for decades. It's basically eating foods high in micro-nutrients and staying away from processed unhealthy foods,' Mr Lemon explained. 'Takeout foods, meat, dairy, and sugars are what I avoid. I look at what has the highest nutritional value, in its most natural form and I eat that.'

'I'm not sure I could do that, my first loves are ice cream and chocolate,' Rachel said, her heart panging at the mention of ice cream.

'You will be amazed when your body is fed the correct nutrients that it needs to function optimally, it will no longer crave junk foods like ice cream. You'll also get sick less, and your body will be a lean, mean, healthy machine.' They all laughed as Mr Lemon fist pumped the air trying to show off his muscular strength.

They settled in and chatted about their sons, and Rachel's heart ached to hear that Travis still hadn't replied to Mr Lemon's message. She checked his Facebook to see that he had indeed read the message, just never replied.

Pulling out her own phone, she found Travis's Facebook profile and looked for where the details of his wife were. She hoped she wasn't anything like Claire as she typed her a message explaining the situation and asking if they could chat.

Soon their tummies were all rumbling, and Mr Lemon went to make them lunch. They had a roasted vegetable salad with salmon. Mr Lemon made sure to include garlic in the meal and lined the plates with uncooked baby spinach leaves, explaining the health benefits of each ingredient. For dessert they had a summer fruit pie, where the crust was made from ground almonds, dates, and coconut instead of ground biscuits or short crust pastry. He filled the crust with a mousse made from soy milk, blended fruit, dates, and mint and topped it off with blueberries, bananas, and strawberries. They were all surprised at how good it tasted.

They chatted and before leaving, Rachel checked Mr Lemon's Facebook account again to see if Travis was online. Still nothing. She checked her own phone and saw his wife had replied to her message.

Hi Rachel,

Thanks for reaching out. I would like to chat to you. Perhaps Skype is a better option? Let me know what time will suit you. Just keep in mind the time difference.

Thanks

Sandy

She made a mental note to reply later, not wanting Mr Lemon to know she'd made contact in case it yielded no fruit.

Rachel hugged her new friend before saying their goodbyes. She hoped the next time they met she would have something good to tell him.

Chapter Twelve

'Hey, Rachel!' Amelia screamed excitedly as they wandered in. 'It's about time.'

'Sorry, I was waiting for Will,' she said as she neared the table they were seated at.

'Hi, Will,' Carlos and Amelia echoed as he pulled out the chair for Rachel to sit. Rachel felt high. Will was unusually affectionate tonight and it was her first time seeing him since their salsa class. She was surprised when he didn't hesitate at the invite for the double date.

The waitress appeared with vodka shooters and set one down in front of each of them. Rachel raised her eyebrow to Amelia. 'Starting already, I see?' She giggled merrily. Amelia winked at the waitress as she handed her a shooter.

'Got to get this party started,' she said as she raised the shot glass.

'Cheers!' they all shouted before they clinked glassed and downed their shooters.

'Another one?' the waitress said, handing them their laser tag vest and gun.

'Perhaps later, I gotta beat the hell out of these three,' Carlos said, replying for them all before standing to put on his vest.

They moved out from the bar into the adjoining laser tag venue. Their waitress opened the door leading into the 'war room'.

It was pitch-black in there, except for some glow in the dark markings on the wall. The TV came alive and a computerised voice began speaking, setting the tone for the battle scene and giving instructions of how laser tag would work. Their guns would fire infrared beams. Their vests were infrared sensitive targets that would sense the beams and make a sound when they were hit. There were zones and targets to hit that would give them additional points as well as allow them to go into stealth mode, so they couldn't be detected or hit.

The buzzer sounded and the door leading into the battlefield was unlocked. They each ran in, trying to find a hiding place, but still be able to prey on their victims.

Will squeezed Rachel's hand as they split and ran in two separate directions. She ran up a ramp through the dark corridors, guided only by the glowing lights giving direction. She could hear Carlo's chubby steps behind her, her heart beat faster as she hid behind a wall and started shooting the moment he came into view.

The thrill took Rachel by surprise as she turned and ran, making sure to shoot at the target in the corner of the room, allowing her to go into stealth mode.

Suddenly she heard a thump and Will screaming for someone to help him. She ran in the direction of his voice. He was crouched over Amelia who laid flat on her back, passed out. The lights all came on. The game organisers must have seen on camera something was wrong.

Rachel bent over and checked her pulse, just as Carlos ran towards them, she was still breathing. Will lifted her in his arms and ran out with her.

'Put her in my car,' Carlos called, but Will just kept running. He threw her in his back seat and Rachel began climbing in with her. 'Let me go please,' Carlos begged.

Rachel moved out and let him in. 'I'll meet you at the hospital,' she said, running towards her car.

Rachel arrived a few minutes behind them and found Carlos and Will in the waiting area.

'How is she?'

'She came around just before we got here,' Carlos whispered. 'I can't imagine anything happening to her.'

Rachel went over and sat with her arm around him. 'She'll be okay, she's strong.' Turning to Will she asked, 'Do you know what happened? You were the first to get to her.'

'No idea.' He shrugged; his face buried in his hands.

Rachel sighed. For now, all they could do was wait.

A few hours later, the doctor came to see them.

'She's okay, it's actually good news,' he said eying their confused expressions. 'She said I should let you know that she's pregnant.'

The shock lingered on for a moment before Rachel broke the silence hugging Carlos, 'You're going to be a daddy,' she beamed. His face was cold as ice.

'How many weeks is she?' he asked, his jaw clenched.

'Around six weeks,' the doctor said, sensing the tension.

Carlos turned and walked away. Rachel moved to go after him, but Will stopped her.

'Let him be,'

Rachel nodded as the doctor told them which room to find her in.

'You go and see her,' Rachel said to Will. 'I'll get flowers and balloons in the gift shop.'

Will nodded as he followed the doctor to the room where Amelia was.

Rachel wondered why Carlos had reacted so strangely. She knew they weren't married, but they were dating long enough for them to seem serious. She wondered if there was something else going on.

Heading back to the room with balloons, flowers, and magazines in hand, she put on her most happy face. They were going to celebrate.

'Hey, mom to be, how you feeling?' she asked, walking into the room. She took one look at Will and Amelia's tear-stained faces and knew he'd told her about

Carlos' reaction. 'Why did you tell her about Carlos?' She grunted at Will. 'She doesn't need that stress now.'

'What was I supposed to do,' he fumbled, 'she asked where he was.'

Amelia closed her eyes and turned her back to them. 'Can I be left alone please? I'll be in here for another few days under observation. Come see me another day. I just want to be alone.'

Will tried to protest, but she just ignored them. Rachel took his hand and led him out the room.

They found Carlos in the parking lot waiting at Will's car for a lift back to the laser tag so he could get his car.

Will walked Rachel to her car as she glared at Carlos. She wanted to ask him about his reaction, but Will kept telling her now wasn't the time, so she decided to wait, but she had a sickening feeling this wasn't over yet.

Chapter Thirteen

Rachel tapped nervously on the desk in her study, listening as the Skype call rang on the other side.

'G'day,' she heard a voice before she saw the face.

'Hi,' Rachel said, smoothing her hair self-consciously.

'Sorry to ask ya to call me in the middle of the night your end, but I can't risk Travis catchin' me talkin' to ya, so I had to do it when he's at the yakka.'

Rachel nodded, taking in Sandy's silky blond hair, thin frame, and thick Australian accent. She felt she needed a separate English dictionary for this call. 'No problem, I fully understand. Have you told him I reached out to you?'

'Not yet. I dunno how to go about it, hey. I thought his oldies were dead. I never knew his dad was still alive until ya sent that message. Imagine my shock.'

'I don't blame him for saying he's dead to be honest from what I've heard.'

'Are ya a member of the family?'

'No, not at all,' Rachel said, feeling relaxed staring into Sandy's green eyes, she seemed so easy going. 'I became friends with Mr Lemon, Travis's dad, and he asked me to help him reach out to Travis on Facebook.'

'Why's it taken him so long?'

'Apparently, he tried before, but he just had no way of going about it. Also, he says he was young and stupid.'

Sandy sighed, covering her face with her hands. 'Yeah, this explains so much about Travis now. He tries so hard to be a good dad to the girls, ya know, but he has this bitterness in him that I could never understand. It creeps up at the strangest of times, especially when my oldies are around. I could never understand it 'til now.'

'It would make anyone bitter, being denied by your father, and watching your mother struggle to bring you up on her own.'

'Yeah, I just wish he'd shared this with me,' Sandy said, running her fingers through her hair. 'So, how'd we fix this, hey? I'm afraid to get involved, what if his father hurts him again?'

'His father's now eighty years old. I think they both need this more than either one realises. Mr Lemon has changed and knows what a terrible man he was. He wants an opportunity to apologise to Travis and to make things right. Yes, he hopes to be a part of your lives, but if Travis won't allow that, he'll accept it. Just give him the chance to explain, you know, to apologise. He's old and I wouldn't want Travis to regret this if anything happens to him.'

Rachel watched as Sandy eyed her… oceans apart. She knew she was asking a lot, but she also saw a desperate wife wanting to help her husband heal from the bitterness he carried inside him.

'I'll have a talk with him,' she said eventually.

'Just give me some time, yeah? I need it to be the right moment, ya know, otherwise he'll just get mad with me.'

'I agree. Keep in touch and let me know how it goes. Let's hope we can both get a happy ending to this.'

'I'll try do a bonzer job of it. I like ya, Rachel, yeah, ya a good person.'

'Thanks Sandy, the feelings mutual.'

'Now, I better get the tucker on the stove, I have a bad habit of yabbering too much,' she said, before saying goodbye and ringing off.

Rachel laughed, Sandy was infectious, and she hoped Mr Lemon would get to know her as his daughter-in-law.

Chapter Fourteen

The water bubbled above the surface, succumbing to the heated pressure beneath it. Rachel stood, robotically, pulling a cup from the drinks trolley in the corner of her office.

She waited. Waited for the temperature of the kettle to settle from its one hundred degrees Celsius. She knew from experience that black tea should be brewed at a maximum of ninety-three degrees.

Reaching for the tea bag, she lowered it into the cup, watching as the tea leaves embraced the hot water and release their potency. She plunged her honey dipper into the liquid gold allowing it to drip steadily into her cup, making circles as it moved down in long spaghetti strands.

It was Monday, and she should have been meeting Amelia for tea, but instead her friend lay in hospital refusing to see her.

Since their botched group date, she'd tried to reach out to her, to comfort her and let her know she was there for her. Amelia never responded. She was tempted to go down to the hospital to see her, but she knew people needed space sometimes to process change.

The ticking of the clock on her wall was her reminder that it was time to see Kailee. It was her last day here in the ward, and Rachel needed to prepare her to face reality after two weeks of being cocooned in safety. Now was her time to emerge stronger than when she arrived. It was time to face the world with all the tools she was equipped with.

She took a sip of her tea before putting it back on the trolley. Sometimes the ritual of making tea was more therapeutic than drinking it. She picked up her notebook and pen and headed to the therapy room inside Ward C where Kailee was.

'Hey,' she heard a familiar voice behind her.

'Hi,' she said, turning to look straight into Ruari's hazel eyes. The image of the honey popped back into her mind, as his eyes appeared to have a golden glow.

'Are you on your way to see Kailee?' he asked, brushing his hand awkwardly through his dark brown hair.

'Yeah,' she answered, tapping her notebook as emphasis.

'I've just come from there. She seems ready to go, excited almost.'

'I think the time here has been good for her.'

'Did you get her to open up more?'

'Yes and no. She talked about some things, but I think she'll learn to trust me more in therapy.'

'Yes, trust is key for any relationship,' he answered, the golden colour in his eyes suddenly clouding over to look like muddy water.

Rachel was tempted to probe, to see if he'd tell her what suddenly crossed his mind, but she knew that would be fruitless. She'd learnt before not to be too personal with him.

They stood in awkward silence before he nodded and walked on. She stared at the back of him as he walked away. He stopped outside the electroconvulsive therapy room as a steward wheeled one of his patients out. He bent down and used the cuff of his shirt to wipe the drool off her face, holding her hand as he spoke to her reassuringly. The patient was still confused after the treatment, but she seemed to relax as he spoke tenderly towards her.

Rachel turned and continued walking towards Kailee, wondering why Ruari appeared to only be so aloof with her. From all she'd witnessed in the hospital, and all that she heard from the nurses, he had a reputation of kindness. Yet never once had she seen that side to him.

She grew angry with him again. In the past eleven years he could have been a mentor and a brother to her, but he chose to be a distant stranger.

Chapter Fifteen

Time was so fleeting. Three weeks had already passed since her parents' arrival, and November was in full swing. Spring was in its final stages of splendour and summer was knocking with all its might.

Rachel wiped the beads of sweat off her forehead as she opened the door to let the satellite TV engineers in. They were here as promised, it was Saturday.

She smiled as she ushered them in, showing them where the TV was. Leaving them to get on with it, she went to pour three glasses of iced tea. One for herself and two for the installers. The air was thick with humidity, and she felt the back of her neck prick in response.

'Something to drink for you both,' she said, laying the glasses down on the coffee table. The cool breeze entering through the open door licked the back of her sweaty neck.

She realised how seldom she left her front door open. Crime was so embedded in her brain that despite living in a secure, eco-estate, she still chose not to leave her door unlocked.

She brushed off the urge to go and close it, knowing full well the cool breeze was a welcome treat for them all.

Picking up the book she was meant to read and discuss with Amelia, she kicked off her shoes and walked barefoot onto her terrace overlooking the nature reserve. She still hadn't heard from her and her heart panged as she tried to focus on the book. Her mobile buzzed in her pocket. She pulled it out and tapped lightly on the screen to see the message in full view.

We need to talk. Can I see you?

It was Carlos.

Sure, we can meet tomorrow at Menlyn Maine Shopping Centre?

Okay, 2pm outside Starbucks.

See you then. Rachel replied, unsure why she agreed to meet with him, perhaps it was because she still had so many unanswered questions about his reaction that night. She wanted so desperately to be there for Amelia, but she still wouldn't return her calls or messages.

Rachel ran her fingers thoughtfully over her phone. Carlos's message made her stomach clench in anxiety. Something gave her the impression of being amiss, and she hoped meeting Carlos would clarify things a little more.

The afternoon wound down as she read the first few chapters, the drilling from the engineers attaching the satellite dish on her roof a welcome distraction from her thoughts. Max and Snuggles were running outside in the garden cornered off from being able to reach them. As lazy and as friendly as they were, she preferred to keep them at bay. Snuggles had a bad habit of lying in wait at people's ankles she didn't like, like a cat about to pounce. She'd nipped at the gardener's calf once, so Rachel knew she had the potential to bite.

She watched Max run around her rose bushes. She checked her watch. On cue, four o'clock. He did this every day at the exact same time. Giggling, she turned to see the installers coming off the roof, they seemed to be rounding up.

Looking back at Max she laughed, she really loved her dogs. People who had never owned a pet couldn't understand how close you could feel to them… like human companionship.

One of the installers tapped lightly on the door signalling they were done. Her tummy growled, reminding her she hadn't eaten since breakfast. Heading inside and closing the sliding door, she made a mental note to bring in Max and Snuggles after his jog.

'So, Ms Johnson, here is your decoder and remote,' he said showing her each device. 'You have one hundred and forty-two channels as well as music channels. You can also connect to WiFi and watch live online streaming.'

'What am I supposed to do with so many channels?' Rachel laughed, thinking of her father.

'Trust me, the more choices you have, the more you actually want.'

Rachel looked at him shaking her head. She couldn't understand why she would ever want more. He chose a channel for her and signalled to his co-worker that it was time to leave. Rachel let them out, locking the door behind them. Moving to the kitchen she made herself a ciabatta sandwich with leftover roast beef, smothered in butter and Dijon mustard, topping it off with some fresh rocket from the garden.

Heading for the couch, she turned up the volume on the TV. The show, *Come Dine With Me,* was a reality show of people having dinner parties in each other's homes for prize money. Her eyes began to doze off, the afternoon sun having acted like a sleeping pill lulling her to sleep.

Her eyes flew wide open in shock as she gasped for air. It was dark, and the flicker of light from the TV brought his features slowly into view as her eyes adjusted. Jack. He was on top of her on the couch stark naked. A look of intent to finish what he'd started years before, rooted firmly in his eyes. She tried to scream and wriggle beneath his weight, he laughed sarcastically.

'No one's here to protect you now, sweetheart,' he growled as he pushed her down deeper into the couch.

Her mind sped at a million miles per second. How had he got in? How did he know where she lived? Where were the security guards at the gate? No one could enter unless she'd announced they would be arriving.

She tried to turn her head as his fist crashed into her face, the echoes of his triumph ringing in her ears.

Everything went dark, it embraced her like a wet blanket, taking the air out of her lungs. The darkness pulled her away from him in deathly defeat.

Somehow, she managed to fight the urging of her own mind to succumb to the darkness, somehow her brain seemed to connect long enough with her body to bring her back to the light. She was dazed, and her vision blurred as the trickle of blood from her nose touched her lips, stirring her senses back to life. The taste of iron in her own blood, forcing her to acknowledge the horror that her nightmares were coming to life.

She could feel his hands around her feet, dragging her limp body through the house.

Rachel kicked, her life depended on it, trying to free her legs from his tight grasp. His rough grip felt like barbed wire against her skin. She knew it was now or never, this would be her only chance to get free. There was no point screaming, her neighbours were too far away to hear anything. The alarm. She remembered the emergency button. The skin on her back tore as he raked her body across the room, aiming for the stairs to take her to her bedroom. She realised he'd cut her top off, probably after he'd punched her in the face. Her mind swam in confusion, how had all this happened so fast? How had this monster found her again? She saw the gleam of the knife in his hand as it caught the moonlight coming in the window. With all the strength she could muster, she flipped her body over, kicking violently until his hands slid off her legs. He laughed, this time a tormenting laugh.

'There is no one to save you now,' he said.

Scrambling frantically, she clawed her way to her feet and ran to the corner of the room where the emergency button was mounted on the wall. He grabbed a hold of her hair, trying to pull her back. She felt her scalp lift fiercely as her head flung back, his knife pressing against her throat.

She pressed into the knife, straining forwards to reach the panic button, feeling the cut it made on her neck. She decided that she'd rather die trying to live than let him have her after all these years.

Her fingers pressed the button just as she felt another blow to her head. The alarm rang loudly signalling to the estate security that she was in trouble. Jack heard the screeching siren and let her go before running for the sliding doors.

Rachel could hear Max and Snuggles barking frantically, stuck behind the fence in the garden. The sirens of the security vehicles grew closer, and Rachel felt herself drift into oblivion. The blood gushing down her neck into a pool at the back of her head.

Chapter Sixteen

The pounding of her head beat like a djembe drum, pulsating through her every cell. Cranking her eyes open she flinched at the harsh hospital lights overhead. Her eyes scanned the room, her heart cried out in fear.

'Hi,' a gruff voice whispered to her right.

Rachel jumped; her peripheral vision skewed by the bandage tightly wrapped around her head.

'You're safe now,' the man said patiently, seeing the fear in her eyes. 'My name is Detective James, and I've been working on your case.'

Rachel tried to speak, but the words got caught in her throat. Detective James lifted her head slightly and brought a glass of water to her lips. He patiently waited as she sucked on the straw.

'Did you catch him?' she croaked eventually, sinking her head back into the pillow.

'Yes.' He nodded. 'We found him hiding in the bushes on the estate.'

'How did he get in?' she asked, beginning to shake at the thought of what had happened, hot tears streaming down her face.

'From the camera footage at the security gate we could see he'd been following you home for a while. Yesterday he used the men coming in to install your satellite TV as a way to gain access.'

'Yesterday?' Rachel questioned confused. 'Is it Sunday already?'

'Yes, you were badly beaten up, so your doctors gave you something to sleep and rest for the last twenty-four hours.'

'I still don't understand how he got into my place. I locked the doors after the engineers left.'

'It seems as if he conned the security to let him into the main access gate, saying he was with them. Then he watched your place and snuck in while you were too busy to notice. He hid in the cupboard in your spare bedroom until they left. Then waited for you to fall asleep before attacking you.'

Rachel looked at him confused, questions running through her head.

'We found his clothes in your cupboard in the spare room. He was still naked when we arrested him.'

Rachel shivered, her heart still racing in fear.

'Is there anyone we can call to come see you while you're in here?'

'My boyfriend Will. His number is on my mobile,' she said, turning her head expecting her mobile to be next to her.

'Your phone will still be in your house, Ms Johnson. The paramedics wouldn't have brought it with.'

Paramedics? Rachel felt overwhelmed. She couldn't remember any paramedics coming to her aid.

'You had a nasty gash on your head, and a cut on your throat. You were unconscious when they arrived.' She could tell he was used to dealing with trauma victims.

'Can you give me Will's full name or phone number, if you can remember it?'

'Will Harris, and his number is …' she trailed off, trying to strain her mind to recall his phone number.

'I'll find him, don't worry. Now get some rest. You will probably be here for a few days. I'll come to ask you more questions when you're a little stronger.' He jotted down Will's name in his notepad. 'Anyone else I can call? Parent perhaps? Close friends?'

Rachel shook her head. If she had the strength, she'd have explained how far away her parents were or how estranged her brother was. She would even have told him how her best friend was in no state of mind herself right now to be visiting her. Instead she just turned away and let the tears fall into her pillow. She was alone. Alone until Will came to see her. For now, that would have to be good enough for now, at least she was safe here.

'When you're discharged, I'll have one of my officers escort you home to give you peace of mind that there is no one in your house, okay?'

'Thanks,' Rachel muttered, fear already snatching her breath away like a vacuum.

Looking at her one last time, Detective James said goodnight, and turned to leave, promising her he would call Will and let him know where she was before the night was over.

Rachel closed her eyes. Everything pained, and Jack's words kept echoing in her head like a movie stuck on repeat. 'There's no one to save you now.'

He was right, this time she was all alone, this time she'd have to fight for survival on her own. She'd survived this attack physically, but now the real fight began. The fight in the battlefield of her mind.

Chapter Seventeen

Will never came. Detective James kept his promise and had a police officer escort her home three days later. When she checked her phone, she saw messages from Carlos asking why she'd stood him up, and she saw messages from Will asking if she were okay. Her sadness grew to anger as she questioned why he'd send her a text message but not shown up at the hospital.

She pushed the thoughts out of her mind and switched her phone off. From now on, she'd do this on her own. She wouldn't beg anyone to be there for her.

She could still feel his hands on her, still smell his breath. Her dried blood cried out from the floor, evidence of the struggle that had taken place. She shivered, wishing Max and Snuggles were there. Detective James had arranged for them to go to a shelter, and he promised to bring them by later. She had a sneaky suspicion it was his way of checking in on her.

He had come to the hospital every day since their first meeting. He found some question or another to ask her. She knew he was just using it as an excuse. She saw the pity in his eyes. She heard the nurses whisper to him outside the door of how she hadn't eaten and that no one came to visit her.

She jumped as she heard a knock on the door.

'Rachel, are you there? I came to see if you're all right?'

Rachel held her breath too scared to move, afraid he'd know she was there.

'Rachel, please, I know you're in there. The security told me you're here.'

Rachel felt her cheeks grow hot with anger. The security had no right to tell anyone she was here. Let alone him.

'How did you get past security?' She answered now, crawling towards the door. 'They aren't supposed to allow anyone in.' She positioned her back to lean against the door. There was a scuffle outside, as if he too sat down and leant against the door.

'Will gave me the access card for the main gate.' Ruari sighed in response.

Rachel let out a sob. Will could give his brother the access card but not drive himself to see her. His rejection hurt her more that the pain of the assault. Was she now so worthless, so defiled, that he couldn't bring himself to even face her? Were all her fears now realised? Is this why she'd never told him about Jack in the first place, because deep inside she knew he would see her this way?

'I have the house key too, but I won't come in unless you open it for me.'

'Go away, Ruari, I don't need you, I don't need anyone!' She spat back in anger.

'Rachel, you can't lock yourself away like this. Let me help you.'

'Help me?' she scoffed. 'You're the last person on this planet I would ask to help me.'

'I know, I deserve that,' he said, his breathing heavy.

They sat there in silence for what felt like hours. 'Did the hospital give you any meds to help you sleep?' he asked, eventually.

'Mmm,' she mumbled.

'Are you taking them?' he asked, his voice laden with concern.

Rachel kept quiet. There was no point lying, she wasn't taking them, and she had no plans to take them. She was too afraid she'd fall so deeply asleep that she wouldn't hear anyone who might come in her home.

'Your office assistant is worried; she's been referring your patients to other psychologists who were available. She didn't know how to get in touch with you.'

Rachel ran her fingers through her bloodstained hair. She still hadn't washed it, after it being bandaged for three days. Her patients. She'd almost forgotten about them. It pained her to think that they were going to be in the care of another therapist, while she herself had to go into therapy. Rachel shivered slightly. She really didn't want to see her therapist. She knew it was compulsory for her to go through a trauma debriefing, and she anticipated that the hospital board supervisor would probably restrict her from handling any trauma related cases for a while going forward. She knew it but she didn't want to accept it. Right now, all she wanted was to wake up from this nightmare with her life back to normal. But one thing it wasn't going to be for some time was normal. She had to make contact with her therapist and schedule an appointment, but she wasn't ready to talk about this just yet.

Sliding her body down to the floor, she curled herself into the foetal position and let her tears run down her cheeks, making pathways on her skin as they left their salty residue behind.

She closed her eyes, aware of Ruari outside. She couldn't understand what he was doing there, why he came. Perhaps Will was worried about her? Perhaps he thought Ruari would be better at helping her? She shook her head violently, banging it against the floor. She didn't need a psychiatrist, and she definitely didn't need Ruari.

'Go away, please,' she pleaded, as loudly as she could muster.

She heard him sigh on the other side.

'Rachel, you can't be alone. Please,' he begged, desperation lining his voice. 'You know how bottling stuff like this only leads to destruction. I don't need to tell you that. You see it in your patients all the time.'

'I'm not a patient,' she spat back, 'and I'm definitely not your patient, if that's what you're getting at.'

'I'm not asking to be your doctor, I'm asking to be your friend, to help you work through this.'

She had a million things to say back to him, a million ways to tell him how she didn't need his friendship. She wanted to scream out that he was a stranger she'd known for eleven years and that there was no going back now. But she felt too weak. Her head began to throb from the stress of trying to target all her anger at him.

'Okay, I'll go,' he conceded, as the silence between them grew.

'I've left something here for you. When you're ready, you can take it.'

She heard him stand and listened as his feet slowly dragged off. She waited until she heard the rumble of his engine start, and his car drive away.

Slowly she stood, the thumping growing louder in her head. Turning the key, she unlocked the door and peered out slowly to see what he'd left.

Bending down she opened the large gift bag and found the box set of all three *Bridget Jones's Diary* movies, a huge, white, fluffy dressing gown, white slippers, a packet of nuts, and a box of chocolates. Rachel lifted the bag and held it in her hands. It was just what she needed.

Slowly, she went back inside, checking three times if the door was locked properly behind her. She couldn't bring herself to watch the movies just yet. She didn't want any noise in the house, just in case she couldn't hear an intruder.

She could feel the paranoia overtaking her mind, bit by bit. She felt it like a cancer eating at her brain. All her training as a psychologist didn't seem to matter now. All the logic, all the knowledge. She lay again on the couch, starring into oblivion, allowing her mind to go blank and block out her thoughts. She was drifting into depression, she knew it, she could even smell it on herself, but she didn't care. It was as if heavy dark clouds had descended and there was no way to remove them.

She closed her eyes, willing the days away, hoping that somehow, she could wake up months from now and this nightmare would all be over. That she'd have her life back, that she could feel joy again.

Chapter Eighteen

Two weeks had gone by and still nothing seemed to change, except for the world around her which she watched daily through the sliding door leading to her terrace. The birds chirped, the butterflies fluttered gently from plant to plant, but she didn't see any of it. She watched without seeing. She existed without living.

Detective James had brought home Max and Snuggles, as promised, and they faithfully sat at her feet night and day.

Rachel sat in the same spot, now wrapped in the gown Ruari had given her. It was the easiest choice to make on what to wear, no thinking required. Right now, she wasn't able to make any decisions. She knew she needed to take her dogs for a walk. She knew she was being unfair to them. But she couldn't bring herself to leave the house. The only time fresh air entered her home was when she allowed them out briefly to use the toilet, then called them back again.

If it hadn't been for the fact that she had no curtains or blinds on her sliding door, she probably would have sat in complete darkness. The light, like every thought, was an overwhelming invasion.

She licked her lips feeling their rough texture beneath her tongue. They were cracked. She'd hardly eaten or drank anything all week. The empty packet of nuts lay on the floor next to the couch, the empty box of chocolate along with it. She'd struggled to eat these past few weeks and had no desire to clean up after herself.

A rapturing knock jarred her from her thoughts. Max and Snuggles jumped and growled towards the door.

'Who is it?' she called fearfully, moving her hand on the couch to feel for the panic button on her keyring.

'It's Ruari, I'm coming in, Rachel,' he said, inserting the key into the keyhole.

The door swung open before she could protest. Max and Snuggles stood barking at him, but neither one closed the gap.

Rachel calmed them down and Ruari came inside, carrying packets of groceries. His eyes clocked the untidy space. There was dog food thrown across the floor, empty glasses, and Rachel's clothes leading in a trail to where he assumed was the bathroom. He noticed the empty look in her eyes.

Ruari locked the door behind him but went and opened the door to the terrace. The dogs immediately ran outside. He turned to see Rachel's pained expression as the breeze pushed its way into her living room, slapping her sunken face.

'I'm going to make us something to eat,' he said heading for the kitchen.

Rachel sat mutely, listening to the cupboards open and shut as Ruari tried to find the pots to cook. She was numb, too numb to even be angry at him for barging into her home and thinking it was okay to take over like this. She was too numb to argue and too numb to even help him find whatever it was he was looking for.

An hour later, he reappeared with two plates filled with chicken noodle stir fry.

'I'm not hungry,' Rachel said as he handed her a plate.

'Eat what you can,' he said, moving to the couch on her left.

They sat in silence, the clinking of their forks the only evidence that any eating was taking place. Rachel was surprised at how hungry she actually was. The food felt like lead in her stomach after days of being mostly empty.

'I'm glad to see you've bathed,' he commented, looking at her still wet hair.

Rachel grunted, it was bad enough having him in her personal space, seeing her looking this way.

'You don't need to do this,' she replied, avoiding his comment, 'I can take care of myself, okay?'

Ruari looked around her living room. 'Judging from the state of things, I don't think you've been taking care of yourself.' His eyes locking with hers.

'Listen, I know you don't like me, so whatever your motive is, just drop it. If Will put you up to this, then go tell him I'm fine.'

Ruari ignored her. Instead he stood and started tidying up the house. He went into every room and opened the windows and curtains to allow more fresh air and light inside. He found a cloth and started wiping her bloodstains off the floor. She still hadn't been able to bring herself to do it after the attack.

Rachel left him to it. She didn't know why. But she had no desire or self-dignity to care. Finally, he came back with two bowls of ice cream.

Rachel took the bowl, tears filling her eyes as she remembered Daniel.

'I didn't know what flavour you like so I kind of did my own thing. If you don't like the added bits on top, just push them aside.' He watched her intently as she stared hard into the bowl.

Rachel moved the spoon around in the ice cream bowl. Inside were three scoops of vanilla ice cream, topped with sugared cinnamon popcorn, pecan nuts, and a squirt of caramel fudge sauce all around the edge of the bowl.

'Thanks,' she muttered, tasting the different flavours as it cooled her throat.

Max came back inside and growled at Ruari.

'You're sitting on his couch,' Rachel said, amused at Max. 'The other belongs to Snuggles, so I suggest you sit on this couch with me if you don't want to be growled at.'

Ruari looked hesitantly at the couch Rachel was sitting on. He was about to take his chances with Max until he started barking.

'Sorry, buddy,' he said quickly, jumping off the couch and moving to where Rachel had suggested. He planted himself as far from her as possible, as if too afraid to be near her.

Rachel looked at him out of the corner of her eye. If anyone should be cowering away, it should have been her. She couldn't understand him. For so many years he'd completely ignored her, yet here he sat, the only person who had bothered to reach out to her, but still he managed to treat her like a plague.

If circumstances were any different, she might have almost found it funny, seeing him pinned so tightly in the corner. It was a small two-seater couch; there really wasn't much further he could run.

Ruari picked up the remote for the TV. 'Do you mind?' he asked, not really waiting for her to answer. He turned the station to a music channel. She'd never even had a chance to try it.

Sounds of Christmas started ringing through the air. No matter how depressed Rachel felt, the sound of Nat

King Cole singing 'Chestnuts Roasting on an Open Fire', just warmed her heart.

'You do know it's only the middle of November, and you're playing Christmas carols?' she said, feeling almost light enough to laugh.

'I believe the only month you don't play Christmas carols is January—' he winked '—that would be overkill.'

Rachel allowed the corners of her mouth to curl slightly into a smile. They sat in silence as the Christmas carols played. She eventually found herself relax and her eyelids became like led, beckoning her to sleep. She couldn't fight it any longer, and she leaned her head against the backrest, aware of Ruari inches from her. Her full stomach weighed in on her and sleep overcame her.

It was the first time she'd slept so soundly in weeks. When she woke, she could hear Max having his afternoon jog around the bushes, and she felt her cheek pain from being plunged into Ruari's shoulder bone. Quickly she moved, seeing how stiff he sat, with both hands clasped in his lap too afraid to touch her.

'Umm, sorry. I fell asleep. I didn't mean to move onto you,' she said awkwardly.

'It's okay,' he mumbled, uncomfortable with her entering his personal space. 'I didn't want to wake you. I need to leave, I wanted to wait for you to wake up before I left. Glad you got some rest.' Ruari stood and turned to go. He then doubled back and inserted the first of the *Bridget Jones* movies into the DVD player, noticing they'd gone untouched.

'How about you watch this?' he said, handing her the remote. Rachel nodded, not knowing whether to thank him or not. She still was unsure of his motives.

He reached into his pocket and laid the set of keys he had to her place on the coffee table. 'Next time I come, I want you to let me in. Okay?'

She nodded, but she knew that would never happen. She was relieved as she watched him walk out the door. He was gone. Gone like everyone else.

Chapter Nineteen

She moved with a steady stride, putting one foot in front of the other. Her ponytail swishing behind her as she jogged. The air was thick and heavy, summer was here, but she kept moving despite the humidity threatening to clog her nostrils.

Her breathing grew more desperate as she climbed up the hill, her mind swirling slower than it had the previous few weeks. Max and Snuggles panted beside her, keeping up with her rhythmic movements.

Rachel stopped at the top of the hill, gasping for breath. It was her third day jogging, her third day out of the house. After Ruari's visit she'd closed herself in again, unable to shake off the darkness. But then it came. The letter.

At first it bore no resemblance to the ones she'd received years before. In the past, the envelope had been red, always red. This time it was white, but the handwriting was unmistakably the same.

Rachel took in another breath, giving a smile to Max and Snuggles as she pushed forward with the final hurdle of her jog. She'd found this daily five kilometre run just what she needed to clear her mind.

Turning the corner, her house came into full view, and she relished the sight of it. A zebra stood grazing in the field adjacent to her home, he looked up lazily as she approached.

She unlocked the door and let Max and Snuggles run past to their water bowls. She grabbed her water bottle from the counter, then sat and stared at the letter on the coffee table.

She opened it again, probably for the hundredth time. The white flap creased from her endless use.

Pulling out the pages, she sat back and began to read its words again.

Dear Rachel,

I know it's been a while since I last wrote. I'd stopped writing because I felt you no longer needed me. I'm writing again because I think, perhaps, you might need a reminder of who you are.

You fought a fight years ago and overcame the torment you faced. You won over fear, you won over low self-esteem, you fought, and you won.

Now, you're in the same fight again. But remember it's a fight you've already conquered, it's a fight you already know the formula to overcome. The only thing you're fighting now, Rachel, is your own mind.

This same mind has grown since then, your mind has helped countless others like you to overcome. Your mind, Rachel, is your battlefield. Do you remember I told you this?

If you give into these fears, Jack wins. He wins. Do you hear me?

The only power he has over you now is the fear he's instilled in your mind. That fear cannot hold you captive. That fear cannot stop you from living. Don't give into it. Keep pushing forward, show him that he has no power over you.

Even if Jack sits in a prison cell for the rest of his life, what good would it be to you, if your mind is locked in that same cell, held captive there with him?

Live your life, Rachel. Live it like you did before and go out there and turn this pain into a way to help others.

Love x

Rachel rose with new determination. Each time she read the letter she felt stronger, more able to conquer her fears. She went to the laundry room and fetched the step ladder she stored there. She felt nervous, she hadn't looked at these letters in years.

Reaching to the top corner of her cupboard, she took down the letters she'd received twelve years before. All thirty-six of them.

She carried the box to her bed and sat down taking each letter out one by one.

The letters had started coming a week after she was attacked in grade twelve. The first month she received one every week, each letter gave her strength to move forward. Soon they started arriving with larger time gaps between them until finally they stopped all together.

She opened the last letter she'd received from him, years earlier.

Dear Rachel,

I hope you're keeping well.

I'm writing today to let you know that this will be my last letter. You seem to be able to live a life without me now. I want you to know that I could never forget you, and there is a place in my heart that beats only for you.

I hope in some way these letters have helped you to find the strength you needed. I wish I had the courage to tell you who I am, but today I realised that could never be, and possibly was never meant to be.

You will forever be in my thoughts.

'Good night, good night. Parting is such sweet sorrow, that I shall say good night til it be morrow…'

Love x

Rachel looked at the quote from William Shakespeare he'd added in there, thinking how apt it was 'good night til it be morrow', it felt like morrow now, because he'd come back to her.

For years after the letters stopped, she'd try to figure out who he might be. She started feeling like everyone she saw was possibly him. Eventually she gave up because if he really wanted her to know who he was, he'd have revealed himself. But now he'd found her once again. Rachel wondered how he knew that Jack had attacked her, or how he knew where to find her?

As grateful as she was for his letter and the strength it gave her to push beyond her fears, she wished he'd just show himself to her.

Rachel wondered if her mystery letter writer was the reason she was never sure about committing to Will 'til death do them part.

Chapter Twenty

The sun streamed in, its rays warm and soft on her skin. The wind danced between the leaves, making melodies as the birds harmonised their tune. Rachel eyed herself in the mirror, one more time, touching the scar on her neck, which was a reminder of that awful night. She reached for the comb and pulled it through her hair, taking in the morning air.

Today was the day she'd chosen to start her therapy. She'd emailed her therapist to schedule an appointment for this morning.

Rachel had last been in therapy while she was studying, and a few years after that, when it was mandatory to see a therapist. Most people didn't know, but psychologists, and psychiatrists were required to go into therapy by law. Since then she was in no need of therapy. She met with the hospital board supervisor weekly to go through her cases, and she would evaluate whether there was any counter transference. To date, she'd been fine. But because of the attack, she wouldn't be allowed to practice until she underwent therapy again.

Last night she'd turned her phone on after three weeks of having it switched off. There were messages from Will asking her if she was okay. Mr Lemon had tried to call her several times, each time leaving a voicemail asking where she was. He seemed more concerned with each call. She knew she needed to call him back, but she'd do that later. It was hard to believe it was the beginning of December and she'd barely noticed the time slip by.

Her assistant, Chloe, had left messages daily, updating her on the patients who had to be handed over to other psychologists. It seemed that Ruari had given her an update on all the details of what had happened, as she spoke with the sickening sound of sympathy in her voice. She said her parents had sent numerous emails, and she'd replied saying she'd pass on the emails to Rachel but hadn't told them where she was.

After listening to Chloe's messages, she returned her call and told her she'd stop by the office today.

Snuggles nuzzled her feet as she set down the comb. Her dogs had been her only companions these past few weeks, but now she had to face the world.

Grabbing the latest letter, she put it in her handbag. She'd take it with her as her source of strength. She'd read it so many times she could recite it word for word.

Dear Rachel,

I hope my letters are reaching you.

For now, since I do not know, I write these in hope that they are, and that you draw strength from them.

I want you to start each day with a joyful heart. Appreciate the small things. For now, focus on the sunshine, the smell of the flowers, the birds chirping in the trees. Find joy in these things. Do not allow your troubled thoughts to rob you of your strength. When your mind goes into the shadows, bring it back to the light. When the clouds descend, force yourself to find something beautiful and think of that thing.

What is ahead of you is far greater than anything that has happened to you.

Rachel smiled. She wished there was a way to reply to his letters, but there was never a return address on them. His letters always seemed so selfless because he asked for nothing in return for them.

Grabbing her car keys, she patted Max and Snuggles and set off to the hospital. It was a new day. She was starting her day off with a joyful heart, just as the letter had asked her to.

The drive to the hospital seemed longer than usual. She had to stop herself from feeling paranoid that someone was following her. It seemed harder than she thought, because she'd look at each car behind her a hundred times if it stayed following her for too long. Her skin crawled with the urge to remind her of her fears, to remind her of Jack's touch. Each time she had to determine to shake it off and focus her thoughts elsewhere. She knew it would get easier with each day, but right now the time seemed to tick by so slowly, as she fought her own mind, her own thoughts.

Trauma was such a defiling thing, because even after the incident it lingered on you like a strong stench. It beckoned your mind to lock itself in the traumatic episode, long after it had happened. It was so easy to get locked in that castle of trauma. Every cell in your body seemed infected with its virus. Every cell seemed to move and shake to its beat. But she knew that she had to move out of that day. Her mind had to break free from its hold. She had to make sure that one moment in one day, didn't poison every moment of every day. She was the only one who could rid her body of the poison. She was the only one who could make new memories and new moments. It was her choice, whether her future would bare the stench of her past or be free from it.

Chloe came running out to greet her as soon as she parked her car. She'd been watching the parking lot from the office window.

'How you feeling?' she asked, touching Rachel sympathetically.

'Okay,' Rachel said, not wanting to go into detail. Chloe sensed her guardedness and chose to talk work instead.

'All your patients have been reassigned to new therapists. Since we aren't sure for how long, I thought it best to find a locum for the practice. We can discuss that after you see Diana,' Chloe said, running alongside Rachel, as she strode into the hospital and stopped at the lift door. Chloe hadn't realised how long Rachel's legs actually were until now. Hers felt like tree stumps in comparison trotting after her in haste.

Rachel nodded mutely, walking into the lift as the doors opened. Diana was her therapist, and her heart thumped at the mention of her name. She wasn't sure she was ready for this. She felt safer in the lift, just her and Chloe, but her heart beat wildly again as she neared Diana's office floor. What if he was there? What if he was waiting for her? Detective James said he'd been released on bail. She'd refused to go to the hearing, sending her lawyer instead. She didn't think she could face that monster. Not yet anyway. The lift jolted as it stopped on the third floor. Chloe instinctively stepped in front of her sensing her fear.

'Come on,' she said cheerfully, grabbing Rachel's hand.

'Hey, you don't have to walk me to her rooms. I know the way.'

'I know,' Chloe said brightly, still not letting go of her hand. Rachel felt the ends of her lips curl into a slight smile. Chloe was sweet, and very motherly, and right now she could do with her cheery face.

They walked in silence down the hall towards Diana's rooms. Rachel resisted the urge to turn her head every time she heard someone approaching. Instead, she'd squeeze Chloe's hand in anticipation of what might be lurking in the shadows. Her heart pounded, her breathing shallow with every step. She knew she needed to breathe normally to prevent a panic attack. She was waging war on her mind and the anxiety was trying to overtake her.

Chloe opened the door to the waiting area in Diana's office.

'I'll stay until Diana is ready to see you,' she said to Rachel, before nodding at Diana's office assistant in recognition.

'No need, I'll be fine,'

Chloe ignored her, taking the seat beside her. The room was silent except for the annoying ticking of the clock mounted on the wall. Rachel hated waiting; she didn't know how her patients waited for her. Right now, every second felt like years as she fought the fears inside of her. Tick tock, tick tock. The rhythm of the clock tried to match the rhythm of her heart, but her heart was running a hundred metre sprint and the clock was stuck in a marathon. She was tempted to scream, to run out of here, and go back to locking herself inside her house. She couldn't handle the sound of her own heart booming in her chest, each beat like roaring thunder. The clock ticked and the minutes passed until eventually the patient in with Diana came out and Diana appeared.

'Rachel, come in,' she said kindly, nodding to Chloe that she'll take it from here.

'Thanks,' Rachel said, grabbing her bag tightly, smiling faintly at Chloe before going into her office.

Chapter Twenty-One

Rachel walked slowly back to her office. The session with Diana had been hard, it was her first time saying it all out aloud. Diana recommended that she come to see her weekly, and that they re-evaluate her going back to work in about three months' time. Right now, she didn't know what to do with all her time. Her phone buzzed in her bag. Getting into the lift she made sure the doors were shut and she was alone before reaching for her phone to check her message.

I'm sorry for being so distant. Please forgive me.

Can we meet for lunch today? Our usual spot?

I've been a bad friend I know. Text me.

Love,

Amelia

Rachel stared at her phone. She was tempted to be angry with Amelia, but she couldn't be. She was her best friend, and she had no way of knowing what happened to her. She knew she had her own issues to deal with. She sent a reply text to meet her at twelve. She needed the distraction anyway. Amelia could tell her all about the pregnancy.

The doors to the lift opened and Rachel quickly made her way into her office, denying her mind the privilege of making her think someone was lurking in the corners. Chloe was sitting there waiting for her.

'How did it go?' She asked, following her through her patients waiting area. It was empty. Rachel's heart sank. She hoped her patients were okay with their new therapists.

'It was fine. I'll see her weekly. For now, get the locum. This place can't carry on sitting so empty,' she said, swaying her hands around the empty room.

Chloe nodded, going back to her desk to get the file with the available locums for Rachel to choose from. Rachel went into her office. She felt exhausted. Her session with Diana had taken everything out of her. She stared at her desk like it was the first time she'd seen it. It was bare except for a pink and white cake box in the middle. Her stomach grumbled, and she realised she hadn't had breakfast yet. She opened it and found a chocolate croissant inside, a piece of carrot cake, and a biscuit in a clear bag, iced to look like a yellow smiley face. She smiled, as the face was so infectious. Picking up the smiley face she added some *prestik* and stuck it to the side of her laptop screen. Chloe knew just how to cheer her up.

With teacup in one hand and croissant in the other, she moved over to the couch her patients sometimes sat on. Kicking off her shoes she sunk into it, starring out of her office window.

She heard her door click open just as she dunked the croissant into the tea and stuck it in her mouth.

'So, you're a dunker, huh?' She heard Ruari ask her in mock amusement.

Rachel frowned trying to swallow the piece now lodged in her mouth.

'Sorry, I didn't mean to startle you,' he said, unaware that his presence was not a welcome intrusion. 'I just came to say hi and to see if you got my goodies, but I can see you've already dug in.' He took a seat in the chair opposite hers.

Rachel swallowed hard. 'Flip,' she muttered aloud instead of in her head. She didn't know they were from him. She'd assumed it was from Chloe, it was the kind of thing she'd do.

'You left this for me?' she asked, realising how harsh her tone of voice was.

Ruari's brow deepened, making it hard for her to tell whether he was angry or not at her brash response.

'Yes, Chloe told me you're coming in, so I wanted to give you a welcome back gift.'

'Welcome back to what? An empty office where I'm banned from seeing my patients?'

'That's not what I meant, Rachel. We were just happy to know you're out of the house again.'

'We? Who's we? You and your heartless brother Will? I always thought you were the cold and heartless one in the family, but I see your brother is cut from the same cloth.'

Ruari's face looked pained as Rachel's eyes stared at him in flaming anger.

'I wouldn't be sitting here if I was as cold and heartless as you claim I am. I was just worried about you and hoped to cheer you up.'

'How is Will?' Rachel shot back, shocked at her directness. She hadn't returned any of his messages, she still couldn't understand his distance. The last message he'd sent her was some feeble excuse of how he couldn't handle emotional stuff and thought Ruari would be better at it. Fat chance! She definitely didn't think Ruari was better at anything, let alone caring for her.

'I think you should ask Will how he is. I don't want to get involved. I just wanted to know you were okay, and by *we*, I meant Chloe and I.' Ruari spoke with a tenderness in his voice, aware that he was probably the easiest person for her to target her anger at.

Rachel sighed, closing her eyes, breathing deeply, she was too tired to deal with any of this. The struggle of trying to overcome her own mind was becoming exhausting as it threatened to overtake her every moment.

She opened her eyes, feeling calmer from her breathing.

'Sorry, I came because I care, not to upset you,' Ruari said sheepishly, running his fingers through his hair.

'I'm sorry too. I'm just trying to get a grip on everything.'

'You're doing really well, so don't be so hard on yourself. You've come out the house, and you've started your therapy. I know you will be stronger soon. Just give it time. You're a fighter, Rachel, I can see it in your eyes.'

'Right now, I'm not sure I'm winning this fight,' she said, looking down at her hands. Ruari knelt down in front of her, careful to keep a safe distance.

'Coming here today definitely shows you're winning. You need to just keep focusing on yourself. Right now, don't worry about Will or work or anything else. You are all that matters.'

'Thanks, and I'm glad you came,' Rachel said, looking into his eyes, she meant it. She'd been so set on hating him that she didn't see he'd been the only person trying to reach out to her through all this.

'Anytime,' he said and stood to his feet. 'Let me get back to my office before Chloe scolds me for hogging your time.'

She smiled feebly as he turned and left. She scanned the watch on her wrist, it was eleven o'clock. She'd have to leave soon to go and see Amelia. She hadn't decided yet if she was going to tell Amelia what had happened, after her session with Diana, she didn't know if she had the strength to retell the story again. She also didn't want to burden Amelia when she had her own thing going on with the baby.

Chloe came in, files in hand and Rachel forced her mind to focus on the task at hand. She'd decide whether to tell Amelia when they were together. For now, she needed to choose a locum who she trusted enough to stand in at her practice. Moving over to her laptop, that still had the smiley face biscuit on it, she wrote her parents a quick email to say she was fine, before going over the files with Chloe. Seeing Ruari made her heart ache for Will, and she wished beyond anything he would just come and wrap his arms around her.

Chapter Twenty-Two

Rachel spotted Amelia first, seated at their usual table, wearing one of her ridiculous Christmas hats. This one looked like Santa trying to get out of a snow globe. Rachel marvelled at how she looked just the same, even though she was probably around twelve weeks pregnant by now. She didn't appear to have gained any weight.

'Hey,' she said in her most cheerful voice, knowing straight away she wouldn't mention Jack and what happened.

'Rachel.' Amelia jumped up, grabbing a hold of her and holding her tight. 'I'm so sorry, I know I should have called you sooner.'

'Hey, don't stress, I knew you needed to deal with everything, and I didn't what to push you.' She knew how it felt to need to deal with something alone. She'd been doing that herself for the past few weeks. If Amelia only knew that she also hadn't tried contacting her because she herself had been locked away.

'I'm starving, have you eaten?' Amelia asked, eyeing the menu. Rachel thought back to the half-eaten croissant she had earlier.

'No, not really, I need to eat. What are you getting?' She checked the menu that she'd read hundreds of times before.

'I think just a roast chicken salad. Trying to keep healthy so I don't gain too much weight,' she said rubbing her tummy.

'Salad will be good for baby. Very nutritious, Let's order, and you can tell me all about it.'

Rachel settled for some macaroni and cheese with a side salad. She needed some comfort food right now. She could feel the hairs on the back of her neck stand up every time someone walked past her. Her instinct was to keep checking her surroundings, and it was taking everything inside of her not to do that.

'So, what's been happening? Are things okay with you and Carlos now?' Rachel asked, trying to focus on Amelia instead of the paranoia prowling in her mind.

'No. We broke up.'

'What? Are you serious? I thought he'd come around after that night. You guys have been together for four years and he just walks out on you?'

'He said he wasn't ready to be a father. What can I do, I can't force him?'

'So, he doesn't want to be a part of the baby's life?'

'That's what he said.'

'Oh my word, Amelia, I'm so sorry. If only I'd met with him when he asked to see me, maybe I could have changed this for you,' Rachel said recalling how Carlos asked to meet with her before the attack. She'd been dealing with so much that she never thought to try message and see what he'd wanted.

'He asked to see you?' Amelia asked, taking a sip of the Rooibos tea the waitress had brought.

Rachel paused, trying to think of what to say. She didn't want to give away why she hadn't met with him.

'Yes, he sent me a text just after my parents went back to Spain, saying he needed to talk. I agreed to see him the next day, but something came up and I didn't end up going.'

'What did he want to talk about?' Amelia asked, her voice suddenly quivering.

'I don't know. The text didn't say, and I never called him again after that.'

'Well, please don't!' Amelia shouted causing Rachel to jump. Her reaction completely unexpected. 'I'm sorry,' Amelia said more gently this time, seeing she'd frightened Rachel. 'I just don't want you to waste your time listening to his lies. If he tries to make contact with you, just promise me you won't respond or take his calls?'

Rachel stared blankly at Amelia, confused about her reaction.

'Promise me, Rachel?' She pleaded with desperation in her voice.

'Okay, I won't. Although, I'd have thought you'd take all the help you can get, if it would get you both back together?'

'I'm past all that. I don't want to get back with him. I don't need him in my life.'

'What about the baby, Amelia? Don't you want the baby to know its father?'

'The baby and I will be just fine without him.'

Rachel saw the fire in Amelia's eyes, and she decided to just back off. It wasn't her life to interfere with, but she'd hoped that Carlos would at least be a part of his child's life.

'So, do you want a boy or girl?' Rachel said attempting to change the topic.

Amelia noticeably relaxed seeing Rachel had let it go. 'I think I want a girl, but right now I'd be happy with anything.'

'Ooh I can't wait to go wild buying all the cute baby stuff.'

Amelia smiled but her eyes told a different story, she seemed distracted and distant suddenly.

'How's Will?' she asked after a moment of silence passed between them.

'He's busy, you know him,' Rachel said trying to brush off the topic of Will. She wished she could tell her best friend everything about the attack, and about how she wanted so desperately to curl into Will's arms and feel safe there. She still couldn't understand his distance. She knew he wasn't one for people's emotional problems, but she never thought he would abandon her this way. Not coming to see her once. Yes, she didn't return his messages, but that was in response to him first rejecting her. She thought their love was more than that.

Diana had told her to give him some space, and to focus on her own healing, but she felt she would have been so much better if he was holding her hand through this, not pushing her away.

'When last did you see him?' Amelia asked just as their food was brought to the table.

'Let's just say it's been a while. I would rather talk about the baby than waste my breath on Will,' Rachel said sternly to end the topic. 'So, when can we start shopping for our little sweet pea?'

'Whenever you're ready,'

Rachel could tell that the baby was a painful topic for Amelia right now, instead of a cause for celebration. She could only assume the issues with Carlos was the reason for this.. She watched Amelia retreat again, pushing the olives aside on her plate. She didn't come across as being herself and Rachel could understand why. It couldn't be easy having the father of your child walk away and not want to take responsibility for the baby. Who did that? It made her quiver with anger. Carlos was making a child grow up wondering who her father was, all because he felt he wasn't ready for a baby. She shook her head in muted disbelief. She'd never have taken him to be so selfish. He always came across so selfless and caring, but she knew all people handled pressure differently, and this clearly overwhelmed him.

Rachel starred at her friend, usually looking so comical in her crazy Christmas hats, now looked so sullen. She wanted to cheer her up and make this a happy memory for her.

'Hey, I've taken some leave from work,' she said quickly, trying to sound nonchalant. 'How about we go shopping for baby stuff tomorrow? Then we can stop by my friend Mr Lemon. I haven't seen him for some time now. Maybe he can give you some nutritarian recipes that will help baby grow nice and strong?'

'Okay, that will be nice,'

They finished their food and paid the bill, opting to take a walk through the park along the river. The jacaranda trees had lost their purple flowers, and the birds chirped merrily to December's tune. The air was thick with humidity as summer took a hold of the Pretoria skies.

Rachel couldn't believe it was December already. This year had gone so fast. Things looked all in disarray now, their Rio plans were thwarted by Carlos and Amelia breaking up. She was tempted to ask Amelia what they should do about it, but she decided not to. The topic seemed too sour on this warm summer's day. Rachel couldn't help but wonder whether or not they should just cancel the trip. She didn't know what future she had with Will after he'd abandoned her. She also wondered whether it was a good idea for Amelia to travel to Rio while pregnant.

Rachel looked over at her. She felt dishonest for not telling her what had happened recently, but she felt justified in her reasons. She knew that they were going into a whole new phase of their lives. Soon there would be a baby accompanying them to their weekly catch-up sessions, and conversation would change to nappies and the cost of formula. Their freedom to do whatever they wanted would also be gone. The baby would bring a whole new dimension to their friendship, but she questioned if they were ready for it.

'So, what's your plans for Christmas?' Amelia asked, bending to pick up a flower that had fallen off a tree.

Rachel stared at her perplexed momentarily. She knew it was December, but Christmas definitely wasn't something that had occurred to her. What would she do for Christmas? Usually she and Will spent time at his parents' home, or they would plan a trip down to Durban to have some time at the beach. This year she felt uncertain what to do. Her heart still felt confused about Will.

'To be honest, I haven't given it much thought. Not sure I've felt the Christmas spirit yet,' she said, noticing for the first time a small bump where Amelia's flat tummy used to be. 'And you?'

'I'm not sure. I guess I'll have to decide closer to the time.'

Rachel smiled weakly. She felt the same. She was living one day at a time now, and Christmas, even though only two weeks away, was still too far away to focus on. She pitied Amelia even more than she pitied herself. She'd be fine spending Christmas on her own, but she knew

Amelia wasn't accustomed to being alone, and she hoped she'd be fine.

'We can have Christmas at my place?' Rachel suggested, realising that might be the solution they needed.

'I'll let you know. I want to see how things pan out first.'

'What things?' Rachel probed, feeling Amelia was being a little cryptic. 'Things with Carlos?'

'Race you to the end of the park,' Amelia suddenly shouted, sprinting off, leaving Rachel feeling vulnerable and alone. She sprinted quickly after her, watching through the corners of her eyes if Jack was around.

'You shouldn't be running in your condition,' Rachel panted as she reached Amelia.

'Who said? I should be running more. Can't be getting fat now.'

She shook her head laughing, still wondering what Amelia meant. She had a sneaky suspicion there was something she wasn't telling her, and she didn't know why.

Chapter Twenty-Three

Amelia cancelled their shopping trip. She messaged to say she wasn't feeling well. Rachel questioned whether that was the real reason, but she decided not to press. Instead she got up, got dressed, and went to see Mr Lemon.

The last time she'd seen him was with her parents. Since her attack she hadn't returned his calls or updated him on her Skype call with Sandy, or Sandy's email earlier this week confirming that she'd spoken to Travis, and that he asked for time to process everything. She felt terribly guilty. She'd befriended Mr Lemon in an attempt to offer some sort of companionship to him, but instead she'd abandoned him.

She considered calling first, but she didn't know how to say sorry over the phone. It felt so impersonal. Instead she made her way to his home, hoping he was there and wouldn't mind her just popping in.

Stopping off at Menlyn Maine, she bought him some Sally Williams nougat. It probably didn't fit into his nutritarian eating plan, but it was the closest treat that she considered 'healthy'. It had egg whites and nuts. That had to be healthy, right? He would just have to ignore the bucket loads of sugar it contained. She thought back to Carlos as she walked past Starbucks. She wondered what he'd have said to her had they met that day. She hoped Amelia wasn't making a lifelong mistake in her determination to not leave the door open for him to someday know his child.

Jack's face popped into her mind and her stomach churned with nausea. She sat down on the closest bench and breathed deeply to still her thoughts. Reaching into her bag she touched the letter she'd received that morning. She still hadn't opened it. She pulled it out and opened the white envelope.

Dear Rachel,

There are two things I want you to do for me in the coming weeks.

First ...

Keep a gratitude journal and write down all the things in each day that you're grateful for. It can be as small as a lady smiling at you in the coffee shop. Notice it, acknowledge it, and capture it by writing it down.

Second ...

Do something fun with someone who makes you smile. Make it memorable. Make it magical. Let the memory last forever.

Keep putting one foot in front of the other. Baby steps, that's all you need. I'm so proud of you, you're doing well.

Remember that 'Hardships often prepare ordinary people for an extraordinary destiny' – CS Lewis.

Love x

Rachel hugged the letter close to her chest. She didn't know why she hadn't thought of a gratitude journal already. It was something she usually advised her patients to do. She stood up feeling her strength return and went to the bookstore to buy herself a journal before making her way to Mr Lemon.

***

The smell of jasmine wafted through the window in Mr Lemon's lounge. Rachel began to relax as she told him of her ordeal over the last few weeks. He was a comfort to her, like a hot mug of milk on a cold winter's day.

He listened intently, careful not to interrupt her as she spoke, watching her closely, making sure she was fine.

He had grown fond of her in their short time knowing each other, and he could tell from the beginning that she was a fighter. Today she proved him right, as he visibly saw her fighting for survival with each word she spoke. It was evident that the hardest part in all this was the loneliness she faced. People had abandoned her in her greatest time of need, and others she'd pushed away, unsure of their commitment to be there for her.

He knew he'd have sat with her day and night had she allowed him, but she was in a vulnerable state and probably unsure who to trust. The two people who wanted to be there for her, Ruari and him, were the two people she barely knew. How sad that those closest to her were nowhere to be found.

Life experience had taught him that it's not always the people you think will be there for you in crisis, that actually are. Usually it's the unexpected ones that reach out to show a loving arm. He recollected countless times that his closest friends vanished when he needed them. Most times it was the kindness of strangers that had helped him. It was a phenomenon he couldn't understand, but one he had come to accept. He grew to believe that God always sent what you needed when you needed it, no matter the means. Perhaps their chance meeting that day at the tea garden was some type of divine destiny? A destiny designed to bring him closer to his son, while giving her companionship when she needed it. Only when you gained perspective on a situation, could you see that there was some greater hand at play with each person you meet.

He thought of her mysterious letter writer and wondered who that could be. Why wouldn't he reveal his identity? There had to be something preventing him from being honest about who he was. There was no other reason for being so mysterious. He just hoped she wasn't attaching herself to someone who would once again disappear out of her life and abandon her.

As for Will… he could tell from his first interaction with him that he wasn't the right man for her. He was a Casanova, and having been one himself, he knew one when he saw one. He couldn't tell Rachel that, she needed to come to the conclusion herself. He just hoped she did soon. She deserved to be loved and Will was not the man to love her.

He watched her usually bright blue eyes look almost navy as she spoke, a flicker of determination evident inside. Her face looked gaunt from lack of food and she fought the tremble in her voice.

'I can't believe this nightmare came back to haunt me after all these years,' she whispered, tears prickling her eyes. Mr Lemon pulled the knitted throw he had on the arm of the couch over her. It was a warm summer's day, but he knew she needed the weight of the blanket to comfort her. She nuzzled into it, inhaling its scent.

'I don't know why there are so many twisted people in this world,' he said gently, sitting beside her. 'I hope they manage to put him away for a long time.'

'I hope so too. The detective seems to think they have enough evidence, including the camera footage to lock him up. I just hope I don't have to testify.'

'If you do, you look him in the face and let him know that he didn't win. Don't give him the satisfaction of thinking you're afraid of him. People like him thrive off the control they exert on their victims. Show him he can never control you.'

Rachel nodded and Mr Lemon tapped her knee. 'Now, let's make something for you to eat. I need to fatten you up,' he said, trying to cheer her up. 'Come, you can help me prepare something.'

Rachel followed him to the kitchen. She was grateful for his kindness and wished she'd reached out to him sooner.

'So, what are we cooking today?' she asked, seeing the herbs growing at his windowsill.

'How about a nutritious feel-good salad?' he said, reaching into his fridge to take out all the ingredients, explaining as he went along. 'I'll add some Goji berries to help you feel better. Goji berries have been used for thousands of years in Chinese medicine. They help increase energy and enhance the release of feel-good hormones. They are your body's little helpers in assisting you handle stress and improve your mood.'

'Sounds perfect,' Rachel watched him add the shrivelled red berries to the rocket and spinach leaves.

Next he reached for a jar filled with cashew nuts. 'These contain vitamin B6 which help with the uptake of serotonin in the body.'

'Mmmm, a natural anti-depressant.' Rachel smiled, seeing where he was going with this meal.

'Exactly. Now I would never suggest to a therapist that anti-depressants are bad, but there is no harm in eating properly as well, right?'

'Definitely. Diet is really important. I tell my patients that all the time.'

'Seems you haven't been taking your own advice,' Mr Lemon said, winking at her.

Rachel smiled weakly. She knew she hadn't been eating properly. She barely had an appetite and had no desire to cook for herself. Preparing a meal with Mr Lemon made eating easier, than doing it alone.

He handed her a knife and she cut up some cucumber, and tomatoes, while he made an almond balsamic vinaigrette. It had roasted garlic, almonds, balsamic vinegar, raisins, dried herbs, and onion powder, which he blended together with some water.

The smell of the roasted garlic had filled the kitchen and they sat down to enjoy their meal.

'So, I have an update for you on Travis,' Rachel said between mouthfuls of food.

'You do? Because I have one too.'

'Oh, my word, okay you tell me yours first,' she said, surprised by his response.

'He sent me a message on that appy thing of yours saying he would like to call and chat to me some time, he just needs time to process everything.'

Rachel jumped up and hugged Mr Lemon, grateful that Travis had reached out.

'I wonder what made him reply after all this time?'

Rachel filled Mr Lemon in on her chat with Sandy. 'You will love her. I could tell she just wants the best for her family. She seems like a good solid wife. Her accent takes some getting used to though.'

'Yes, that Aussie accent is different. Hard to believe those were once British inhabitants.'

Rachel laughed, feeling relaxed in Mr Lemon's home.

'So, what's your plans for Christmas?'

'Normally, Will and I do something together or with his family, but now I don't know.' Rachel's voice trailed off. She really didn't know what to do. She needed to see Will and discuss everything with him. They couldn't just avoid each other. They were either in a relationship or not.

Mr Lemon seemed to read her thoughts.

'Do you still want a relationship with him after he abandoned you?'

'That's what I need to decide. I guess I'm hoping he can convince me of his reason for doing so. I'm not sure I'm ready to throw away eleven years so easily.'

'Only you know if it's worth fighting for.' Mr Lemon gestured, wondering if it was just a fear of loneliness that was holding her back.

Rachel sat back and sighed. She needed to decide quickly because they were both in limbo right now. She wondered what was going through Will's mind. Did he still want to be with her? He did say that he'd only kept his distance because he didn't know how to handle the situation. Maybe it was as simple as that. Maybe she was reading too much into the situation? It had hurt her, but maybe she could see past it.

Sipping her iced ginger tea, she decided to surprise him and visit him later that evening. It was time to face up to this once and for all.

Chapter Twenty-Four

Her heart thumped. It was night. It was dark. She was outside, alone, driving to see Will, determined to see what fate lay before them.

A bright light jarred her from her thoughts, as a car flashed its lights at her. She knew she was driving slowly, but she felt it was easier to tell if she was being followed that way. The car overtook her, hooting loudly. She shook. She was driving at sixty kilometres per hour, which was the speed limit here on Dam Road, but this guy was clearly in a hurry. The road became dark again. No cars behind her. That was good. She was safe.

Breathing a sigh of relief, she looked to her left, seeing the moon scamper across Rietvlei Dam, as the wind blew over the water. In the day she was able to see ostrich, zebra, and rhinos walking these fields. She recalled when Will and she had gone for their game drive in the nature reserve that surrounded the dam. They'd just started dating, still young and naïve, talking about all their hopes and dreams for their future. Young love. What a sensation. Free from pain, free from heartache. You could love without reservation, without responsibility. It was almost a blissful affair that you got to only experience once. Back then they had no bills to pay, no responsibilities. No stress from work or life. They lived in oblivion to each other's faults and failures. Back then they were perfection to each other. Young love. It doesn't last. It changes.

Change must come. Love was supposed to develop from blissful oblivion to security. A deep rooted knowledge that when you saw past the bliss, and you were faced with reality, that you still chose each other.

They'd been at the edge of that choice for some time now, but they never seemed to take the plunge.

There was a sweetness in loving someone in spite of their faults. She saw it in her parents. Yes, they fought. Yes, they frustrated each other at times. But they came back together afterwards. True love said: Even when you're at your lowest, ugliest point, I still choose to love you. Even when you think you're unlovable, I find things to love about you. Love is a choice, not an emotion. Those who discovered that secret had love that lasted a lifetime. It brought a deep rooting that was unshakable. Rachel realised she wanted that, and she was willing to make the first move, to let Will know that she'd choose him, even when he failed her. She'd choose to love him, even if he should have been unlovable.

She parked her car outside his apartment and reached in her cubby hole for the keys to his place. This would be the first time she would ever be using them. Grabbing her handbag, she checked all her mirrors one more time to make sure no one had followed her and got out to go and see Will.

The key shook in her hand as she inserted it in the keyhole. She didn't realise she was this nervous. She could see the light flicker from the TV in his lounge, so she knew he was home. Turning the key, she opened the door.

Her heart stopped. The scene seemed to play out in front of her in slow motion. She blinked hoping she was mistaken. Will jumped up off the couch, grabbing his pants off the floor.

'Rachel, what are you doing here?' he questioned. She couldn't tell if he was angry or just alarmed, his dark eyes illegible. Her ears began to buzz as her eyes fixated on her.

'What is she doing here?' Rachel questioned him; her voice hoarse. Will turned to where she was looking, and they both waited for her to say something. Amelia just starred, a strange amusement bewitched her face, as she watched Rachel's disgusted expression.

'Rachel, I can explain,' Will mumbled, grabbing her shoulders, and moving her over to a couch to sit down. Rachel's eyes never moved from Amelia, who was still getting dressed.

'How do you explain sleeping with my best friend?' Rachel screamed, jumping off the couch and banging Will on his chest. He held her back, as she started to move towards Amelia. 'How could you do this to me? You're supposed to be my best friend! How could you sleep with my boyfriend?'

Amelia snorted. 'Listen, I'm leaving. Will, you can fill her in. She was going to have to find out at some point.' Turning to Rachel she said 'What did you expect? Did you think you could treat Will like shit and he'd never look at someone else?'

'Treat him like shhhh…' the word wouldn't even come out, as Rachel felt the shock ooze through her body.

'Amelia, just go, you aren't helping,' Will said sternly before sitting Rachel down. 'We need to talk.'

'Oh, now you think we need to talk?' Rachel was screaming again, a new wave of anger erupting as Amelia left. She could have sworn she heard Amelia laugh before closing the door.

'Listen, I need you to calm down so we can talk about this civilly.' He covered his face with his hands. 'This isn't how I wanted you to find out.'

Rachel got up and walked to his kitchen to get some water. Her hand was shaking, but she sipped the water, trying to steady herself. When she was ready, she made her way back to the couch and sat down.

'Spit it out.'

'It started some time back.' Will sighed. 'Around the time we were meeting to decide on the holiday destination. Amelia started texting me, and I guess I didn't turn her away. I should have told you; I know. Instead I entertained it. I was wrong.'

Rachel seethed. She and Amelia were friends. How did she not see this coming?

She nodded slowly to let Will continue. 'It started off kind of like an emotional pity party for us. She complained about Carlos and I complained about you. To be honest, looking back I guess I made you seem worse that you were. I enjoyed the attention I got from her.' Rachel nodded mutely. She'd heard it all in her therapy with her patients. Most affairs started off emotionally at first. People rarely just hopped into bed with a complete stranger.

'Well, I guess, I don't have to tell you where that led. She came over one day, and well, you know,' he said, his voice trailing off.

'Did Carlos know?' Rachel asked, wondering if she was the only idiot in the dark.

'He doesn't know it's me, but he figured out she was having an affair when he found out she was pregnant. They hadn't slept together in months, so he knew the minute the doctor announced it.'

Rachel gasped as the reality dawned on her. The baby, she'd forgotten about the baby. Her chest pounded, 'So the baby is yours?' she asked, trying to make her mind think that Will was one of her patients, to stop herself from lunging forwards to throttle him.

'Yes,' he said, so softly, that if she hadn't seen his lips move, she wouldn't have heard him.

Rachel let his words settle deep like a submarine in dark waters. Her boyfriend was the father of her best friend's baby. She thought of Carlos and wondered whether he'd figured out it was Will and was trying to tell her that day he asked to meet with her.

'So, you were just going to continue the affair and tell me when? Was I to find out when I was holding Amelia's hand in the delivery room?'

'No. When I realised it was my baby, I knew I was stuck with her. I knew I had to break it off with you, but I was waiting for the right time. Then you got att....' Will stammered,

'Attacked, Will. I was attacked in my home, while you were off shagging my best friend.'

'Yes,' Will answered trying to take a hold of her hand, but she pushed him away, 'and I'm so sorry for that,' he whispered, sticking his hands under his legs. 'When I found out you were attacked, I told Amelia I couldn't be with her. I told her she had to bring the baby up alone. I just couldn't do that to you. Tonight was actually the first time I've seen her since your attack. She just rocked up on my doorstep.'

Rachel's mind went on auto-replay, of how Amelia had asked her in the tea garden if she'd seen Will. She was probably just sussing out the situation to see if she could get him back.

Memories of their other conversations rewound in her thoughts, where Amelia would try to push her to make a decision about her future with Will. She'd been trying to break them up.

'Does Ruari know all this? Is that why he came to the house?' Rachel suddenly felt furious and embarrassed that Ruari was probably in on it the whole time. Prepping her for the inevitable break-up.

'No. He would kill me if he knew. I just told him I was bad at these emotional things and thought he should see you instead. I suspect he knows something's amiss because he keeps grilling me about you every time he seems me.'

Rachel sat back in her chair. Grateful at least Ruari wasn't a part of their lies. She couldn't face one more fake person pretending to be someone they weren't.

Her head began to pound. She'd lost her boyfriend and her best friend in one moment. The loneliness swirled around her like a tornado, sucking the air out of her lungs.

'So, I guess after eleven years this is how it all ends?' Rachel whispered, the tears falling across her face.

Will looked up at her, his face strained. 'Rachel, this isn't how I imagined things to be. I'm sorry. I really am. You deserve better than me.'

Rachel wiped her tears and stood to leave. For some reason she felt relieved, as if the noose that had been around her neck had just been cut.

'I hope Amelia is all you dreamt she could be,' Rachel said letting herself out the apartment. Will watched her leave.

The drive home felt arduous, but it felt freeing. She was alone. Yes. But she felt revived to start again. She was free to be who she wanted to be without the guilt of having Will to try to please. During their relationship she'd felt as if she'd sacrificed who she really was, to try to become someone he might love. Not anymore. It was a new day, and she was determined not to allow anyone to change who she was. Not Will, not Amelia, and definitely not Jack.

Chapter Twenty-Five

He watched from the shadows as she wrote in her journal. She clearly had read his letter. He smiled, content, loving how she listened to his every instruction.

If only she knew who he really was, she might not be so willing to comply.

He sank slowly into his seat, his eyes not moving from her. The waitress approached him to take his order, but he waved her away, the coffee he sipped on was all he needed as he watched, he waited.

He knew she wouldn't recognise him sitting here, he made sure of it, with his navy-blue cap, and large dark sunglasses. He even went through the trouble of wearing clothes twice as big to disguise his build.

She looked in his direction and his heart skipped a beat. She was beautiful.

Slowly he lifted the cup to his lips, trying not to make any sudden movement to jar her from her thoughts. He watched as she wrote frantically at first, then slower as she calmed down.

He could sit here all day and watch her. Her hair hanging loosely in its ponytail, touching the nape of her neck, her eyes creasing at the corners as she concentrated. He knew her better than she knew herself.

Standing up, he threw some money on the table, before taking one long last look at her. He wanted to go over and reach for her, but he had another idea. There was something he needed to give her first.

Chapter Twenty-Six

She watched as he gulped down the dark brown liquid. The air abuzz with Christmas cheer like a sickening sweet toffee. His face paled in comparison to how she remembered him, pained by the thing that united them.

'I figured out it was him the next day, after I found out she was pregnant,' Carlos was saying, chomping on the chocolate chip cookie he'd ordered at the Starbucks counter. 'I'd gone to the hospital to try to talk to her, when I saw him there kissing her.'

Rachel's stomach hurled. The thickened air weighing down her nostrils. She fanned herself wishing it wasn't so dam hot.

'I thought I was seeing things at first. Or misunderstanding what I saw, but no one sticks their tongue down their friend's throat, right?'

Rachel nodded mutely, the heat forcing a bead of sweat to trickle down her back. 'So, I called you. I thought you should know. It was only fair. They were doing it to both of us,' he said, wiping his own sweat off his brow. 'I've been angry you know, heartbroken and all that, but now I'm just numb. Numb, yeah that's the word.'

Rachel felt it too. The numbness. She'd called Carlos asking to meet, almost wanting to hear it from him, as if that would make it more real. Yet here she sat, pools of sweat gathering at the base of her bra, and all she felt was numb.

'Why on God's green earth did we choose to sit in the bloody sun? Can we move inside?' Carlos asked, wiping his face with the Starbucks serviette.

Rachel nodded as they grabbed their cups and found a seat in the air-conditioned store.

'Flip, my brain was frying back there. I feel like I can think now,' he said, wriggling into the green cushioned seat.

'So, what took you so long to call me?'

Rachel sighed. There was no way she was going to confide in Carlos about all her recent events. Yes, they shared a common pain, but she didn't trust him. She knew she had trust issues, but she was fine with that. It was safer, or so she thought.

'I was busy, and I didn't get a chance. Then I met with Amelia and she told me you broke up with her because you weren't ready to be a father.' Rachel watched as Carlos grunted. 'She made me swear not to contact you. Only after I caught them at Will's place did I know what had happened.'

'I could tell she was acting shady for a while. Flippen glued to that phone of hers. I was suspicious, especially when she kept making excuses why we couldn't have sex. One moment she'd be cold like an ice-queen with me and then the next she was hot as hell. The mood swings drove me bananas.'

Rachel nodded, recalling how Will did the same to her. Only thing was she didn't read enough into the signs.

'I guess I kind of knew Will and I weren't meant to be together,' Rachel said aloud. 'Otherwise I probably would have fought more for his love and attention. I was kind of fine with the distance, you know?'

Carlos let out a slow whistle. 'Eleven years, that's a long time, Rachel.'

'Yes, but now it's time to move forward.'

He reached across and squeezed her hand. 'How about we meet each other in a year's time and fill each other in on the progress?'

'I like that idea,' Rachel said, squeezing his hand in return. 'Let's hope we have happier stories to tell.'

'Well, it's up to us to ensure we do.'

'So, what are we going to do about this holiday?' Rachel asked.

'I'm still going. So, it's up to you if you want to join me. No bloody way I'm letting those two rob me of a holiday.'

'What if they decide to come as well?' Rachel asked wide eyed.

'I'll plant some cocaine or something in their luggage and get them arrested before they can touch down.' Carlos laughed as Rachel high fived him.

'Good plan.'

'So, give it a think, and if you still want to come, then say the word.'

'Thanks, Carlos. I'll let you know.' Rachel smiled, uncertain what she wanted to do. Rio would be nice, but she wasn't sure she wanted to go on a trip that would only remind her that she'd broken it off with Will.

They settled into a familiar chatter about Christmas, she'd decided to spend it alone. What choice did she have now?

Chapter Twenty-Seven

Her phone buzzed on the coffee table. It was the front gate security. What did they want on Christmas Eve? Rachel picked up her phone and tapped the green circle on her screen.

'Hello,' she answered, listening as they spoke. Nodding slowly, she felt her heart quicken. 'Okay, let him in.'

Moving to the door, she waited until she heard a car stop in front of it. Neatening her hair nervously, she opened it.

'Daniel, what are you doing here?' she said, as he got out of the car. Rachel ran outside and threw her arms around him.

'I'm here to see my sister,' he said cheerfully.

She took his hand and led him inside the house, trying not to ask why the unusual visit. Max and Snuggles ran up to him, he knelt down allowing them to sniff him. It seemed they sensed he was family as they nuzzled into him gently. She locked the door and went to the kitchen to make him a Nespresso. He followed her and made himself comfortable at the kitchen counter.

'Mom and Dad told me what happened to you, squirt. I'm so sorry.'

Rachel stopped still. She wished they hadn't done that. She had only just built up enough courage to call and tell them about the attack.

She moved again, busying herself with the task at hand, not answering him.

'I left her, and I'm not going back this time.' He spoke softly.

'You left Claire?' Rachel asked, shocked.

'Yes. After Mom and Dad called, I told her I needed to come see you. She started this huge fight with me about it. I just packed my bags and walked out. I've abandoned you guys for too long, hoping someday she would come around. But if she can't have compassion for you after this, then I don't want to be with her anymore.'

Rachel went and threw her arms around him. 'I'm glad you finally stood up to her.'

He squeezed her tight before releasing her to get back to her coffee making. 'Still two sugars?' she asked, as he looked up, his eyes finding hers.

'Yes, please. I'm sorry I wasn't here when it happened.' He looked around the room trying to picture the scene.

'I'm just glad you're here now.'

Taking their filled cups, she walked them into the lounge and sat down on the sofa. 'Do you want to talk about it?' he asked, not wanting to push her.

She nodded. Taking a deep breath, she began to tell him all the horror she'd been through with Jack and then with Will and Amelia. She told him about her mystery letter writer and how he had given her strength to recover. Daniel listened mutely, his brotherly radar on high alert, he was determined not to let her get hurt again, and he was worried this mysterious writer might do just that.

'So, what's the plan now that you've left Claire?' Rachel said, moving the topic off her nightmares.

'I'll check into a hotel until I figure things out. Knowing her, she'll fight tooth and nail for the house, and I just want to be done with her, so she can keep it.'

'You'll be staying with me until you figure things out. No way my brother's staying in a hotel.'

'Are you sure, squirt?'

'I need company, Dan. I'm lonely, and I could do with the shoulder to lean on. I think we could both benefit from the TLC.'

Daniel nodded; she was right. They needed each other now more than ever.

Chapter Twenty-Eight

Rachel slept soundly knowing her brother was in the house.

They'd spent the evening pulling out all the Christmas décor she'd failed to put up and worked to make the house look a little more festive. With no gifts for them to put under the tree, Rachel had baked biscuits late into the night while Daniel slept, and stuffed them in stockings, hanging them next to the tree. She'd also roasted a lamb with all the trimmings and baked a Malva pudding to take over to Mr Lemon later today. He had called a few days before inviting her to lunch. She knew he was a nutritarian, but he'd encouraged her to bring her own food, which she was more than happy to do. Christmas wouldn't be Christmas without some wholesome fatty food.

'Merry Christmas, squirt,' Daniel said, coming into the lounge. Rachel smiled, it was good to have her brother with her, safe and sound. 'It smells great in here,' he said looking around. Rachel smiled as she reached behind him and gave him a Christmas stocking.

'Merry Christmas, Dan.' She smiled, as he took out a cookie and sampled it. Leaning over he wrapped his arms around her.

'This is the best Christmas I've had in years. I actually woke up this morning realising I get to see my sister again.'

'I'm glad to hear that.' Rachel grinned walking arm in arm with him to go into the kitchen to make them a coffee.

'So, what's the plans for today?' He opened the door for Max and Snuggles to come in from their morning jog outside.

'We'll go over to Mr Lemon's around twelve o'clock. Until then, we get to just relax.'

'So, who is this Mr Lemon?' Daniel asked sitting on the floor allowing Max and Snuggles to lick him all over.

Rachel was overjoyed. He seemed so much more relaxed than the times she'd seen him before. Preparing the coffee, she told him all about how she'd met Mr Lemon and about her mission to reunite him with his son Travis.

'Will he mind you bringing me along?' Daniel asked, aware that he was gatecrashing their Christmas lunch.

'I called him last night and told him you'd be coming. He is more than happy to have you. Do you want to Skype Mom and Dad?' Rachel asked setting the coffee down in front of him.

He nodded as she grabbed her laptop and called them.

'Merry Christmas, Mom and Dad, I have a surprise for you both,' she said into the camera, walking around the counter to bring Daniel into view. Peter gasped, as Mary's lips quivered.

'Merry Christmas, Mom, Dad,' Daniel said, putting on his bravest face.

'Merry Christmas, son,' they both chimed in.

Rachel filled them in briefly of what had happened, and Mary sobbed softly. 'I'm so happy you're with Rachel and you're together for Christmas,' she whispered.

Daniel chatted to them, and Rachel moved away towards the ringing doorbell, giving them some privacy.

She opened the door to find one of the security guards standing there with a letter for her.

'This was delivered for you, Ms Johnson,' he said handing her the white envelope.

'Thanks, Samuel,' Rachel said taking the letter. 'Did you see who brought it over?'

'One of the DHL delivery guys gave it to the night shift last night, with strict instructions that it must only be given to you today.'

She sighed as she watched him turn around and leave. She'd hoped she could find out who her mysterious letter writer was, but he seemed to be determined to keep his identity hidden.

Opening the letter, she sat back on the couch to read it. Her heart aching, as she realised how attached she was getting to these letters again.

Dear Rachel,

I just wanted to wish you a Merry Christmas and to give you this ...

Rachel stared at the blank page that followed confused. What did he want to give her? There was nothing there.

The knock at the door startled her again and she ran to see who was there.

'Ms Johnson, sorry, I was meant to also give you this,' Samuel said, handing her a yellow and red DHL delivery bag.

'Thanks,' Rachel muttered excitedly, closing the door and sitting back on the couch to open the bag.

She gulped as she saw a Browns Jewellers box inside the bag. Opening the chocolate brown and gold box, her heart pounded as she caught sight of the necklace inside. Her hand ran over the white gold chain and the five diamonds set in place to symbolise the Southern Cross. She caught sight of another letter in the bag, opening it, she whispered aloud as she read.

Dear Rachel,

This is my Christmas gift to you ...

The Southern Cross, which is only visible from the southern hemisphere. It was used by ancient Mariners to guide them home. I hope this will be a reminder to you that you will never lose your way.

Merry Christmas.

Rachel held her breath pulling the chain out of the box before clasping it around her neck. Her heart secretly hoped that if anything it would help her find her way to him.

'Wow, expensive gift,' Daniel said coming around the couch. 'Who's it from?'

'Remember I told you about my mystery writer?' Rachel said, handing Daniel the letter to read.

Daniel read it silently and smiled at Rachel before sitting next to her. His mind far away as she babbled on about her gift. He was sceptical about this guy, whoever he was. Almost to a point of anger. It seemed he was toying with his sister's feelings when she was most vulnerable. If he really cared about her, why wouldn't he just fess up and say who he was. Instead he kept Rachel guessing, hoping, and wondering. And now this? A necklace worth tens of thousands. This was clearly someone with money to splash on whomever he chose.

Rachel glowed as she told him again the story she'd told him last night. This guy seemed to give her hope, but if he'd disappeared on her before, who's to say he wouldn't do it again? If he hadn't come forward after all these years, what made Rachel think he'd come forward now? Was he just some weird creep messing with his sister? Daniel found it hard to believe this guy genuinely cared for her, and if he did, what was holding him back from revealing his identity?

He sat idly watching her, determined to protect her this time. He had failed her relentlessly in the past. Her first attack, then the second. Her bad relationship with Will and now this. No. This time whoever was around had to get through him first. This time, he was her protector. No one else.

***

Mr Lemon beamed as he opened the door to Rachel and Daniel.

'Merry Christmas, my dear,' he said, kissing Rachel on the lips, 'And welcome home to you dear, Daniel.'

'Thanks,' Daniel said, instantly warming to Mr Lemons' ease and fatherliness.

'Come on in.'

Rachel entered as Joanne grabbed her in a warm hug.

'Lovely to see you again,' she said to Rachel before moving over and embracing Daniel, ushering them towards a seat.

Daniel and Rachel smiled at this loving couple. They both felt like they were with their second parents.

'So, how's things going with Travis? Any progress?' Rachel asked.

'Actually, he called me this morning to wish me merry Christmas.'

'Wow, talk about good tidings.'

'Yes, it was. I was surprised. The conversation was a little stiff. I think he is still trying to grapple with the idea of talking to me, but I could hear his dear wife egging him on in the background to keep trying. She seems sweet. She also chatted to me.'

'I'm so glad to hear that. She's amazing. She sends me WhatsApp voice messages at least once a week, you would swear we've known each other for ages the way she babbles on in those messages,' Rachel said, happy for this new turn of events. 'Did he let you chat to the girls?'

'No, not yet. He says he isn't ready for that. He needs to see if he can trust me again.'

'I don't blame him, Albert,' Joanne interjected, 'I know it hurts, but you have what, thirty years to make up for, just be patient.'

They moved over to the dining room table, where Mr Lemon had set out all the food, including what Rachel brought. He had made a grilled salmon with eggplant cannelloni in a pine nut romesco sauce. She giggled as she saw Daniel try to hide his apprehension towards the food. Especially when Mr Lemon encouraged him to try the kale, apple, and cranberry salad.

'Don't worry, just use my food to mask the taste,' Rachel whispered as he dished a healthy helping of Rachel's roast lamb and macaroni and cheese.

'Thank goodness you made this,' he whispered back, trying not to let Mr Lemon hear.

Rachel laughed. Mr Lemon's' food was really delicious once you got stuck in, but at first glance, it sure didn't look that way.

'How are you doing, Rachel?' Mr Lemon asked concerned. She'd told him briefly about Will and Amelia the night before.

'Much better, I have my brother back with me, and I have this.' Rachel touched the necklace around her neck.

'That's beautiful,' Mr Lemon commented, taking a closer look.

'It's from her mysterious writer,' Daniel said in a protective tone, dripping ever so slightly with contempt.

'Aah, I see,' Mr Lemon said, noting Daniel's tone, and agreeing with his protectiveness. They were definitely kindred spirits on that matter, he could tell. 'Well, let's hope you find out who this chap is, my dear. No sense receiving gifts from a stranger you've never met.'

Daniel nodded a little too obviously, and Rachel sensed their caution. She knew she was allowing her heart to wander into hopeful places with this unknown person, but was it so wrong to feel this way? Was it wrong to want to meet the person who had been a part of her life secretly for so long? Surely, he couldn't be bad? Surely, he must have her best interests at heart? Her heart felt conflicted.

'What's your plans for tomorrow?' Joanne asked, trying to change the topic. She could sense the tension as Daniel's jaw clenched.

'I'm thinking of taking Daniel to Sun City. Can you believe he's never been?'

'Oh, then he definitely deserves a trip there,' Mr Lemon said.

'Why don't you both join us?' Rachel offered. 'We're going up to the resort to spend the day at the Valley of the Waves.'

'Wouldn't miss it for the world,' Mr Lemon said, 'You're up for it, my darling?'

'Absolutely. At our age we accept every invitation we get.'

'That's settled then, it's a date. Tomorrow we take over the world.' They all laughed as Rachel's stomach knotted. No one knew her fear of being out there, exposed to Jack.

Chapter Twenty-Nine

The two-hour drive to the Sun City Resort was just the relaxation they needed. The sun scorched, and the aircon chocked under its fierce rays.

Rachel shuffled around, trying to find the coolest spot. She couldn't wait to dip into the water at the Valley of the Waves.

The car pulled up to the gate, they handed over their money for the entrance fee before Daniel drove them into the parking area.

Daniel looked excitedly at Rachel, feeling as if they were teenagers again. Grabbing their bags that had their towels and costumes inside, they made their way to the sky car that would take them up to the main entrance.

Rachel wrapped her arms around her brother as the glass sky car ascended slowly. The view emerging the higher they climbed.

She looked around, breathing in the air of this magnificent place, located between the Elands River and the Pilanesberg. Just two hours away from the main cities of Pretoria and Johannesburg. The resort reeked of luxury and never ceased to amaze her, built in 1979 by hotel magnate Sol Kerzner.

The sky car came to a stop and they stepped out. The walk up the ramp to the Sun City main entrance let them into the building and its sheer volume. The magnificence of the room caught Rachel's breath as she looked around at all the shops and restaurants. The place looked just the way Rachel remembered it. It buzzed with excitement and they followed the signage to the Valley of the Waves. People were everywhere, eating, chatting, and shopping excitedly, moving in various directions to do what they came here to do.

There was an array of activities available to guests and day visitors alike. Golf, the zoo, game drives, or simply relaxing in the pools.

They made their way past the stores, past the cinema until they ascended an escalator that looked as if it was moving them into a long-forgotten cave. The space grew smaller and the light dimmer as cave man drawings flanked the false rock formations on either side. Finally, the light returned as they exited the building onto a bridge, bordered with huge elephant statues on either side. The sun burnt their skin as they walked past the security into the infamous Valley of the Waves.

The Valley of the Waves was, to Rachel, what made Sun City so appealing. In a place where the ocean was a six-hour drive away, they managed to create the beach right here. It contained a six thousand five hundred square metre wave pool with hydraulic mechanisms that generates waves of nearly two metres high every ninety seconds. It was a phenomenon. The waves fizzled out onto a sandy seashore that resembled the best beaches in the world.

'Hey, you made it,' Mr Lemon said cheerfully, as they approached the spot he had reserved for them.

He looked strange in his Billabong board shirt, cap, and T-shirt. 'Joanne made me buy these,' he quipped, seeing Rachel eye him strangely.

'Aah, that explains it. You're the one with style,' Rachel said hugging Joanne.

'I'm not that hip and happening. I didn't even know about Facebook, my dear, so these branded swimwear things are definitely not a part of my wardrobe.'

Rachel laughed hugging him warmly. 'Well, I'm glad Joanne is bringing you back into the twenty-first century,'

'My thoughts exactly,' Joanne said. 'I can't be hanging around an old man all my life.'

Laughing, they greeted Daniel and made their way to the change rooms to get into their costumes.

The air was thick and humid, and the floor was hot under their bare feet, as they walked towards the mouth of the Lazy River.

The Sun City attendant helped them all into the water and onto their blow-up tubes.

Rachel laughed at Mr Lemon's witty humour. She felt happy. Today she was with people she loved, and she tried to forget the horrors of her recent past. Panic hadn't completely left her, and memories of Jack still threatened her. Her overactive imagination drifted to images of him trying to drown her, and she forced herself to push the irrational thought out of her mind. No one was harmed or had drowned here, she had to believe she was safe.

She knew that if she insisted of living in fear, he was exerting power over her even in his absence, and she wanted to be free from his grip.

The day wound along, and they all got some burgers to eat.

'So, how was that slide you just went on?' Mr Lemon asked Daniel.

'It was epic. It's called the Temple of Courage, and it's a seventeen meter drop down into the splash pool below.'

'Not my scene,' Rachel said.

'You're just chicken, what slide did you end up going on?' Daniel asked.

'Umm the Mamba Tube slide.'

'Oh my word, squirt, you really are chicken.'

'Am not,' Rachel said punching him in the arm. 'I just don't like my stomach ending up in my mouth.'

'That's the best part,' Mr Lemon said, 'you should try it. If it weren't for my age, I would have been up there with Daniel.'

'I'm with Rachel on this one, sorry gents, but no way I'd go on that thing, even if I were forty years younger.'

'Time for a selfie,' Rachel said pulling out her camera to position it to get all of them in seated at the table.

They all cuddled in and Mr Lemon beamed the widest when she screamed, 'Cheese' making them give their corniest cheesiest smile. Tapping her phone to see the pic she smiled up at her friends. They were beginning to feel more like family. More like her safe place.

'This is one day to keep in the memory banks,' Joanne said. 'Please tag me in that pic on Facebook.'

'What, you're on Facebook?' Rachel said.

'You bet ya. Can't let this old bag be picking up chicks on there without me keeping my eye on him.'

They all laughed. Rachel found her on Facebook and tagged them all in the pic.

She touched her necklace thoughtfully. He had asked her in one of his letters to do something fun with someone who makes her smile. *Make it memorable. Make it magical. Let the memory last forever.*

Today she'd done something fun with people she loved, and the memory of this moment would last a lifetime.

They finished up their food before getting back into the water. Daniel dared her to try one of the slides, but she definitely didn't have the stomach for it. Instead, she and Joanne lay on the sand while the men went to the waves. Rachel's mind couldn't help but wander over to him, and she scanned the crowd wondering if he was near. Touching her necklace, she hoped it would help her find her way to him.

Chapter Thirty

Rachel packed frantically. Her mind spinning at a million thoughts per second.

'Are you sure you're going to be okay alone here?' she probed Daniel. Guilt lining her lips.

Daniel stood at the door of her room watching her, amused, the steaming mug of Nespresso he'd made her still untouched on her bedside table.

'I'm grown, squirt, I'll be fine. The question is will you be okay?'

Rachel groaned. She was so annoyed with herself. How had she forgotten that she had this Mind Institute conference to attend in Switzerland?

Chloe had called her early that morning asking what time to meet her at the airport. Seriously? Sometimes

Chloe managed to be the worst office assistant known to mankind. Could she not have reminded her weeks back of this trip?

Daniel laughed, moving out of the room to go pack her some croissants for the road. Snuggles and Max, unamused by the sudden movements, came off their beds, and went to lay in the sun outside instead.

Rachel tried to find everything warm she could to pack. She felt so unprepared for this trip. She'd booked it in June. At the time it seemed like a good idea. It was offered mostly to therapists and she decided to book Chloe for the trip as well. She hated travelling alone, so she always tried to take someone along. Looking at her situation now, she was so happy she'd thought to take Chloe and not Amelia. What a waste that would have been.

Shoving as many clothes in as she could muster, she scanned the agenda Chloe had screenshot over to her. She could see she'd need an array of formal and informal clothes. The annoyance rose once more. Now she was leaving Daniel. She didn't want to leave him, and she didn't have the right clothes for this.

'Geez,' she muttered, looking through her cupboard. Who expects you to wear formal gowns in below zero temperatures?

Grabbing whatever she could, she threw it in the suitcase, and shoved it closed. 'I'll see what I can buy there,' she said to herself.

'What was that?' Daniel asked, coming back into the room with her car keys in one hand and a brown bag filled with a croissant in another.

'I'm just trying not to panic. Reminding myself there are shops in Switzerland too.'

He laughed, lifting her bag and moving her out the house.

Rachel bent to kiss her dogs, explaining that she was leaving them for a while. They seemed to understand, and she seemed to calm down.

'At least you can keep them company,' Rachel said, following Daniel out the house.

'Yeah, you just go and enjoy yourself on your Mind retreat.'

Relief washing over her as she heard her own laughter. 'It's not really a retreat. It's more like workshops designed by a brain expert. He gets a bunch of healthcare experts in the field together from across the world, and all those minds then design the best programs to offer in different sectors of the market.'

'Okay, I'm lost?' Daniel said, putting the bags in the boot.

Rachel laughed. 'Never mind. I feel awful leaving you on New Year's Eve. Honestly, I'd rather be here with you than off with Chloe.'

'I'll be fine. Promise. The time alone will be good for me. Give me time to process and all that.'

Rachel eyed her brother, looking for any sign that he was unsure about being alone. None.

'Okay, if you say so.'

'I do. Now go have a break. I think it's actually just what you need.'

She sighed aloud, hugging him before getting into the car. Perhaps it was just what she needed. Fresh air, new faces. Away from the memories of this place.

***

His eyes gleaned her. She looked particularly beautiful today in her pale pink cotton T-shirt and dark blue skinny jeans.

Her golden-brown hair bouncing over her shoulders as she spoke to her assistant. The annoyance visible on her face. He muffled his laughter watching her, enjoying his position of anonymity.

His eyes scanned the nape of her neck, and he felt the warmth rise within him, she was wearing it, the necklace. This was his only way of being as close as possible to her. For now.

He looked away for a moment, guilt shadowing his glance. He wondered what she would do if she found out who he was. Was it worth risking their relationship doing this?

It had all seemed like a good idea years before, he didn't know how else to get her out of the depression that had overcome her. There were times she came too close to finding out who he was, and he knew then he had to stop. It had broken his heart to stop, to walk away, but it seemed like the right decision at the time.

Until it happened again. The attack, that monster, who he vowed he would kill if he ever laid his hands on him.

The letters felt like the only way to reach her again. If he hadn't found out on his own what happened, he knew she would have never told him in time for him to help her. The real him. The him he feared she would hate forever if she knew he had been writing the letters to her.

He would have to stop again. He couldn't risk her finding out his identity. He couldn't risk it, there was too much to lose.

He stared at her again, blinking back the tears. He failed to protect her twice. He failed.

Chapter Thirty-One

Rachel starred at the itinerary, her bare feet rubbing against the plush carpet. Three days had passed in an exhausted blur. She hated travelling. If it weren't for Chloe and her constant chatter, she'd have hated it all the more.

She looked around the room, panelled in scented swiss pine, she was told it had a calming effect to alleviate stress, reduce your heart rate and facilitate sleep. She was already a believer. Moving towards the balcony, she opened the glass sliding doors, it was her first time staying in Interlaken, and already she loved being here. The air was crisp and cold. It had a way of instantly relaxing you.

She stepped outside; her breath caught in her throat at the cold. She should have put her slippers on, but she moved forward, nonetheless. It was 3 degrees, and she would have frozen had it not been for the three layers of thermal clothes she had bought yesterday.

They'd arrived two days earlier, exhausted from the flight and had gone straight to bed in their hotel. She'd been too tired to even appreciate the spectacular views of the Eiger, Mönch and Jungfrau mountain ranges that appeared everywhere she turned. The next day had been spent shopping for warmer clothing, what she brought hadn't prepared her for the below zero temperatures at night.

Today, however, was time to go to the workshops. She was grateful there was no time zone difference between South Africa and Switzerland, it made the journey less exhausting.

Rachel checked the time, it was eight o'clock, she was due for breakfast with Chloe before attending the first workshop. She still grappled to believe it was a new year. It felt as if she'd missed it, being on a flight the entire time.

Chloe was easy to spot with her thick black hair, and bright red scarf.

'Good morning, sleep all right?' she asked as Rachel sat opposite her.

'Yes, it's extremely quiet here, best sleep I've had in years.'

'So, what's the plan for today? I see we can choose our own workshops to attend. Where are we headed off to first?'

'Chloe, I didn't bring you here for me to dictate to you the entire time. You choose whatever session you want to go to, no need to follow me around the entire time.'

Chloe sighed, relief setting in. 'Thanks, boss, because all these brain profile sessions and setting up course material sessions will just drain me. I'll stick to the more fun ones, like Pilates in the freaking snow.'

Rachel laughed. 'I thought as much. Good thing they have a mix of things to do. I'm going to focus on the strategy sessions. I like the thought of getting involved in making a difference to how the world views mental health.'

'Mmm,' Chloe said, unconvinced, as the waitress set down their breakfast.

'Sorry, I ordered for you; hope you don't mind.'

Rachel shook her head as she cut into the Zopf. It was a rich white bread baked in the shape of a braid, which she lathered with butter and jam.

'Aren't you having some cold meats?' Chloe asked, pointing to the platter to choose from in the centre of the table.

'I'll stick to the jam and butter for now,' she said, sipping on her steaming hot chocolate.

'Do you think we'll have time for sightseeing with this insane schedule?' Chloe asked, eager to see more of Interlaken.

'We'll see.' Rachel didn't want to commit to anything, although she'd already made plans for the two of them to go sledging tomorrow night, for now she wanted to keep it a surprise.

Chapter Thirty-Two

The day had gone by quicker than Rachel anticipated. She loved the interaction with the people and therapists from different countries. She enjoyed being able to choose which sessions to attend. Because of this, she actually hadn't seen Chloe all day except during lunch. All the sessions where held in different parts of the massive resort they stayed in, and she enjoyed the scenic walks moving from venue to venue.

There were many other therapists and specialists from South Africa, many she recognised, but she mainly kept to herself unless the instructor forced them to interact.

She felt bad neglecting Chloe this evening, after all, she had forced her to come on the trip with her, but she didn't feel like eating at the hotel's restaurant, as stunning as it was. She wanted to experience the sights and sounds of the city on her own.

Walking through the streets, she marvelled at how clean everything seemed. The sounds of the city were so different with the locals speaking mostly German, English, and French. Her tummy growled and she searched the streets for somewhere to eat.

Seeing a sign on an old gothic styled building say *Bierhaus* she decided to go inside. Since German was pretty close to the South African language: Afrikaans, she knew that must be a pub.

Entering the dimly lit pub she decided to sit at the main bar on the far end of the room, where all the locals seemed to gather. She wasn't much of a drinker but decided to be adventurous, anyway. She was shocked to see that one shot of whisky was twelve Swiss francs, which in South African currency could buy you around six McDonald's meals. She chose to drink the Glenlivet twelve-year-old single malt scotch whisky which promised to have notes of vanilla, lemon, toffee, and honeysuckle. She wasn't sure how those contradicting flavours were even all possible in one glass.

'Drinking alone?' she heard a female's voice beside her as the bartender put down her drink. 'Vinita-Jax,' the red haired twenty-something year old said, sticking out her hand to shake Rachel's.

'Umm, Rachel,' she replied, caught off-guard by the sudden introduction.

'Fancy some company?' Vinita-Jax asked, making herself comfortable in the chair beside her before asking the bartender to give her whatever Rachel was having.

'Do I have a choice?' Rachel felt amused that she appeared to attract people wanting to be friendly with her. The reminder of Amelia made her heart pang.

'Well, unless this seat is taken, I would say no,' Vinita-Jax said, taking a sip of the whisky, before licking her lips. 'I can definitely taste the vanilla, and lemon,' she said mockingly.

'Yes, and I the toffee and honeysuckle,' Rachel teased back. She liked her already. 'Do you live here? Your accent's very British,'

'Definitely don't live here. I'm from London, up here on holiday with some friends, but they bored the crap out of me, so I decided to go out on my own. And you?'

'From South Africa, here on a working trip for the Mind Institute.'

'Oh, I've seen all the banners up at the hotel. Rather annoying if you don't mind me saying, the last thing I want to see when on holiday is the hotel I'm staying in being taken over by some company.'

'I agree, even if I'm a part of it. So, I'm sure you get this all the time, but how did your parents come up with your name?'

'Yip, get that every day,' Vinita-Jax said still eager to tell the story, 'My parents had these two dogs, who were their 'babies' before I came along. Apparently, they couldn't figure out what to call me, so they decided to make up a name that had both their dogs' names in it. Vinnie and Jack. That's how I got named, after their dogs.'

Rachel laughed so hard, she almost spat the whisky onto the bar counter. 'Somehow they chose well, it kinda suits you.'

'I had no choice but to make it work,' she said laughing. 'The worst part is people just kinda call me Vini for short. The whole Vinita-Jax thing is too long for people to pronounce, much to my parent's annoyance, as they feel like people are disrespecting the memory of Jack.'

Rachel giggled and gulped down her whisky. Her nose beginning to tingle.

'So, are we eating or not?' Vini asked scanning the menu. 'How about a snack platter for two, unless you want a full-on meal?'

'Platter for two sounds good,' Rachel said, noting how confident Vini was.

'Two more whiskies and a platter for two,' Vini called over to the bar tender who nodded. They signalled to him they were moving to sit in one of the booths.

Rachel snuggled into the semi-circular suede booth in the corner of the pub, a pendant lamp just above their heads over the pine table.

'Love the necklace,' Vini said, seeing it catch the light as they sat.

'Thanks. I love it too although I have no idea who it's from.'

'What do you mean?'

Rachel told her new pub buddy all about her mystery letter writer as well as about Jack, Will, and Amelia. She didn't know whether it was the whisky making her spill her guts to a complete stranger or the fact that she knew she would probably never see her again.

'Are you insane?' Vini said, after hearing how she got the necklace. 'How do you know this actually isn't Jack sending you these letters? Oh my word, Rachel, this is exactly the kind of thing a psychopath like him would do. He would get such a kick out of seeing you secretly fall in love with him.'

'No, it can't be from him. I won't believe that. I don't think he'll have it in him to do that, and he would have mentioned it when he came into my house. It would have been something for him to boast about, but he didn't say anything.'

'So, who then? It must be someone you know. How else would he know where you live, and that you got attacked again? I don't think it's the person who helped you in school. That makes no sense, because he could have just called you up and spoke to you the first time it happened. Why write these secret letters?'

Rachel's mind went back to the night she'd been saved from Jack's first attack. Why didn't she see his face? Vini was right though, he didn't appear to be much older than her, so if it was him, it wouldn't make sense to write her letters. He would have called or sent a text message or something. Letter writing was so old fashioned, not many people did that anymore.

'Argh, anyway, I rather focus on how pretty the necklace is,' Rachel said, trying to force her mind off him.

They both gulped down their second whisky and signalled for another. The wings and ribs were a welcome addition when the waiter set them down on the table.

By the third whisky Rachel could have sworn she could taste the vanilla, lemon, toffee, and honeysuckle. Perhaps she needed to be drunk in order to taste it. Chuckling to herself, she stood up to dance on the small wooden dance floor next to the DJ. She hadn't even noticed the DJ before.

Vinita-Jax came running up right next to her, singing at the top of her voice, 'come on come on turn the radio on...' as Sia Furler's song blast through the speakers.

They giggled... twirling around, singing with their fourth whisky in hand. Rachel felt herself start to lose control and the floor seemed miles away, her head spun from the lights, and the baseline pumping like a heartthrob in her ears. Her head found the floor, and everything went black, Vini was screaming for help somewhere in the distant nowhere.

Chapter Thirty-Three

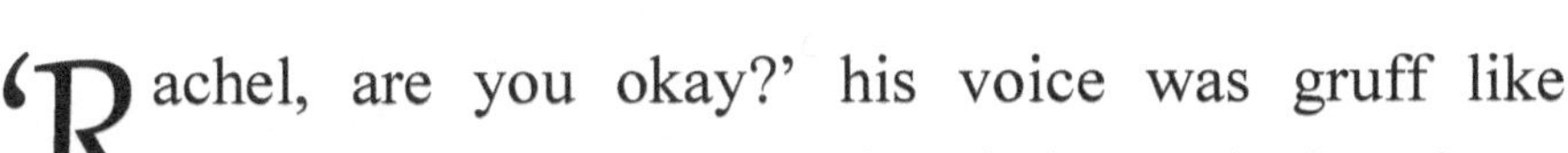

'Rachel, are you okay?' his voice was gruff like sandpaper, panic rising as he tried to make her sit up.

Rachel strained to open her eyes, but her head hurt too much, and she slouched back down shutting them again, trying to gather her thoughts. She was in Switzerland, in a pub, her head throbbing as if someone had hit her on the back of it. She pried her eyes open, forcing them to come into focus, to find a familiar face, and then she found it, leaning over hers, his hand behind her head, his breath skimming her skin.

'Ruari,' she said, her brow deepening in confusion, 'what are you doing here?'

'That doesn't matter now, are you okay? Do you think you can sit?'

She nodded, feeling foolish. Of all the people in the world to find her when she was drunk, it just had to be Ruari. Her cheeks turned bright pink, Vini knelt beside her offering some water.

'Geez, Rachel, you gave me a fright there, you just dropped to the ground with no warning. Talk about a memorable first dance,' she said, winking at her playfully. 'Good thing this handsome chap came to our rescue. One of your friends from the Mind Institute?'

Rachel grunted. She took a sip of water. Ruari was in Switzerland for the conference too. What luck? He must think she's so unprofessional getting piss drunk at a work event.

'Let me help you up,' he said, picking her up into his arms.

'Hey, put me down,' she screamed, wriggling in his arms, annoyed at the gesture.

'Listen, Vinita-Jax, I'm going to take her back to her room. She's in no condition to walk back herself.' He tossed money on the table. 'That should cover it.'

Rachel's head spun as he walked her out of the noisy pub into the quiet streets outside. She wanted to protest, to kick herself free, but she knew she was in no condition to walk. Her stomach hurled from the numerous glasses of whisky, and she silently prayed she didn't throw up all over him.

She breathed deeply, inhaling the fresh night air, and his masculine scent. Her eyes closed as she allowed him to carry her back to the hotel.

'What's your room number?' he asked, shifting her slightly in his arms as they entered the hotel foyer.

'Two zero nine,' she said, embarrassment colouring her cheeks again.

He climbed the stairs with easy strides, his strong arms firmly carrying her limp body.

'You could have taken the lift,' she muttered, annoyed at how easy he made this seem.

Ignoring her, he continued to her door before gently lowering her and sitting her on the floor in the hallway.

'Where's your key card?' he asked, seeing she had no handbag.

Rachel reached inside her jacket and pulled out the card from the inside pocket. Handing it to him, she watched as he inserted the card until the green light indicated he could push it open. He stuck the card into the wall socket to activate the lights before coming back and lifting her into his arms again and laying her on the bed.

'Thanks.'

He grabbed a bottle of water from the bar fridge and put it on the nightstand. He didn't utter a word. Instead, he pulled off her shoes and pulled the duvet over her. Sitting next to her he put his face in his hands.

'Rachel, you need to be more careful, okay? We're in a strange city. You can't be hanging out with strangers in a pub getting drunk. What if I hadn't come in when I did? What if I wasn't the one bringing you home tonight? I don't want anything happening to you. Okay?'

Rachel nodded, struck by his caring nature which she was privileged to see more of lately..

'I guess I just wanted to feel free, you know. Forget all the things that have happened recently.'

'I understand that but find safer ways to forget. Don't put yourself in more danger trying to run away from your thoughts.'

'What were you doing in the pub?'

'I sat with Chloe for dinner in the hotel, and she mentioned that you messaged to say you were going out on your own. I kind of knew you would do something like this, so I walked into every pub looking for you. I came into the Bierhaus just as you got up to dance. Good thing I did.'

'Thanks.' Rachel felt grateful he found her. He was right, anything could have happened to her. What if some creep like Jack tried to take advantage of her in that state? She knew her actions were risky, but she had so desperately wanted to get away from it all. To feel normal again, not haunted by her past.

'Now get some rest, I'll tell Chloe not to wake you in the morning, best to sleep this off.' He reached the lamp on the nightstand, switched it off before brushing strands of hair out her face and tucking the duvet cover around her.

'Goodnight, Rachel, I'll see you in the morning,' he said walking out the room.

Rachel lay there in the moonlight, her mind still reeling. It had been a fun night with Vinita-Jax. She didn't regret the laughter and friendship she had for a moment. Ruari was right though, drinking so much wasn't a good idea, but the taste of freedom she'd gotten tonight made her want to live a carefree life again. Perhaps this time, just with a little less alcohol.

Chapter Thirty-Four

Rachel dragged herself to the spa. Chloe had called her telling her to meet her at noon. Her head still throbbed, even after taking numerous pain pills.

The hotel spa was beautiful, a glass dome set in a private garden with panoramic views of the snow-capped mountains.

'Hi,' Chloe said, standing when she entered the spa foyer. 'I hear you had quiet the night on the town last night,'

'Ruari?'

'Yip. He gave me a lecture that I cannot let you out alone again, and I'm not to disturb you unless your life depends on it. Does he know he isn't technically your brother-in-law anymore, he can let go of the over concerned act?'

'I know, it's a bit much especially since he never acted like a brother to me when I dated Will. Anyway, let's forget about him, I need this massage. What did you book?'

'Since you left me to go party with some vixen person, I shouldn't be booking you anything, but you do pay my salary so I'll suck it up and tell you I've booked a Clarins full body massage and facial.'

Rachel kissed Chloe on the cheek, chuckling to herself, and wondered what Vinita-Jax would think of being called Vixen.

'Thanks, Chloe, I'm sure you're benefiting from this yourself?'

'You better believe it; no way am I booking a massage for you and not one for myself. Do I look crazy? Company trip, company perks,' she said, flashing Rachel's card in front of her.

Rachel giggled; she didn't mind at all.

'I have a surprise of my own for you later, so it will be payback for the massage.'

'Oh no, am I going to like it?'

'I'm not sure, but it's payback for your big mouth if you don't.'

Chloe's jaw dropped in mock horror as the spa therapist came to take them to their treatment rooms. Rachel quickly pulled out her phone and typed a quick message to Ruari.

Thanks for helping me last night. I would like to show my appreciation. Can you meet Chloe and me in the hotel foyer before dinner?

Rachel held her breath as she watched the screen say he was typing a reply. This was actually the first time she'd ever used Ruari's phone number, even though she'd had it for years.

No need to thank me, but I'll see you there. RH

Well at least he didn't sign off as Dr Harris she thought, laughing to herself. She could live with RH.

***

'So where are you taking us?' Chloe demanded as they stood waiting for Ruari.

'You'll see' she said, a smirk on her face.

'Hey,' Ruari said, coming up behind them. 'So, what's this all about?'

'Glad you're dressed warm,' Rachel said, still trying to adjust her mind to the fact that she and Ruari were being nice to each other. 'We're off for dinner to a different place. This time I'm taking both my bodyguards with me to ensure I don't misbehave.' She winked mischievously at them both motioning for them to follow her outside.

Chloe and Ruari exchanged glances. 'Please not another pub,' Ruari begged, walking next to Rachel as Chloe walked on the other side.

'Nope, not another pub, I'm done being a drunk damsel in distress for one night. Tonight, I might be a damsel in distress for another reason.'

'Rachel!' Chloe screamed. 'Can you just put me out my misery and tell me where we're going?'

'We're off to Niederhorn.'

'Oh no you didn't. That's the sledging place. Have you lost your mind? I don't want to die a frozen death in the Swiss Alps, and they find my body years later frozen on the banks of the mountain.'

'Chloe, you are so dramatic.' Rachel laughed. Ruari shoved his hands in his pockets keeping in steady pace with them heading towards the mountain railway which would take them to their destination.

'Feeling scared there, Ruari,' she said teasing him.

'I'm up for the challenge. Although it really wasn't how I planned on spending my evening.'

'Were you hoping to curl into bed watching soccer in your fleece pyjamas,' Rachel teased, loving him being the butt of the joke.

'Yeah, because you know, I wear fleece pyjamas. The ones with a huge panda printed on them.'

'Just the way I imagined it.' Rachel boarded the train.

'Starlight sledging, hey?' Ruari sat down next to her and Chloe took the seat behind. 'Didn't take you as the adventurous type?'

'New me, new beginnings, time to take chances.'

'Nice, I like it,' he said smiling warmly at her, making sure their shoulders didn't touch. He still seemed to want to keep his distance from her.

They spent the rest of the ride in silence until their stop at Niederhorn.

'First we eat,' Rachel informed them. They walked quickly towards the Berghaus, the icy breeze chilling their bones.

They settled into the cosy dining room, which was decorated with sheepskins, above the lights of the Bernese Oberland. The tradition was to have fondue before the thirty-minute sled down to Vorsass. Chloe entertained them with her stories of the sessions she'd attended in the last two days. She'd managed to find herself in every leisure session there was and avoided the workshops all together. Rachel felt guilty for missing the workshops today, but that whisky had left her in ruin for most of the day. If it wasn't for Chloe booking her the massage, she might not have ventured out at all.

Ruari disappeared and came back with some dynamo run head torches for them.

'Wanna make sure I can see you both properly out there,' he said.

'The sled run is marked with lights, you know.' Rachel protested before putting on her head torch.

'I'm not taking any chances. There might be bears or something waiting for me on the way down.'

'My thoughts exactly,' Chloe said, 'Thanks for this, at least we can scare them off with the bright light.'

Rachel laughed. 'Geez, guys, I thought you were both supposed to be my bodyguards, yet you're more afraid than I am.'

Ruari and Chloe looked at each other and shrugged as they made their way to the start.

The instructor began his induction for the sledge ride. 'This is a Davos-style wood sled. This type provides you with the best ride and control for the long sled runs and even works in deep snow.' He sat in the sled and demonstrated how they were to use their body weight to steer the sled. 'Braking is done by digging your heels in the snow,' he said, digging his heel into the snow as emphasis.

They hired some helmets and goggles and set off to where people were already sledging.

'Hallo! *Geh aus dem weg bitte. Wir gehen sofort durch.*' She heard someone scream in German.

Ruari grabbed her and lifted her out the way, just in time as someone came flying past her on their sled.

'What the heck, you got to stop picking me up and throwing me around!'

'Sorry. He screamed for you to get out the way, so I moved you.'

'I didn't know you speak German?'

'I don't, I just know enough to get around. I had a German friend growing up who taught me the basics.'

Rachel nodded breathlessly, as they sat down at the start line. There was so much about Ruari she didn't know.

The ride down was exhilarating. They giggled and screamed finding their footing and tried not to tumble over. At the end was a cable car that took them back up to the top for them to start all over again. They all went up and down several times before finally deciding to go back to the restaurant for the *gluehwein* they'd been promised by the instructor to warm them up. Gluehwein, or mulled wine, as was the English term, was also common in South Africa, but the taste was completely different due to the different recipes being used.

'This is warming me up nicely,' Chloe said breathing into the mug. 'I'm heading over to the bar, there are some cute guys there looking in my direction.'

Rachel turned and looked over her shoulder to where Chloe was headed. Her eyes met Ruari's as she turned back around. He was eyeing her protectively. She couldn't understand when he became so protective over her.

'Listen, no need to worry, I won't be getting all drunk on you again,' she said into her mug, as it warmed her hands.

'I know. I'm just wondering if you're okay. I know what happened with Will.'

Rachel looked away, her eyes filling with tears. It was strange to talk to him about Will. With strangers, it felt easier because they didn't know the history, but he knew it all. He had been around all these years.

'I'm sorry, Rachel. What he did was wrong. He's my brother, but I want you to know I never agreed with how he treated you, and I definitely don't agree with him sleeping with your best friend.'

'And getting her pregnant,' Rachel whispered, as her eyes found his again.

Ruari reached for the serviette and handed it to her as her tears betrayed her and escaped onto her cheeks.

'Will said you kept giving him a hard time about me. I didn't know you cared,' she said, wiping her tears.

'I knew he was lying to you about where he was. I just didn't know what he was up to. I had my suspicions but no proof. That day in my office when you asked me about the camping trip, I was so angry, because I knew there was no camping trip, and I hated being dragged into his lies.'

Rachel starred at him, remembering the moment and how angry he seemed.

'I thought you were angry with me because I dared to mention something personal at work.'

'No, how could I be angry at you? I was angry with him for lying to you. I wanted to tell you, but I felt it wasn't my place.'

Rachel nodded, it all finally making sense.

'When did you find out about him and Amelia?'

'After you caught them together. He asked me to give him your key back so he could come and see you but I told him I gave it back to you. That's when he told me what he'd done.'

'I don't know who I feel more betrayed by, him or Amelia.'

'Amelia made the first move, but Will didn't stop her. They are both equally to blame. You deserve better than Will, and I hope you see that now.'

'I wish I'd seen who he really was years ago, it would have saved me so many wasted years.'

'I know,' Ruari said, running his fingers through his hair. His hazel eyes changing to shades of chocolate flickers. 'It's hard when the person is your brother, you know. I have all these conflicting feelings to be loyal to him. Family over friends, and all that.'

'I understand. If it were my brother, I guess I would have done the same thing.'

'I tried to talk some sense into him. It was the only thing I could do. But he just wouldn't let you go, and he just wouldn't stop treating you like some second-grade citizen. I hated it, but I didn't know how to tell you without you seeing me as the bad guy. Shooting the messenger and all that, you know.'

'Makes sense. Thanks, Ruari, and all along I thought you were the terrible sibling.' Rachel watched as her comment appeared to cut him deeply. 'I'm sorry, I didn't mean it to sound harsh.'

'It's okay,' he said eventually. 'I deserved that, I've been a jerk and for that I'm sorry. Do you think we can put the past behind us and at least be friends?'

She starred at him for a long time before nodding her head. He was the last person she thought she would be agreeing to be friends with, yet somehow in these last few days she felt that in a parallel universe it could be possible. 'Friends.'

Chapter Thirty-Five

'Today's workshop's going to allow for a bit of fun. We'll learn to mix the new with the old. Tradition with technology. Our intelligence with artificial intelligence.'

Rachel looked nervously, she listened intently to the lecturer. She'd been in serious workshops all day and this was her last session. She'd chosen this class because it described how it would teach you to embrace new methods of therapy with your patients, yet here she stood holding onto a base drum, listening to a man with long curly hair, feeling a little out of her comfort zone.

'Now I want you all to drum along with me and sound it out. Ta, ta-ta-ta, ta, ta,' he said in rhythmic procession sounding out the taps they had to make on the drum.

'That's great. You're a little out of sync, so we'll try that again. Watch and listen, it's important to get the timing right. Ta-ta-ta, ta, ta, ta-ta-ta,' he said again beating the drum.

Rachel followed suit, seeing Ruari struggle with the beat, he looked up at her and smiled. Her stomach did a strange flip as her eyes met his. After last night, she couldn't get their conversation off her mind. It was as if she'd met him for the first time.

They had talked way past midnight, leaving Chloe to go back to the hotel with her new bar buddies. He was so intense, and so kind. She wondered why she never saw that side of him before.

Looking at the instructor, she wondered what made Ruari choose this workshop. Maybe he was tricked into thinking it was something else too.

'Right, now I want you all to come up here on stage,' the instructor said, reaching for Ruari's drum and handing him a tambourine instead then whispering something in his ear.

They all made their way up the stairs to stand on the stage. Rachel's heart beat faster as Ruari pushed his way to come stand next to her.

'Hey, fancy seeing you in this class,' he whispered.

'Yeah, I didn't think this would be your kind of class,' she replied, smiling up at him.

'The instructor doesn't seem to think so either, I've been banned from the drum for missing the beat. I'm now downgraded to the tambourine.' She chuckled and he pretended to be hurt.

'Now, I would like you to listen to this piece of music I'm about to play,' the instructor continued. 'This music has been produced not by a human but by artificial intelligence.'

Rachel listened to the sound, amazed that technology had gone so far that no human being had been a part of the song's production. She could feel Ruari next to her, almost trying to ensure their shoulders didn't rub against each other, even though they were all packed on the stage like sardines.

'Now, I'm going to play that AI song again, and I want you all to play your instruments to the beat I've taught you. Think of yourself in a performance, imagine an audience watching and let's see if we can make beautiful music together with this AI music.'

Rachel sat down and banged her drum while Ruari stood beside her tapping his tambourine. He seemed more comfortable with it, sticking to the rhythm.

They all listened as the song took on a whole new vibe. She understood now, how this demonstration showed them how to mix the old with the new.

They spent the rest of the workshop perfecting their beat, with the lecturer stopping at certain points making sure to give them pointers on how to follow this ideology in treating patients of different backgrounds and preferences. Finally, the two-hour session ended, and Rachel felt her stomach begin to rumble.

'Hey, Rach,' Ruari said, brushing her hand as he tried to get her attention. 'I heard there's a great restaurant not far from here. Was wondering if you would be interested in joining me there for dinner? You know, instead of eating the same old food the conference has prepared for us here?'

Her eyes flicked over his, seeing once again how they changed colour. Right now, they looked like honeycombs, his gaze intensified waiting for her response.

'Sure, but I need to let Chloe know I'm going to be ditching her again. Although, I think she might be ditching me for her new friends, anyway.'

'My thoughts exactly,' Ruari said, combing his hand through his hair nervously. 'Want to meet me in the hotel foyer in an hour?'

'Sure,' Rachel replied. He shoved his hands in his pockets, smiled sheepishly and walked towards the door. She reached for her handbag before heading for her room. He felt different to her somehow. She didn't know how one night could take her from hating him to agreeing to dinner. Something had changed, and she didn't know what it was.

Chapter Thirty-Six

Ruari walked beside her. They roamed the streets looking for the restaurant, their breath making mist clouds as they spoke. There seemed to be a comfortable ease in their conversation that had never been there before.

Ruari recounted a story about how he and his friends would sneak into the local cinema to watch movies until late at night without paying for it.

'It's a skill you know,' he said, 'getting past those attendants at the door. The only downfall is you don't get to have Coke and popcorn because it's harder to run carrying that if you need to.'

'Did you ever get caught?'

'Yes, all the time.' He laughed. 'But then we'd just go to the next cinema where they didn't know us, and sneak in again, until eventually we ran out of cinemas to sneak into because we were on the blacklist at every one.'

'How old were you?'

'About twelve, which looking back was really dumb, because attendants are trained to watch that small children don't go into age restricted movies, and here were us three sneaking into restricted stuff. At that age, though, you think you're invincible.'

'Tell me about it. I can remember thinking I knew it all. Life sure has a way of bringing you down to size, though.'

Ruari nodded. They rounded the corner, falling into a comfortable silence. Rachel noted how he seemed so much more relaxed than she knew him to be when they walked past each other at work.

They entered the restaurant. It was beautiful, rustic, and cosy. Each chair had a knitted blanket on the back for customers to use as they dined.

Ruari pulled out the chair for her and covered her legs with the blanket before settling down beside her, his eyes briefly skimming her. They picked up the menu to scan the contents, both trying to hide the obvious connection they felt.

'Know what you want to eat?' he asked after some time. She nodded and the waitress came and took their order, instrumental music filling the air and making her relax even more.

'So, what made you become a psychiatrist?' she asked, watching him stretch out his legs under the table, being careful not to bump into hers.

'I had a friend in school who suffered from depression. None of us knew at the time. He was the coolest guy in the group. Some days he wouldn't come for lunch, but that was the only odd thing about him. He always seemed so happy and kept the group alive. One day we got to school, and he wasn't there. The principle called our class together and told us he had committed suicide. I just couldn't understand what happened.' Rachel nodded, hearing the pain in his voice at the memory. 'I vaguely heard her say he was depressed, and I went and looked it up, trying to see how I'd missed it. Apparently, his parents were getting a divorce. He never told us. He hid his depression and pain under this façade of false joy. We found out later that those days he didn't rock up for lunch, people would see him sitting in the stairwell crying. Yet us, his closest friends, never knew. I guess after that I just wanted to see how I could help other people going down the same path, so being a psychiatrist seemed like the best way.'

Rachel watched him with fresh eyes. He was so different to his brother. She couldn't believe she never knew this side to him before. Will was so self-absorbed and vain, and Ruari was so giving and selfless. She'd spent so many years thinking he was cold hearted, but all along it was the complete opposite.

'What made you become a psychologist,' he asked, interrupting her thoughts. Rachel closed her eyes for a second, wondering if she could even confide in him of the horror she'd faced on her matric dance night. That journey to overcome, and the letters she'd received from her mystery writer were what made her want to help others who were in pain.

'Let's just say that it's for similar reasons to yours.'

Ruari nodded, sensing she'd put up her guard. He watched her play with her golden hair, twisting it around her index finger before looking up at him, in an effort to push back the memory that just flooded her thoughts.

'Any chance you're up for a movie after this?' he asked, trying to change the subject. 'I hear they have some amazing German options at the cinema.'

'Since you know German, I think you can be my translator,' she said winking at him.

'Forever at your service, ma'am.'

They finished their food and paid the bill before bracing the cold again to walk towards the cinema.

Rachel was relieved that there were English movies. She didn't know why she'd believed his joke, but she really had expected them to all be in German. He bought her a Coke and popcorn and they made their way into the cinema.

Settling into the chair Rachel realised that this was the first time in years she was actually going to watch a chick-flick. 'Thanks for not trying to talk me into some action movie,' she said, remembering how Will would force her to watch whatever he wanted.

'Real men watch chick-flicks,' he said, bumping her shoulder playfully. She noticed he jarred slightly when he realised that he'd touched her and moved to the other side of his chair. Strange. There were some things about him she didn't think she would ever understand.

She slouched into her chair, ready for the movie to begin, relieved that for once, going to the movies wasn't a stressful event. After so many years with Will, she'd stopped doing things she liked. She'd almost laid them aside to keep the peace with him.

Ruari looked over at her and smiled. She felt safe. The safest she'd felt in months, with the most unlikely person. No Jack, no Will, just Ruari, just peace.

Chapter Thirty-Seven

The shrill of her scream echoed through the rooms of the hotel. Ruari ran back panic gripping his every fibre. He had just walked her to her room seconds before after their movie.

His knock on the door was so brash, his fist pounding in desperation to reach her. Waiting a second he jiggled the handle, fear grabbing his throat. He couldn't bear the thought of anything happening to her.

'Rachel, open up, are you okay? It's Ruari,' he called out as the hotel manager came running down the hallway.

'We just received a call from Ms Rachel that she was in danger,' he said urgently before slotting the key card into the door to unlock it.

Ruari fell to the floor at the sight of Rachel sobbing in a ball by the toilet door, scooping her up in his arms he whispered reassuringly that she is safe before sitting her down on the couch adjacent to her bed.

'Ms Rachel, I'm Matteo, the hotel manager, are you okay, ma'am?'

Rachel's sobs grew louder as she pointed towards the edge of her bed.

'Ma'am, was someone on your bed?'

'Jack,' she said finally, his name coming out as a shrill from the back of her throat. 'Jack was in my room.'

'What? Where is he? Did he touch you, did he hurt you?' Ruari said desperately, taking a hold of Rachel.

'He… he… left that on my bed…' she stuttered lifting her finger feebly in the direction of her bed.

'What did he leave, ma'am?' The hotel manager asked, looking at the bed confused.

Ruari sighed as he realised what Rachel was referring to.

'Do you mean the towel art on your bed?'

The hotel manager frowned as Rachel nodded in agreement.

'Ma'am, that was done by the cleaner It's something we do for all our guests.'

'But,' Rachel stammered starting to realise she'd overreacted. 'But why would they put a heart with rose petals and an elephant, like they know I'm from Africa?'

'Because we give them that information. We ask them to do something to make you feel at home. If you noticed, the other days there might have been no towel art but there were others things in your room to remind you of home, like Rooibos tea,' he said pointing to the coffee station.

'Oh,' Rachel said, embarrassed by how panicked she'd become.

'Thanks, Matteo, I'll take it from here,' Ruari said, indicating he could leave.

Matteo nodded before saying goodnight and letting himself out of the room.

'I'm sorry for being so silly. I can't believe I thought it was Jack.'

'After what you've been through, it's only natural to feel that way.'

'Thanks,' she said feebly. 'I feel so shaken up. I was doing so well. I'd almost forgotten he existed. Now I feel as if he crept under my skin in one second.'

'You'll have setbacks, Rachel, it's normal, what matters is that you rationalize your thoughts and remind yourself that you are safe.'

'I'm scared, Ruari. What if he knows where I am?'

'He doesn't, trust me, but I can sit here while you sleep if that would make you feel better?' Rachel nodded as Ruari moved to sit next to her on the couch. 'Go lay in the bed, I'll be right here,' he said reassuringly.

'I'll rather sit here with you if that's okay?'

Ruari nodded. He reached for the duvet on the bed and covered them both, ensuring there was distance between them.

Rachel curled up in a ball and rested her head on the armrest, aware of his presence next to her, and his every effort to be close to her but still keep his distance. He still made no sense, but tonight was not the time to try figure it out. She closed her eyes and succumbed to sleep as it lured her in like bait to a trap.

Chapter Thirty-Eight

She leaned back into the couch, the steaming mug of coffee warming her frozen fingers, her mind betraying her with thoughts of Ruari. She sighed. He had been so kind this last week. It was as if she was with someone else.

'Penny for your thoughts?' Chloe asked, walking towards her. She blinked twice. How did she even begin to tell her that Ruari was on her mind. 'Still recovering from last night's scare I think,' she lied. Well, half lied.

Chloe gave her a tight squeeze before going over and unzipping her dress cover.

'Listen, I know Ruari sent me here to keep you company today, since you weren't up to going for the workshops, but it's our last night, and I will not let you miss this dinner tonight. Jack is not worth you losing your mind over. So, get up, you *are* going to shower, we *are* getting all dressed up, and we *will* be going to dance the night away.'

Rachel cringed; she couldn't imagine anything worse than dressing up. She just wanted to curl up in a ball until their plane left tomorrow morning.

Chloe stood with her hands perched on her hips flared out like a peacock.

'Okay, okay, I'm getting up,' Rachel said grumpily. She knew she wasn't being fair to Chloe. Her mind wondered over again to Ruari, a smile curling her lips. She recalled how they'd both jumped in shock when they realised they'd somehow landed up snuggling together in the night. If it had happened with anyone else, she would have giggled through the moment, but he was so horrified, that she didn't know what to do as she watched him jump off the couch and call Chloe and bark at her to get there immediately. The minute she arrived he mumbled his apologies to her and bolted out the room.

Rachel moved into the shower, the warm water cleansing her memories of Jack. Chloe was right, he couldn't steal her joy again. She touched her necklace, wondering where *he* was and if he knew she wasn't in South Africa. She'd messaged Daniel several times asking if any mail had come for her, and every day he gave her the same annoyed answer that there wasn't anything. She hoped the only reason for that was because he somehow knew she wasn't around. She couldn't bear the thought of him disappearing on her again. Times like last night, she wished it was him holding her as she slept instead of Ruari, she knew he wouldn't have run the minute she touched him, or would he?

***

Rachel looked around at the crowd. Chloe had already deserted her to mingle, or should she say flirt? She nodded and smiled as she recognised some people from the sessions during the week. She couldn't believe it was her last night here already. This trip had been the change in scenery she'd needed.

Lifting a glass of Champagne from one of the passing waiters, she took in the elegantly decorated conference room. The lights were dimmed, the tables had chandeliers hanging above them that looked like blue ice crystals. She loved the winter wonderland look. It reminded her of the movie *Frozen*, but a far more sophisticated version.

'You look gorgeous,' she heard Ruari whisper behind her at the nape of her neck. She smiled and turned to look at him.

'Thank you.' She blushed. 'You're looking good yourself.' She eyed his black and white tuxedo.

He nodded towards the tables indicating they should take their seats. She could feel his eyes penetrating her as he walked one step behind her. She had to admit, this dress really was stunning. Royal blue velvet that clung to her every curve before flaring slightly at the bottom. It came with a cape that was lined in ice blue silk, that just hinted at its existence as she walked. It had been her best find on their shopping spree when they first arrived. She looked down self-consciously at her cleavage, hoping for the first time, it wasn't too revealing.

'So, who do you think the *Idea of the Year* will be going to?' Ruari asked, pulling out the chair for her to take her seat.

'Definitely not me.' She laughed. 'I didn't come up with any world changing ideas this time around.'

'Neither did I.' Ruari sighed, a competitive edge seeming to rub against his poised demeanour. 'I was way too distracted to even concentrate on the sessions.'

'Distracted?'

'Umm, yeah, let's just say, not really into it,' he said, trying to hide what he really meant. Rachel shrugged and let it go. The lights dimmed and the music started, the MC took to the stage.

The evening wound down as people dined and danced. Rachel declined every dance she was offered by every male in the room. She couldn't understand whether she had a 'pick on me' sign on her forehead or what. She scanned the room looking for Ruari. He had disappeared ten minutes earlier, shortly before the dancing had started. She wondered if he was hiding from the dance floor or from her. Soon, the MC came back on stage and announced for them to take their seats, it was time for the guest of honour to speak. Rachel blinked hard when she saw Ruari taking the podium, she scanned her program to see how she could have possibly missed seeing his name there but realised they hadn't stated the name. They'd kept it a surprise.

Rachel laughed at Chloe as she signalled her excitement at seeing Ruari up on stage, she felt proud for him.

Ruari's speech was captivating, he shared with the audience the same story he had told her of why he went into psychiatry. He also shared some studies he was currently working on, trialling new drugs with several pharmaceutical giants to try to find medication with less side effects for patients. She was so proud as she listened to him speak. The sincerity and compassion in his voice captivating his peers in the room.

'Hey, you didn't tell me you were the guest of honour,' she said when he took his seat next to her after a standing ovation.

'Yeah?' he asked mockingly. 'I'm sure I mentioned it.'

'You were phenomenal,' she whispered, as the music started again.

'That means a lot coming from you. Wanna dance?' She took his hand, allowing him to lead her to the dance floor. She could see the frustrated glares of the men she'd refused earlier who'd begged her to dance.

She allowed herself to melt into his arms as the Boyz II Men's 'Doin' Just Fine' played. She could feel him gently touch the base of her back as he moved her in time to the music.

'I think you should sing this song to Will,' Ruari said eventually.

Rachel nodded knowing how right he actually was. She was really doing just fine without him. In fact, she couldn't even say she missed him anymore. 'I guess it was over long before I knew it was. He was never there for me, always consumed with his own life. It just got worse as the years went on, you know?'

'I know. I'm glad you've seen him for who he really is. You deserve someone who will cherish you, Rachel, not someone who will break your heart.'

She breathed deeply, his arms tightening around her. She still couldn't reconcile this man holding her so close, with Will's brother she'd known all these years. False perceptions were a strange thing. They really skewed your perspective of someone.

Chapter Thirty-Nine

The room air was humid and dense. She sucked in her breath like a thick milkshake.

'So glad to have you home, squirt,' Daniel said handing her a glass of iced tea.

She took a sip and tickled Max's belly. 'I can definitely say the same except for this insane heat wave?'

'I know right? It's thawing you out from icy Switzerland,' Daniel teased. 'You were knocked out last night, your snoring even woke Snuggles and me up.'

'Sorry, big brother. That flight had me buggered.'

'Feeling any better today? Ready to go and see Mr Lemon? He's been driving me nuts with his nutritarian food. Keeps sending me messages to come pick up dinner and when I get there, I'm stuck with no meat.'

Rachel laughed. She knew her brother was a typical South African male; he definitely loved his red meat.

'I'm up for the visit, let me just go take another shower, I'm already hot and sticky after the first one.'

***

'Rachel, dear, you look so well rested,' Mr Lemon said, engulfing her in a hug.

'I'm a little tired , but I definitely feel better in my soul.' She smiled, her heart lighter after their trip. She hadn't realised how the change in scenery and her friendship with Ruari had lifted the burden she'd carried for so long.

'So, where's Joanne?' Daniel asked, taking a seat at the restaurant table.

'She should be here any minute. She spotted some décor or something in the shop next door. She loves to shop.'

'I see that desire doesn't grow dim with age,' Daniel said amused.

Joanne joined them soon after and Rachel filled them all in on her trip.

'Vinita-Jax sounds lovely,' Joanne said, after Rachel told them about her drunken ordeal.

'Oh, she was. I wish I'd gotten her phone number, but after passing out, that definitely was the last thing on my mind.'

'Aah, my dear, now it's my turn to tell you about this amazing appy thing called Facebook. Did you know you can look people up on this thing?' Mr Lemon said winking at Rachel.

'Mr Lemon, how far you've come.' Rachel laughed, pulling out her phone and looking up Vinita-Jax. 'Well she definitely is the only person by that name on there,' Rachel said, clicking to send her a friend request.

'How's things going with Travis?'

'It's going slowly, my dear. I'm not putting any pressure on him. These things take time. I just wish I'd mended things many years earlier, but no sense living in regret, hey?'

'You've made great progress so far, so don't be hard on yourself, Albert,' Joanne said tenderly, turning to Rachel. 'How are things with you, Rachel? Do you think you can forgive Will and Amelia?'

'I think I can. I've realised that we were never meant to be in the first place. He came into my life when I needed a distraction, and he became a safe crutch that stayed. I just wish I'd realised sooner that he wasn't the one.'

'Yeah, I feel the same about Claire,' Daniel said. 'What a waste of my life. She's been messaging me asking me to take her back, but I just keep ignoring her messages. She definitely won't change, and I've decided that the next woman I'm with must love my family too, and not just me.'

'Do you think you'll both jump into relationships again soon?' Joanne asked.

'I do hope so,' Daniel said. 'I still believe in true love.'

'Mmm, agreed, son,' Mr Lemon said thoughtfully.

'And you, Rachel?' Joanne pressed.

'I don't know, to be honest. I have so many walls built up inside and right now I feel that's safest.'

'I think when the right man comes along you will know, squirt. He'll be the one to melt those hard to reach places. When that happens, you will just know.'

Rachel touched the chain on her neck. She wasn't convinced for her own love life, but she did hope that

Daniel would find someone to love him. After what he had experienced with Claire, she knew he deserved someone who would cherish him. She just didn't feel that was possible for her right now.

Chapter Forty

Rachel leaned back in her chair and looked out at the sunrise. She'd been back in her office for an hour already excitement brewing at her first day back at work.

Diana had given her the all clear a week ago, and today was her first official workday. She'd made an early start, hoping to beat Chloe to the office so they could discuss her schedule for the next few weeks.

'You're bright and early,' Chloe said interrupting her thoughts. 'Excited?'

'Yeah, I'd say that. It's been too long.'

'Tell me about it, I was dying without you. Trust me, I'd rather work with you than grumpy old Dr Potter.'

'Was he that bad?'

'The worst, Rach. He was demanding and frustrated the crap out of me. Please don't leave me again.'

'But I hear the nurses love him?'

'Maybe the old *tannies* his age, but to the rest of us he is a drag. He is good with the patients though, just me that wanted to kill him.'

'Well, I'm glad to be back. Now tell me what's the plan?'

'I've got patients booked from this afternoon. We just thought you should ease into it this morning.'

'We?'

'Well, Ruari and I.'

'You told him I'm back? Geez, are you two besties now since Switzerland?'

'I thought we were all friends? He cares a great deal about you, Rach, so do I. You know that, right?'

'I guess. It's just weird being his friend. It's like I'm waiting to be woken up and realise this nice guy thing is all an act.'

'I can assure you it's no act, Rach. I've gotten to know him since your attack, and he is probably the best guy I've ever been around. They kind of don't make them that way anymore you know?'

'Ooh, sounds like you're in love with Dr Harris,' Rachel teased.

'I might be.' Chloe laughed. 'But I doubt he would look twice at me. Word around the hospital is that none of the nurses who know him from way back in varsity have ever seen him date anyone. They've all tried their luck with him and failed.'

'Well, you might be the one to crack his heart,'

'Trust me, if I did, I would be the envy of the entire hospital staff.' Chloe laughed.

'I struggle around him, to be honest. We chat on WhatsApp often now, but I keep thinking that at the end of the day he is still Will's brother.'

'Give yourself time, Rach. You need to get over Will, and maybe being Ruari's friend is a way to do that. Once you get to really know him you will see him for who he is and the connection to Will might fade over time.'

'I sure do hope so, Chloe. Otherwise I might need to end this friendship.'

'Listen, try hook me up with him before you do.' Chloe winked.

'That's a deal,' Rachel said laughing. She could see why the staff found Ruari handsome. There was no denying he was in fact gorgeous. His features couldn't have been more far removed from Will's; whose looks could be described as average next to Ruari. But she'd never taken note of his looks because she was always so focused on being annoyed with his personality, which she knew now, she'd misinterpreted. His eyes though were another story. They felt like they owned her soul every time she looked into them, and she couldn't understand why.

'Thinking anything good?' She blushed, Ruari's voice disturbed her thoughts. She was sitting on the couch in her office waiting for Chloe to bring her breakfast, not realising how much time had passed, or that Ruari had come in and caught her thinking of him.

'Trust me, they aren't worth mentioning,'

'So, Chloe invited me over for breakfast,' Ruari said, motioning to Chloe bringing in the food.

'Mmm, I see,' Rachel said, realising this crush Chloe had on Ruari was going to be impacting her life too.

'Are you ready for your first day back at the grind?'

'As ready as I'll ever be. To be honest, I didn't realise how much I loved my job until I had to walk away from it the last few months.'

'I completely get that. I think there are few people who can put their heads down at night and truly feel like they made a positive difference in the world that day.'

'Yes, that's true, and I'm ready to feel that way again.'

'Can you guys stop gushing over your jobs please,' Chloe chimed in, 'I'm starving.'

'Me too,' Rachel and Ruari echoed.

Rachel noticed the light on her phone signalling there was a message unread. She clicked to open it.

Rachel, we need to talk, it's Sandy. Do you think you can Skype anytime soon?

Yes sure, just having breakfast, will call you just now. Rachel replied.

'Who's that?' Ruari asked.

'Please tell me it's someone asking you out on a date.' Chloe joked.

'You wish. It's just Sandy wanting to Skype, will call her just now.'

'Hey, did Vinita-Jax ever respond to the friend request you said you sent her?' Ruari asked.

'Yeah, actually she did. That girl is crazy. She sent me pics of her bar hopping in Italy.'

'Making friends with strangers again I guess?' Ruari mused at the memory of their first encounter.

'Yes, and getting them drunk.'

'I'm sure not everyone had a handsome man come carry them back to their room like you did, Rach,' Chloe said.

Rachel blushed as her eyes met Ruari's. So much had changed since that night, she could never have dreamt she would casually be sitting here eating breakfast with him.

'Good thing I came because Vini would have just kept dancing with someone else,' Ruari teased, trying to fill the silence that suddenly appeared.

Rachel nodded; she was grateful he had come that night. It felt like destiny, the kind of destiny Mr Lemon always spoke of. This moment felt like a piece of the puzzle of her life was slowly starting to fit together.

'Well, I better get to my patients, and you better call Sandy,' Ruari said, rising and clearing their take-away packets and containers.

'Geez, thanks for reminding me, I almost forgot about Sandy.' Rachel jumped to her feet and logged onto Skype on her laptop.

The room filled with silence as Ruari and Chloe left her alone, and the familiar jingle of Skype pierced the room.

'G'day, Rachel,' Sandy said into the camera.

'Hi, Sandy, good to see your face again.'

'Yeah, mate, likewise.'

'So why the urgent call? I hope it's not bad news. Is everything going okay with Travis and Mr Lemon?'

'Yeah, that's actually why we're calling.'

'We?'

Sandy smiled as Travis's face came into view.

'Hi, Travis. Wow, great to finally meet you.'

'Yeah, I guess you're the girl I should be thanking for connecting me with my father.' Rachel noted how his accent was still mostly South African, compared to Sandy's thick Australian accent.

'Well, I hope I did a good thing?' Rachel asked, still unsure what was going on.

'That's why we're calling you. Travis wants to surprise his dad with a visit. What ya think?'

'Wow, Travis, that's a big step.'

'Yeah it is. But we've been talking for some months now, and we even talked him through how to download Skype. Talk about a mission. But he eventually got it and has been skyping the girls too in the last week. I just feel a real connection with him. I can see that he's changed and is sorry for what he did. I have some business I need to wrap up in SA, so I thought I would bring the girls over to meet him. Sandy has convinced me time is of the essence, and she's right. I can't take it for granted that he'll be around forever, so I want to come over.'

'That's the best news I've heard all year.'

'Well, we're only ending January now so there's not much to compare it to,' Sandy joked.

Rachel smiled, if only Sandy knew what the last twelve months had entailed for her, she would understand.

'Okay, so tell me how I can help?' Rachel asked, as Travis began to fill her in on the plan. She just hoped Mr Lemon's heart could take this. She realised she might need help getting this plan together, and she knew just who she wanted to help her with it.

Ruari.

Chapter Forty-One

Ruari walked beside her. The breeze licked their sweaty skin while they hiked in the Moreleta Nature Reserve. Rachel took in the view. It had been a gruelling summer, the long grass now a lush green from recent rain.

She loved it here, the beauty, with zebra; impala; blesbuck; springbok, and ostrich grazing beside them along the hiking trail.

'So, how are we going to get Mr Lemon all the way out there for this surprise?'

'I'm going to pretend it's my birthday.'

'Geez, Rach, didn't take you for the kind of girl who lied,' Ruari teased.

'What choice do I have? I've considered including Joanne in this idea, but I don't think she'll keep it to herself.'

'Yes, you're right. She would probably get too excited and spill the beans.'

'Look at you, talking like you know her.'

Ruari laughed. 'I might as well, I've listened to you tell me all about them ever since Switzerland.'

'True and you'll be meeting them soon at my fake birthday party. You better buy me a gift.'

'A fake gift or a real one?'

Rachel slapped him on the shoulder. 'You know what I mean.'

'Which way?' Ruari asked, pointing at the different hiking paths.

'Left, it's the easier one, and more shaded. I'm roasting like a tomato here already.'

'Yip, that much is pretty obvious,' Ruari teased.

Rachel shot him a mock angry look. They'd been out here for half an hour, but in this heat, it felt like an entire day. She could imagine how she must look, her hair wet from sweat, her cheeks red despite her efforts to protect them by wearing a cap. Ruari, by comparison, was turning golden brown, his skin shimmered as the sun gleamed on the beads of sweat. She wished her skin could look that radiant being scorched by the sun, instead she looked like a lobster just thrown into boiling water.

'How long will Travis and his family be down for?'

'A week, but we'll be at the venue together for three days. I can't wait to meet Sandy. She's like the sister I never had but always wanted.'

'Glad you've had people around you, Rach. You've been through a lot.'

Rachel touched the Southern Cross on her neck. The one person who had helped her through this was *him*, and she hadn't received any letters from him lately. She couldn't understand why.

'Anything else you need my help planning?'

'No, you've done enough already. Thanks for your idea on the venue. I don't know why I never thought of it.'

'It's a long drive out there though.'

'Yes, but it will be oh so worth it.' Rachel stopped for a breather and took a sip from her water bottle.

'Want to pose with the ostrich?' Ruari asked, taking out his phone. The ostrich was grazing close to her leg.

'Do you think this thing is going to bite me?' she whispered. 'I hear they have quite the snap on that beak?'

'I'll save you, don't worry, just say cheese,'

She plucked up the courage and stood next to it, smiling into Ruari's camera.

'Take one together?' she asked after he had clicked.

He nodded, moving to stand beside her and turn the phone into selfie mode. 'Everybody say, *cheese*,' he said.

The ostrich flared its wings behind them, just as he clicked.

'Perfect pic,' Rachel marvelled. 'You're the ostrich whisperer.'

'More like the perfect memory,' he said smiling down at her. Rachel felt it again, that feeling he was pulling her into himself every time their eyes met.

Chapter Forty-Two

Even by her own standards, this was breathtaking. Rachel stood on the porch and looked out at the panoramic view. Of all the lodges in the Sabi Sands Game Reserve, Ulusaba Rock Lodge had to be the most spectacular.

Her heart quickened in anticipation, the sun beginning to set over the South African bushveld. Ruari should be here any minute with Mr Lemon, Joanne, and Chloe, and if all went as planned, Travis and his family should be arriving soon after.

She was glad she'd asked for Ruari's help to plan this reunion, she had to give him credit, his idea to come here was the most spectacular of all. The staff were busy setting up for her fake birthday party, which was in fact, Mr

Lemon and Travis's reunion party. This jaw dropping ten bedroomed lodge, was now reserved exclusively for them.

Her hand trailed over the chocolate brown leather couch. The living room had an earthy smell of straw and cow hide. The soundtrack nestled in the breeze of birds chirping, buffalo running, and lions roaring. She went out onto the deck, leaning on the balustrade next to the infinity pool, her eyes a wonder at the endless view of nature untouched. Nature in its perfect form… the way it was created to be.

Sabi Sands was deep in the bushveld, bordering the infamous Kruger National Park, and out here, with the setting sun and the animals roaming around them, there was no more magical a setting for a father and son to reunite.

When they'd pitched the idea to Travis, he agreed that this had to be the destination. This tranquil space would allow him the opportunity to get to bond with his father, surrounded by people who were rooting for this relationship to heal.

'All set, squirt?' Daniel asked coming up behind her. 'This place is phenomenal.'

'It really is. I'm so glad I trusted Ruari with this idea.'

'So, I'll finally get to meet the infamous Ruari tonight? I hope he's nothing like his twit brother.'

'Trust me, he isn't. I think you will get along just fine.' Rachel smiled at Daniel as he left her to go back inside. He had become so overprotective of her lately. It was good to have him with her after all these years.

They'd driven up to the lodge early that morning to make sure everything would be ready and perfect when the guests arrived, but her thoughts for most of the day were about *his* letter.

Since Christmas, she hadn't heard from him, and there had been an aching in her heart wondering where he'd gone to. Until last night, when a new letter was left by a courier with the security personnel.

She went to her room; she'd already unpacked and her dress for this evening lay neatly on the wooden four poster bed. The bed was adorned in cream linen with a sheer net draping the sides. She reached into the cupboard, drawing out her handbag. Her fingers found the smooth paper, the letter, her only connection to him. Feeling her body tremble, she opened the envelope to read the pages within. The now all too familiar text.

Dear Rachel,

I write to you feeling conflicted. For so long I've not known what to do.

I need to be as honest as I can with you, and I hope somehow in your heart you will one day learn to forgive me.

Rachel, I've toyed with the idea of coming clean, of revealing to you who I am, but right now I see no hope of that working out.

Because of this, I have to stop writing to you. I can't leave you with false hope while I figure things out. That would be gravely unfair on you. If life were different, perhaps, if I were braver, I would have told you who I am a long time ago. But it's too late now. I stand too much to lose. So, for this reason I will walk away. I will not write another letter and I hope this time, there will never be a need for me to even consider it again. I was wrong, so wrong, to even start.

Just know that there is someone out there who cares deeply for you, who just wanted to help you during a difficult time. Someone who wanted to see the sparkle come back in your eyes.

*I hope one day the Southern Cross can bring us together,
but through different circumstances.*

*'Goodnight, goodnight, parting is such sweet sorrow. That
I shall say goodnight till it be morrow.'*

Love x

Rachel let the tears pour down her cheeks, her hand
holding onto the chain around her neck. She'd spent all of
last night going over his letter in her mind, wondering why
he thought he couldn't tell her who he was.

This morning she'd woken burning with anger, she had
started to feel that at some point, somehow, they could be
together. She knew the idea was crazy, because she had no
clue who he was, and he had never actually ever *said* that.
But in her heart, she couldn't bring herself to believe he
was anything but a good man who she could spend the rest
of her life with. She so desperately wanted to meet him, to
know him, to love him, but now he had robbed her of that
opportunity. She didn't know whether hating him or loving
him was the easiest route her heart should take.

'They're here.' Daniel burst into her room, jarring her
thoughts.

'Thanks,' she muttered, grateful that her back was turned to the door so he couldn't see her tear-stained face. She hadn't told Daniel about the letter. She didn't know how to. She knew that he would tell her it was for the best. But how could he think that? How could anyone know what was best for her?

She shook her head in an attempt to remove the cloud that was hovering there. Today was Mr Lemon's day and she was determined to celebrate this moment with him. Nothing would steal it from her. Not even *him*.

Chapter Forty-Three

───────○───────

'Rachel, dear.' Mr Lemon beamed. 'Happy Birthday.' Rachel looked bewilderedly at him, before snapping back into focus. The lie. This was the only lie they could think of to get him to come on an over five-hour drive to the game reserve.

'Thanks, Mr Lemon, I just keep getting younger.' She winked at the others as he bent down and kissed her cheek.

'This is for you, dear, from both of us.' Joanne smiled, handing her the birthday present. 'Happy birthday.'

'It's a Gladiolus flower and symbolises strength. Plant it in your garden, and whenever you look at it, remember the strength you have now after all you have been through,' Mr Lemon said, nodding at the plant.

'Thanks, it means more than you'll ever know. I don't think I would have gotten through it without everyone in this room.'

Daniel came and put his arm around her. Even though Rachel felt bad for lying to Mr Lemon and Joanne about her birthday, she definitely was grateful for the gift they gave her.

'You're evil,' Chloe whispered as she hugged Rachel.

'What choice did I have? I couldn't think of another excuse to get him up here,' she whispered back.

'Let's hope he doesn't take his gift back,' Ruari chimed in.

'You're both just as guilty for going along with me. Neither of you could come up with any better idea.'

They both laughed, taking in the space around them.

'Geez, this place is stunning!' Chloe said. 'Ruari, you will be planning my for real birthday party, at least I know you have taste.'

They giggled, grabbing a welcome drink from one of the waiters.

'It's good to be back in the bushveld. Forgot how peaceful it is around here. Far from the hustle and bustle of the city life,' Mr Lemon said already seated on one of the oversized couches. 'So where do we leave our bags?'

Daniel showed them all to their rooms, and Rachel quickly checked her phone to see Travis had texted to say they'd be there within the hour. Her heart thumped as she waited for what was to come.

'Are we all set?' Ruari whispered behind her ear.

'Yip, they'll be here in an hour.'

'Okay, great. When they're here, you make sure Mr Lemon is out by the pool, then I'll sneak them into the lodge.'

'I hope he doesn't get too much of a shock,' Rachel said, worried about his age.

'Do you think we should let Joanne in on the secret now, maybe she can advise us how best to go about it then?'

'I still think she'll tell him.'

'Okay, let's just stick to our original plan.' Ruari said, as they made their way to the rooms to get dressed for the party.

***

Chloe was on her second cocktail by the time Rachel went out to the pool, whose water shimmered in reflection to the nights sky.

'You look beautiful, squirt,' Daniel said. She was dressed in a champagne pink strapless summer dress, her hair hanging loosely across her shoulders.

'Exquisite,' Ruari whispered.

'Hey, don't get any ideas with my sister,' Daniel said before walking off to talk to Chloe.

'Your brother has been grilling me from the moment I came out here.'

'About what?'

'Will and you, and me and you.'

'But there isn't a *me and you*,' Rachel said, feeling her stomach flip.

'Try telling your brother that. He thinks I'm here with ulterior motives.'

'And are you?'

'Seriously? You think so little of me?'

'I'm just making sure. A girl can never be too careful, you know.'

'I would never do anything to hurt you, Rachel. I mean that. Since I've met you, all I've done is try to protect you. I spent your entire relationship with Will trying to make sure he didn't hurt you, because I always suspected he had the potential to cheat on you. Unfortunately, all my efforts were pointless, because in the end, he did just what I feared he would do.'

'I appreciate you, Ruari. I've never said it before, but in this last month, you've become the closest friend I have, and I couldn't imagine this moment without you.'

'Thanks,' Ruari muttered, embarrassed by the intensity of her words.

Rachel felt her phone vibrate in her hand. 'It's time, they're here. Will you go and let them in?'

Ruari nodded… beelining for the door. Rachel made her way to Mr Lemon and put her hand on his shoulder, turning him away from the view of the lounge, and making him instead face the night sky.

'Mr Lemon, I have a little confession to make. Today isn't my birthday. I used it as a lie to get you to drive up here. The truth is, there's another reason we all came here today, and that reason is you.'

Mr Lemon looked down at Rachel bewildered. 'Me?'

'Yes. But not just you,' Rachel said looking back to see if they were here. She gently reached for his hand and turned him back around. 'We're here for you and Travis.'

Mr Lemon began to tremble as Travis came towards him, throwing his arms around him.

'Travis… my son, it's you, it's really you.'

'Yes, Dad,' Travis said, letting him go. 'And I brought my family here to meet you too.'

Tears filled their eyes as they watched Mr Lemon reach down and hug his grandchildren for the very first time.

'Sandy, I have you and Rachel to thank for this,' Mr Lemon said, as he embraced Sandy. 'I never thought I would get the opportunity to be in the same room as my son again, let alone his entire family.'

'*Your* entire family, Dad. This is now your family too.'

Rachel grinned and Mr Lemon introduced them all to each other. She couldn't have been happier to be here, reuniting Mr Lemon with his family.

'You've done a great thing here today, Rachel. You've bridged decades of pain, into one moment that has changed the landscape of this family's history,' Ruari said, handing her a drink.

'Thanks, Ruari. I didn't plan on doing anything special. I just planned on helping an old man find some peace but knowing him has brought me more peace than I could have imagined. So, I think it's he who has done something great for me, and not the other way around.'

'You've reaped the kindness you've sown, Rachel.'

Rachel smiled, she was grateful she had friends like these, and more grateful that she got to share this with Ruari and not Will. If Will were here, he would have sarcastically told her he was glad the project was finally over.

'Rachel, it's so good of ya to arrange this entire trip here in the bush mate. It's a beauty.' Sandy beamed, grabbing Rachel in a hug.

'And you must be Ruari, yeah? Rachel's told me so much about you.' Ruari shook her hand, locking eyes with Rachel.

'I told her you helped me with the planning,' Rachel quickly explained.

'Aah, the planning, yes. Great to meet you, Sandy. I feel as if I know you already,' Ruari said before he excused himself, leaving them to catch up.

'Well, we make one hell of a team, don't you think? Who'd have thought we'd pull this off,' Sandy said winking at Rachel.

'A hell of a team. I'm so glad it's worked out so well.'

'Travis forgiving his father has changed him, ya know? It's like I'm married to a new man. But listen, before I start jabbering on, let me go splash my face a little, it's been a long drive up here.'

Rachel nodded, it felt strange speaking to her in person after all these months of talking over the phone. She could only imagine how this must feel for Mr Lemon who had waited decades for this moment. Right now, her heart was overwhelmed with joy. Just a few months ago she was assaulted, alone, and rejected, yet here she stood today, surrounded by people who she loved dearly.

Rachel watched as Chloe grabbed Daniel's hand and got him swaying to the beat of the music. She laughed at how frivolous Chloe was. One moment gushing over Ruari, and the next flirting with Daniel. Both men were just too polite to turn her away, so they instead were gracious enough to entertain her innuendos.

'This evening turned out better than we planned,' Travis said, putting his arm around Rachel. 'Thanks for this, I'm eternally indebted to you.'

'Don't mention it, I'm just glad it all worked out in the end.'

'This place is gorgeous by the way. I can't wait to see it during the day.'

'Ruari's choice, and I must say he did a great job,' Rachel said, nodding in Ruari's direction as Chloe tried to get him to dance with her. They both chuckled at the scene. Ruari tried the best he could to let Chloe down graciously.

Rachel looked around at her friends, each relaxing in the starlight sky with the sounds of the animals grazing below echoing in the vibration of the music.

This place was spectacular, and she made a mental note to thank the staff for their hard work in decorating the deck area for the party. There were wooden tables laden with canapes and cocktails; fairy lights hung along the walls but their light paled in comparison to the stars that pierced the clear sky above.

The beauty of the surrounding needed no human intervention, and she could see why the décor in the lodge captured the bushveld, bringing the outside in, with its rustic wooden furniture, heavy fabrics in burnt orange and yellow ochre. Tomorrow they would go on a safari to see the big five.

'Can I steal you away for a dance,' Ruari said coming to stand next to her.

'Are you going to get me slapped by Chloe?' Rachel laughed, seeing right through his strategy.

She relented and went to dance with him.

'Chloe's sweet, but she isn't my type. I don't know how to tell her that.'

'Don't worry about her, she's harmless, trust me. She finds every man she meets attractive and a challenge to overcome.'

'Gee, thanks, I'm starting to feel like a piece of meat here.'

Rachel laughed as they swung to the rhythm of the beat.

'Who's up for a swim?' Sandy asked. 'The girls have gone to change into their cozzies. Rach, Ruari, you guys wanna join us?'

'I'm all prepared, I have my costume on already,' Rachel said, going towards the infinity pool and dipping her toes in to test the temperature. 'Water feels perfect for a swim.'

'I'll go get my shorts,' Ruari said, heading for the room.

'Ya know he's got the hots for you?' Sandy said, as Rachel took off her dress and dipped into the water beside her.

'No way, Sandy, it's nothing like that. Ruari is like a brother to me, in fact, he's my ex's brother, so it would be a little weird if we were anything more than friends.'

'I know what I see when he looks at you, and there ain't nothing wrong with it in my eyes.'

Rachel laughed it off, but her mind began to wonder if there was any truth in it. She knew she'd grown so close to Ruari, and she didn't want anything to mess that up.

'Mate are you swimming with your T-shirt on? Travis asked as Ruari got into the pool with them.

'Yes, Ruari, some of us want to see you without some clothes on,' Chloe called from the other end of the pool.

Rachel watched as Ruari unperturbed jumped into the pool with his T-shirt on, ignoring Chloe's comments. .

Chapter Forty-Four

The strong African sun beat boldly on their backs as they jumped into the safari vehicles waiting for them outside the lodge.

Rachel put on her sunglasses, adjusting from barely any sleep and the shooters Chloe had them drinking well after midnight. Right now, she regretted why she'd chosen to book the earliest safari the game reserve had to offer.

Mr Lemon and Joanne were the only two who looked fresh as a daisy. They'd gone to bed soon after everyone had jumped into the pool.

Rachel felt as if Mr Lemon looked somewhat younger this morning. A newfound spring in his step as he ran around at breakfast, chasing after his granddaughters.

It warmed her heart to see how much they loved their grandfather, and that finally they had a chance to meet the man reformed.

Rachel reached for the camera as they neared a leopard that sauntered lazily towards their vehicle, the guide whispering to them to be as silent as possible.

This was her first safari. She wished her parents were with her , they would love this experience. The wilds were something they all took for granted, having lived here all their lives. Coming back here would definitely be on the cards for their next visit.

The driver moved on slowly, pointing out the birds and animals around them. The air was dry and hot circling them as they drove along the pathways carved out in the grass from vehicles gone before them.

She heard the elephant's trumpeting vibrate in the air before she lay eyes on him. His thick, rough, grey skin, so rugged, so strong, stretched across his ginormous body. It amazed her how such animals lived in this land she called home.

Rachel's eyes fell on Sandy as the vehicle moved them deeper into the bushes. She remembered her words about Ruari and wondered if she may be right.

Ruari hadn't left her side the entire evening after getting into the pool, and if she were honest, she hadn't wanted him to. They'd talked about Jack, and she confided in him about the pain she'd felt all these years. She shared with him how Jack's attack on her in high school had tainted her self-image, and being able to sit in her bikini like that was a point it had taken her a long time to reach.

Ruari had been so gentle in how he engaged her, listening attentively and reassuringly. She knew he was a trained professional, but somehow it felt deeper than him seeing her as a patient in those moments. She felt this overwhelming connection to him, as if their souls were connected in a way that defied space and time.

In all her years dating Will, she'd never opened up to him or anyone else the way she opened up to Ruari last night. She felt safe with him.

Her mind felt like it had layers. One layer remembered Will, one Jack, another Ruari but the deepest layer couldn't stop from thinking about *him*.

She woke up dreaming of him, that his arms were around her and they were lying in bed listening to the roar of the lion. In the dreams she tried so hard to see his face, but it's always hidden from view. His skin touching hers felt so familiar, as if she knew him. How she longed to know him. She wished there was a way for her to find out who he was.

She had called the courier company, after receiving his last letter, begging the manager to tell her who paid for the delivery. They refused, even after her desperation turned to anger.

She'd confided in Sandy last night about the letter, and she seemed to think it could be someone she knew, someone close to her, even Daniel or her father. She had to admit, it would make sense if it were them. They both knew enough about her to be able to reach out to her and send them, but somehow, the profile didn't fit. Her father perhaps, but definitely not Daniel because Daniel didn't know about her first attack. Or did he? Had he found out, and started writing the letters as a way to reach her when he knew Claire wouldn't allow him to? But then why did he seem so annoyed when she received the necklace?

The necklace, her hand came up to touch it. She couldn't bring herself to take it off. Even if he chose to leave her, the Southern Cross would remain around her neck.

She shook her head, thinking about Daniel. It couldn't be him. If it was him, then she really didn't know her brother at all because that would be a really cruel thing to do. And her father. Was he really capable of doing such a thing to her? Her father? The one who had helped her through those first few weeks of torment. The same father who had held her in his arms and lulled her to sleep. Could he write her such letters? Why would he need to do something like that? Why would anyone?

Rachel closed her eyes for a second as the vehicle came to a halt allowing the buffalo to go past. Sandy had even suggested he could be married, or it could be a woman. Rachel shook her head. No! She couldn't believe that, she would have known if it was. Did she really want to know who this beautiful stranger was or would knowing taint everything she held dear to her?

She allowed her fingertip to play with the diamonds around her neck. If only she knew who he was, maybe then she could let go of this necklace. Until then, he, whoever he was, and she believed it was a man who loved her, had managed to lift her out of her darkest moments, and give her hope again. She refused to think that his motives were anything but good. She refused to allow the memory of him to be tainted, but she also knew that she couldn't live in hope of finding someone who had never wanted to be found. She couldn't miss out on her present, chasing after ghosts.

Her eyes fell on Ruari, sensing her gaze he turned to smile at her. That look that made her feel like the planets shifted every time his honey glazed eyes met hers.

Chapter Forty-Five

'Oh, my word, Rach, I could have died from sheer embarrassment,' Chloe said, her face still covered in mud, and dung, and who knows what else.

Rachel laughed as she wet the sponge again and tried to wash Chloe's face.

'We were all just shocked that's all.'

'Yeah shocked and then rolling in fits of giggles.'

'What did you expect? You just plopped over the edge of the vehicle, camera in hand, and then next thing we know you're in a pool of mud.'

'I was trying to take a close-up shot of the birds.'

'Trust me, we all can imagine how close up you were trying to get.' Rachel laughed wiping her face. 'Why didn't you just use the zoom function on your camera instead of leaning in so close?'

'I couldn't remember how, and I couldn't afford for the moment to pass me by. Remind me again why we can't just go back to the lodge so I can bath and get this stuff off me?'

'Because we planned on having lunch here. The chefs have gone out of their way to prepare Mr Lemon food he loves. We can't just leave, it's another half an hour's drive back there.'

'Argh, now how am I to get Daniel to ask me out for Valentine's Day looking like this?'

'What… my Daniel?'

'Yes. Why so shocked, didn't you notice we connected last night?'

'I thought you had your eyes on Ruari? Don't get too hung up hoping for Daniel. He's still recovering from Claire. I doubt he is looking for anything serious right now.'

'Ha, Ruari. I gave up on him when I saw he only has eyes for you, and as for Daniel, I'm not looking for anything serious either.'

'Ruari does not have eyes for me,' Rachel protested.

'Rach, I think you're the only one who doesn't see it… honestly. It's so obvious. His eyes follow your every move. He finds any excuse to be near you.'

'We're just friends and I think he's got this overprotective brotherly thing going on or something.'

Chloe sighed, swatting Rachels hand away. 'Now listen here, Rach, I'm only going to tell you this once, because seriously, you can't be that blind. Ruari ain't got no *brotherly love* for you. He got the: *I want to sweep you off your feet kind* of love, and you're the only one who refuses to see it, but more than see it, you're starting to feel it too. I've seen how you look at each other, smiling like you have some secret conversation going on when no words are spoken. Can you just admit that he's grown on you, and maybe, just maybe, you could feel more for him than just friendship?'

Rachel turned to dip the sponge back into the enamel bowl filled with water. She didn't know what the point was of even trying to wash the sponge. The water now was as muddied as her heart felt.

'Okay, Chloe, I admit, there's something there. I do feel it. But I don't know if I can allow anything to happen.

Imagine me dating him, and then I go to meet his parents, only… they're Will's parents. Do you see where I'm going with this? Imagine the family dinners with Will, Amelia, Ruari, and me. Those won't be awkward at all, huh?'

'Who cares if they're awkward at first? You'll all get over it. If Ruari can make you happy, why don't you give him the chance? That guy would move heaven and earth for you. Don't you see it? Will never looked at you the way Ruari does. Shit, I don't think anyone has ever looked at me the way Ruari looks at you.'

'I don't know, for now, let me just enjoy this long weekend and not think of all this. I don't think I'm up for it.'

'Just remember what I said. Don't shut out true love when it's knocking at your door.'

Rachel gave Chloe's face one last wipe over before hugging her, mud and all.

'Thanks, Chloe, I'll think about it.'

They made their way back to the unlit fire pit. Chloe made sure to plonk herself next to Daniel, and she motioned to the empty cushion next to Ruari. Rachel moved slowly towards it. Feeling self-conscious to sit next to him. It's like everyone knew something was brewing between them, but she was the one acting like it didn't exist.

'I see you got christened with some mud too,' Ruari said, reaching up and gently touching the side of her face. Rachel blushed as she saw his muddied fingers.

'Must have rubbed onto me when I was trying to clean her up.'

'She sure was a sight for sore eyes, covered in mud. Although, with the way she smells, I definitely think it was way more than mud.'

Rachel laughed. 'Well, welcome to the party, because now it's on your fingers,'

'Rather me than you being covered in it,' he said, looking deep into her eyes.

She looked away; his gaze too intense. She could feel the colour rising up from her neck and she hoped her cheeks weren't too pink already. She cursed those shooters last night, because today she'd left the lodge without any make-up.

As if sensing her thoughts, Ruari reached for a stray hair and brushed it behind her ear.

'You look beautiful, Rachel.'

Her tummy flipped as his touch felt like an electric current.

'Thanks,' she muttered, unsure how to handle the moment.

The chef came to her rescue inviting them over to the table that was laid out with lunch.

'On this side, we have some nutritarian dishes prepared specially for Mr Lemon. I would have you know that Mr Lemon is still renown to us young chefs. He's spoken of like a legend, taking over game reserves like ours to cook exquisite meals for the rich and super rich. They tell stories here about you, Mr Lemon, of how you could land by plane on the airstrip and start barking orders to the staff. So, it's an honour to cook for you today, Chef. I hope I did you justice.' Mr Lemon nodded, his eyes filled with tears. 'And for the rest of our guests… who would like some carb filled meaty food, we are doing a braai for you on the other side.'

'I think I'll be heading for the braai meat,' Ruari said pulling his nose up at all the vegetable dishes laid out for Mr Lemon.

'I think I'll join you.' Rachel laughed, seeing Travis and his family trying to embrace nutritarianism.

They dished their food out and all sat eating in a comfortable silence. The sun beginning to make its way down towards its resting place.

'Wanna join me for a walk?' Ruari asked as they finished their meal.

'Sure,' Rachel said. He reached down to pull her to her feet.

'Beautiful day out here, hey?'

'Yes, thanks for helping me with all the planning, Ruari. I think this surprise was a definite success.'

'Sad we all have to leave tomorrow.'

'Well, some of us have patients to see on Monday.'

'Listen, Rach, about Monday. I know you mentioned you used to go to tea with Amelia on a Monday, and I was kind of wondering if you and I couldn't maybe start our own Monday tradition? I could clear my diary in the afternoons if you're up for it?'

'Sounds great, I would really like that. What would you want to do?'

'Well, how about each week we take turns to try to find the perfect picnic spot, and we go and have a picnic? This week I'll kick it off. Are you game?'

'I would love that.'

'Great,' he said, walking slightly closer to her, allowing his fingertips to graze hers.

Rachel's heart pulsated in her chest. His touch felt like home to her. She felt him pull away and keep a safe space from her, but the look in his eyes told her another story. It told her that all he wanted to do was hold her and never let her go.

Chapter Forty-Six

The warmth of the sun danced on her skin as morning broke through the curtains.

Rachel stretched out enjoying the earthy smell of the wood that surrounded her in the lodge. Yesterday had been magical with Ruari and they'd walked and talked for hours until finally they were summoned back to join the others.

She'd loved every moment with him, his voice growing huskier the more they spoke and confided in each other. She felt as if she was finally starting to see the person behind the mask.

Ruari had told her of a girl he'd fallen in love with in high school, and how he'd felt she was the person he was destined to marry one day.

'So, what happened in the relationship?' she'd asked.

'Oh, we never even dated,' he had laughed back. 'I don't think she knew I existed.'

'So, you mean to tell me you didn't even try ask her out on a date?'

'Are you mad? She was way out of my league. I didn't stand a chance. I just hoped one day she would notice me.'

'And did she?'

'Yeah, she did eventually, but not in the way I hoped. I guess I realised that I was a chicken, and she deserved someone with the guts to ask her out.'

'So, that was it, you gave up on love? Is that why you've never dated anyone?'

'Hey, who told you that?' he had protested.

'Office gossip,' she said with a twinkle in her eye.

'Well, unfortunately the office gossip is true. Yes, I never dated, as in a serious relationship. I had flings here and there, but nothing serious. I just didn't want to waste my time on the wrong girl, you know? I always believed that when I met the one, she was for keeps, and I would give her my heart and soul.'

Rachel warmed at the memory; it had felt as if he was talking about her when he'd spoken. She just hoped she wasn't imagining it.

She got up lazily and made her way to the shower, before putting on a safari green A-line dress and heading out to the deck to soak up some African rays and animal soundtracks before heading back home.

Her eyes scanned the living area as she walked through, secretly hoping to see Ruari out by the deck so they could have one last chance to talk before heading back to their everyday lives. The time out here had felt so magical and tranquil, and she hoped the spell wouldn't be broken when she went back home.

Disappointment twisted her heart when she saw he wasn't there. Probably still sleeping after his game of monopoly with the boys last night.

Rachel grabbed some orange juice the staff had put out for breakfast and went to the balcony to take in the glorious views and tried to spot more wildlife.

Looking around, she picked up the binoculars that lay on the viewing deck. They had a beautiful vantage point being tucked into the mountains, overlooking the bushveld. She eyed the watering hole that guests could use to swim in.

Peering through the binoculars, she noticed a familiar figure dipping in the water. She zoomed her binoculars in and her heart leapt. It was Ruari, down by the water having a morning swim. She felt like a stalker watching his bare skin emerge from the water, his muscles immaculately defined from his shoulders down to his torso.

She recalled how he'd refused to take his shirt off to swim the other night and wondered what he was so shy of.

Putting the binoculars down, she breathed deeply, fighting the urge to take one last secret look at him. Eventually her pounding heart relented as she brought the binoculars into focus on him again. She felt her breath catch in the back of her throat; her body suddenly stiffened.

One his back, was a tattoo of the Southern Cross and the words clearly visible *'til it be morrow'*.

Chapter Forty-Seven

Rachel was back in her own bedroom, sleep evading her for most of the night. She still couldn't believe it, the person who had written her all those letters was Ruari. How on earth did she never suspect him all along?

When she saw his tattoo, she knew immediately what it meant, she didn't need an explanation. She'd grabbed Daniel and forced him to drive her back home immediately, without saying goodbye to anyone. Daniel had eventually stopped on the way and forced her to spill the beans on what had happened.

'It's Ruari, are you sure it's Ruari?' he had questioned her.

'Yes, it's him, Dan, he has the same cross tattooed on his back as this necklace, can you believe it? And the words, *til it be morrow* which are the same words he wrote in two of the letters when he decided not to write to me anymore.'

'What do you mean *not writing to you anymore*?'

She'd pulled out the last letter he'd sent her, and sunk down into the car seat, giving Daniel time to read it.

'Oh, my word, Rach, it was him all along,' Daniel whispered as it dawned on him.

He sent Chloe a message saying he wasn't feeling well, and they had to leave. Knowing she would pass the message on to the rest of the group.

'So, what are you going to do now? Are you going to confront him?'

'I don't know, right now I feel like I can't even breathe. I have a million questions running around in my head, like why he did this, and what the hell has been going on in his head all these years. Was he sitting around waiting for Will to break-up with me so he could swoop in and take his brother's girlfriend?'

'Rach, that doesn't make sense… you started receiving those letters before you met Will. So, it's more like Will stole *his* girl.'

'I was never *his girl* in the first place. I don't get it. This is all too much to deal with.'

They'd driven the rest of the journey in silence, both caught up in their own thoughts and questions.

Rachel heard her phone vibrate; it was another message from Ruari. This was probably the fifth one since yesterday. First, he asked her if Daniel was okay, then he asked if they arrived home safely, then the messages became frantic, asking her why he can see she's reading his messages and not responding, so she stopped reading them. She didn't know what to say. She didn't know how to tell him she didn't want to see him.

She knew that was a tall order since they worked in the same building, and she knew she needed to tell him before tomorrow, otherwise he would be at her office door first thing planning the picnic they were supposed to be having.

Why hadn't he told her he was writing the letters? Why didn't he say something when she started dating Will? Or after? They had so many countless moments together recently where he could have said something, even hinted, but instead he kept it hidden from her.

She remembered how she thought he was watching her, following her. For goodness's sake, he even transferred to the same hospital as her. Her heart wanted to believe that he was always just trying to protect her, but her head was making her feel angry instead.

Rachel sat at her window with the duvet wrapped around her. Max and Snuggles came in, sensing her distress and sat at the base of her chair.

'Do you want some coffee, squirt?' Daniel asked, coming into her room with two cups already in hand.

Sitting beside her, he handed her one. 'So, have you decided what you're going to do?'

'I have to tell him I know who he really is. I would never be able to keep it a secret. I can't pretend like I don't know, it's just too huge.'

'Do you think you can forgive him? Isn't that what he asked for in his last letter? I think he knew that one day you would find out, and you might hate him for it, but I think you need to give him a chance to explain.'

'You sound like you're defending him, and you don't even know him.'

'I saw enough this weekend to know he really cares about you. Trust me, the way he looks at you, Rachel, you're his entire world, even I can see that.'

'Right now, I feel like I *am* his world, but not in the way you're thinking. I think Dr Harris needs a psychiatrist of his own.'

'I don't think so, squirt, I just think he handled it all wrong. He probably did what he thought was best at the time.'

'Dan, it's been thirteen years. Do you get that? Thirteen years of someone writing me letters, seeing me at varsity, at work, at his home with his family, and never once, not once, telling me he was the same guy writing to me.'

'But those letters were your saving grace, sis, you told me that yourself. Surely that can't suddenly be a bad thing? He didn't do anything wrong; he was trying to help you.'

'This from the same brother who thought my mystery letter writer was going to hurt me.'

'Well, I wasn't wrong there. But now I've met the guy, I don't think he had bad intentions, like I thought initially. I just can't see that in him, and I know deep down, you can't either.'

'I need some time for things to settle down, I need space to process it.'

'Just don't make him a villain in your head before you know the entire story, okay?'

'I'll try, no promises.'

Daniel shook his head, and stood up, trying to get the dogs to go downstairs with him, but they both stayed put.

Rachel reached for her phone, reading the last few of Ruari's messages, his desperations making her heart ache as she sensed his concern.

She began to type, not knowing what their future would look like after this.

Ruari, I know you're the person who has been writing me letters all these years, I saw the tattoo on your back. Right now, I need space and time to process it all. Please don't make contact with me. I don't know if things can ever be the same again between us. Please respect my wishes. Rachel.

Rachel breathed deeply as she pressed send, her heart thumping in her chest. It wasn't long before his name popped back on her screen.

Rach, please just let me explain. Give me a chance to explain please. I can't do it on a text message. Please just meet me tomorrow like we planned, and I'll explain everything.

Rachel shook her head furiously; he just wasn't getting it.

No, Ruari, I don't want to hear your explanation. Please just leave me alone. When I'm ready to talk to you, if that day ever comes, I'll message you.

She tapped send, her hands shaking with rage. Her phone pinged.

I'll respect your wishes. I hope someday you find a way to forgive me. Love x

Her heart sank as she read the last two words. The same sign off that she'd read in every letter he'd sent her. How could she reconcile that person, with the person she knew while dating Will, and the man she'd started falling for?

Chapter Forty-Eight

The air permeated with the sickening scent of Valentine's Day. Puffy red and white balloons, rose cheeked lovers, and annoying love songs filled every corner of the earth.

Rachel exhaled, wanting to rid herself of these cupid germs that alluded to some notion of perfect love, and fairy-tale endings. Love was no fairy tale and she definitely had passed this delusion in the last few days.

It had been hard trying to come to terms with what she'd learnt, but eventually, she realised that even if she forgave Ruari and gave into her feelings for him, it was destined for failure. There was just no way she could spend the rest of her life seeing Will and Amelia and their baby at every family gathering, reminding her of the betrayal.

Everything was so messed up and she wished so desperately it could have been different.

What if Ruari was the brother she met first, the first one she fell in love with? Would they have had a fairy-tale ending? Would love have knit them together and never let them part?

She'd spent so many nights laying in her bed and sobbing. Sobbing for what could have been, sobbing for what never will be. She absentmindedly touched the Southern Cross on her neck. It was the thing that would always bind them together, and even though she decided it could never go any further, she still felt that they'd shared a connection that could never be broken. It might have ended in heartbreak, but it was a reminder too of her strength and the fact that she'd overcome great sorrow.

'Rachel, hi.'

She turned as she heard a familiar gruff voice behind her. 'Detective James, so good to see you,' she said.

'I've been meaning to give you a call and see how you're doing. Work's just been a little crazy.'

'Yeah, I know the feeling. Wanna have a cup of coffee if you aren't in a hurry?'

'That would be great,' he said, placing their orders at the Starbuck's counter.

'So, what are you doing drinking coffee alone? Shouldn't you be on a date or something, Detective?'

'Call me, Shaun, please.' Rachel nodded. 'I should be asking you the same question?'

'I'm not so sure it's written in the stars for me. And you?'

'Haven't met Mrs Right yet, and I hate days like today. All these starstruck lovers.'

'I feel the same.'

They made their way to a table in a quiet corner. Starbucks wasn't the popular place to take someone on a date, so at least they had some privacy.

'Jack's trial starts tomorrow. The prosecutor's called me as a witness. She says you chose not to testify?'

'I don't want to see his face again. They found enough evidence from other people who came forward, so they don't need my testimony.'

'Yes, that's true. He left such a long trail of broken people in his wake. I just wished they'd stopped him as a teenager instead of dismissing your case back then. It

357

would have saved many women from being assaulted by him. When we arrested him, one of the radio stations ran with the story, and that was when people came forward with more evidence. One of his ex-girlfriends told us she was so terrified of him she helped him stalk and trap one of the women he raped.'

'What? Are you for real? That's terrible. I'm glad we finally have this monster once and for all.'

'You're very fortunate, Rachel. You were saved twice. I know your ordeal was still terrible, and it still shook you, but imagine if you hadn't been rescued. What then? He was hell-bent on destroying you, I could see it in his eyes. You were his first victim, the one he never got to conquer.'

Rachel shivered, she knew that look in his eyes all too well, and Detective James was right, she was fortunate. She'd been saved. For the first time she wondered whether the man who saved her was in fact Ruari.

'So, will you be at the trial?'

Rachel shook her head. 'I can't bear to look at his face. My brother Daniel will be going in my place.'

'Trust me, we've done everything we could to ensure he gets convicted.'

'Thanks, detective… I mean Shaun, I never got to thank you properly back then. You were very kind to me, you treated me with care and respect, and I am eternally grateful.'

'My heart broke to see you so alone, Rachel, I hope things worked out for you in the end?'

Rachel sat back, her fingers drumming against her coffee cup. 'It did. So much so I sometimes find the love confusing.' She thought of Ruari.

'Be grateful for that love, Rachel. I see many victims who are like you were back then. Completely alone, and it's not because no one loves them, it's because they stopped knowing how to let anyone in.'

Rachel looked at the detective and nodded, she knew all too well what he meant. She was grateful for the love she had from her family and friends. Despite the hard times she'd faced in the last few months, she had her brother back, and she had Mr Lemon, Joanne, and Chloe, and yes, for a time she even had Ruari, but now it was time to let that one love go, she would hold on to the others.

Chapter Forty-Nine

Rachel walked slowly through the market. Her rose gold sandals catching some hay as she walked from stall to stall. It was good to be out again at the Hazelwood Food Market. She was meeting Chloe and Daniel for lunch. They'd started dating and things were going well for them.

At first, she was a little apprehensive about it, but as the weeks went one, she realised their feelings were more genuine than she thought, and she chose to put aside her fears of her employee dating her brother and things going south. She really hoped that never happened… she couldn't bear having to go to work every day listening to Chloe pining over Daniel or coming home to Daniel pining over her.

She checked her watch; she still had an hour before they were due to arrive. She'd come early hoping to find some treasures of her own here.

'Hi, Rachel,' she heard a faint voice behind her. Rachel felt goosebumps on her arms. She'd always imagined this moment and wondered what would happen when she was faced with the day that she had to see Amelia again. She swung around nervously, conscious of the fake smile plastered on her face.

'Amelia, hi,' she said, her smile trying not to betray the feelings of hurt she had inside.

'Nice to see you again,' Amelia said, her tummy protruding out now; there was no denying she was pregnant.

'You're looking good. How many months are you now?' Rachel asked, even though she knew the answer. She'd been keeping track.

'Six months,' Amelia said feebly. Rachel nodded. 'Listen, Rachel, I'm sorry about all this. I know how wrong I was to go behind your back with Will. I really miss our friendship. You were my best friend, my only real friend in fact. If it's any consolation, Will and I are no longer together, he dumped me for some teacher at his school.'

'Amelia, I've forgiven you, but I don't trust you anymore. How can I? You say I was your best friend, but you definitely weren't a friend to me. Friends don't do what you did. I opened up to you and shared my feelings and apprehensions about Will, and you took all that information and used it against me to get him to be with you. I'm sorry it didn't work out with you both, more for the child's sake than for the two of you, but I don't think I could ever trust you again.'

'So, is this it? Are you going to walk out on me like my parents did and like Carlos and Will did?'

'What your parents did was wrong, you were their child and they should have managed their divorce better to protect your emotions. But as for Carlos and me, we are not to blame for the relationship ending, you are. If you can't see that, then you need more help than I thought. And about Will, did you really think that a man who cheated on his girlfriend of eleven years wouldn't cheat on you just because you're pregnant?'

Amelia looked away but finally her eyes met Rachel's. 'I guess this is goodbye.'

'I guess so. I hope you give your child the best life, because he or she definitely deserves more from you.'

Rachel watched as Amelia walked away, her head held high as if nothing was amiss. Rachel felt like someone had punched her in the gut. She'd been dreading this moment since the day she'd found them together. She never knew how she would react, but right now she felt this was the best decision she'd made. Amelia still didn't seem to grasp the impact her actions had had on everyone around her, and Rachel hoped that she grew up enough to be a good mother to the baby. She also hoped that Will came to his senses and at least was a part of the baby's life, even if he chose not to be with Amelia.

Rachel wandered through the stalls until finally she spotted Chloe and Daniel.

'Hey, love birds, how's it going?'

Daniel kissed Rachel on the cheek. 'We're good, squirt, you look a little pale, what's wrong?'

Rachel filled them in on her encounter with Amelia.

'The cow, she got what she deserved,' Chloe said angrily. 'What outcome was she really expecting after the stunt she pulled?'

'I just find it sad that she's so delusional, but anyway, she and Will are my past, I need to focus on my future now.'

'Listen, squirt, about your future, have you decided what you're going to do about that holiday you paid for to Rio?'

'I think I'm just going to try get as much money back for it as I can.'

'Any chance that I could buy it off you? Chloe and I would like to go away together, and where better than Rio, right? I can just buy another ticket for her, what you do you say?'

Rachel nodded; she definitely had no intention of going to Rio. 'Let it be my gift to you. I'll message Carlos and tell him you'll be going. I think he would love the company.'

'Thanks, squirt.'

'So, how's the trial been going? Does it look like they'll convict Jack?'

Chloe and Daniel exchanged glances. 'Listen, about that, I, well actually we, think it would be really good if you came to court to see for yourself?'

'Why would you suddenly think that's what's best for me?'

'Just trust us, okay? Please. We'll explain when you're there.'

'I really don't think I can face seeing Jack's face. His voice still haunts me.'

'I know, but we feel it would bring you some sense of closure. You would also get to see the other woman who have come forward, perhaps you can all find strength together to put this behind you,' Chloe said.

'I'll think about it, okay? I've come so far these past few months, I don't want seeing him to be a setback,' she said, her hand instinctively touching the pendant on her neck.

Chapter Fifty

The silence swirled around her like a tornado, all she could hear was the howling wind of her own thoughts. She hadn't heard from Ruari since their text messages, and she was grateful he had respected her wishes, but on the other hand, as the days stretched on, she wished he would find her and help her thoughts make sense.

Seeing Amelia had stirred a deep desire to find true love, she realised, she'd never known it with Will. The *forever love* Mr Lemon kept telling her about. She'd spent the last few days reading the letters Ruari had written her, and she was trying to reconcile the man who wrote the letters with the man she'd begun falling for.

Daniel kept trying to convince her to at least give him a chance to explain, but right now, she didn't know if his explanation would change anything. Even if he confessed that he wrote the letters, and even if his intentions were good, would that excuse him from not telling her the truth once they started getting to know each other? Not once did he give any hint that he was the author of the letters.

If she'd married Will, would he just have left her with the mystery for the rest of their lives?

She stood up and straightened her clothes. She had to muster up all her strength, because she would be going to court to face her biggest fear, Jack.

She shivered as she brushed her hair into a tight bun and finished up her make-up. She'd chosen a white shirt and navy skirt. She knew she looked more like she was going for a business meeting, but it was the only thing that made sense to wear.

Opening her drawer, she pulled out a blue and white scarf, and wrapped it around the scar on her neck. She wouldn't give Jack the satisfaction of being able to see the scar and know that he put it there.

'Ready, squirt?' Daniel asked coming into her room.

'No, but that's not going to stop me.'

'What made you change your mind?' he asked, helping her put on her navy jacket.

'I thought of what Chloe said about the other woman being there. How could I shy away when even worse things have happened to them? I need to face my fears and start really living my life. I guess I didn't realise how this was still holding me back until I was so dead set against going to face him.'

'It's understandable, you went through a lot, and mostly by yourself, but today you aren't alone, I'm with you.'

They drove to the courtroom in silence, they were early, but she'd decided she wanted to get inside and be seated before Jack was brought in.

Her skin crawled as she walked inside and sat on one of the hard, cold wooden benches. She could sense the history… the decades of convictions, but also decades of criminals being set free to go out there and destroy more people.

Her eyes connected with some other women sitting in the third row, and she knew they were the victims too. She could tell from their trembling hands, but hard cold faces. They were here for justice, just like she was.

Her palms grew sweaty as they brought Jack in, he locked eyes with her, a smirk filling the corners of his mouth, he licked his lips, never taking his gaze off her.

She felt her spine tingle, and her muscles grow rigid, she could feel the cold knife against her neck, and taste the blood on her lips, but she sat still, not allowing herself to be the first to avert her gaze. She kept her eyes on him for as long as he kept his eyes on her.

Finally, he walked on, and she saw him try to instil the same fear in every victim seated there. Each woman, just like her, refused to give him the satisfaction of seeing them quiver at the sight of him.

Daniel wrapped his arm around her, holding her close to him. The judge came in and the proceedings began. She found strength in watching the other victims get up to testify, listening to them recount the horror of what they faced. They were all overcomers just like her, and as time went on, she began to feel her stomach relax, and the fear that had been lingering in her all these months began to evaporate.

She no longer needed to be a prisoner to this fear. She was a survivor, but more so, Jack could only hurt their physical bodies, she still had the power to overcome the pain, the torment, the memories. It was her inner power, her true self, that he could never steal from her. Her mind was finally free from him. She knew he never needed to occupy even a corner of her thoughts any longer.

After what seemed like forever, they adjourned the court, and Rachel stood to leave. Jack turned to look at her and then looked behind her. 'He can't protect you forever,' he yelled as the police officers pulled him away.

Rachel turned to look at who Jack was referring to, and her eyes locked with his, it was Ruari, sitting at the back of the courtroom.

'This is why I wanted you to come here today,' Daniel whispered in her ear. 'He's been here every day. He's never missed a session. Jack looks at him with such hatred, probably remembering being punched by him in high school.'

'You mean Ruari was the person who saved me back then?'

Daniel nodded.

Rachel allowed the tears to fall, as she made her way towards him. 'I didn't know it was you who saved me in high school,' she said when she reached him.

Ruari reached down and cupped her face in his hands. 'I would do it all again for you, Rachel, I just wish I could have done more. I wish we could have had him locked up a lot sooner.'

Rachel allowed him to bring her close to him, she laid her head on his chest, as he wrapped his arms around her, holding her tight, his heartbeat resounding in her ears. This was home, he was her safe place.

Chapter Fifty-One

'I need you to explain why you never revealed yourself from the beginning?' Rachel asked. They were seated in a coffee shop not far from the courtroom. Daniel had gone back to work, leaving Ruari and Rachel to catch up.

'On the night of your matric dance, I offered to chaperone because I was part of the old boys' club. I felt something was off with Jack, the way he kept looking at you, so I kept my eye on him all night. At one point, I got distracted, and when I turned back he was gone. I went looking for him and that's when I heard your screams. After that night, I was so filled with guilt. I could have stopped it all from happening if I'd never taken my eyes off him. Jack told the detective working on your case that I was the one who beat him, and that we were just having a fight over you. I tried to convince them it was a lie, that he had attacked you, but Jack stuck to his story, his father had a pretty powerful attorney, and eventually they threw the case out for lack of evidence. I felt like a failure, I'd failed you.'

'So that's when you came up with the letter idea?'

'Soon after, yes. Looking back now, I wish I'd just signed my name on the end or sent you an email instead. But I thought at the time that anonymity was the best way to do it. Writing old-fashioned letters seemed like the only way I could ensure you couldn't trace it back to me. I desperately wanted to help you, I didn't want what happened make you want to harm yourself or commit suicide like my friend did.'

Rachel nodded, recalling the pain she'd seen in his face when he'd told her about his friend's death. 'So, I guess after starting the lie, you didn't know how to come out of it.'

'I hoped someday I could, and the day you came to my parents' house, when I saw you in the lounge, I thought you were there to see me. I thought you'd figured it out.'

'Until Will walked in and you realised we were dating?'

'Yes,' Ruari said, looking down at his hands.

'I'm sorry, Ruari, I can only imagine how hard that must have been. I honestly had no idea you were the letter writer.'

'I know. I just hated knowing you were dating my brother, when I could see he was more concerned with himself than anyone else.'

'So, you decided to let it all go then?'

'Yes, that's when I wrote you the last letter. It's also when I got the tattoo. I decided to leave it be, and that if you were meant to be in my life, then it would fall in place. I thought I'd try to take care of you from a distance. The more I tried, the more I resented Will for how he treated you.' Rachel nodded, sensing his protectiveness. 'When Will told me about the second attack, I hoped that I could help you as me, but you refused to let me do that. So, I decided the only way I could get you out of that house was to start writing the letters again. I knew that it worked.'

'And it did work, Ruari. It's what got me to find my strength again.'

'I know, but I wish I'd found another way. It was foolish of me to do it again. It could have gone either way. I was being irresponsible. Especially when I realised that I didn't know how to tell you who I was.'

'Yes, you had yourself in a tangled web there,' Rachel mused.

'So, I stopped writing them, I wanted you to get to know me as me, and it was going so well until you saw that damn tattoo. I've regretted going down there to swim ever since.'

'I'm sorry I didn't give you a chance to explain. I was just so confused and torn apart. I felt like I could trust you and then suddenly it felt as if that trust was ripped away. Until I saw you today and realised you were in my life all along, just as different people. Always there but wearing a different façade.'

'Yes, like the chameleon in my office. Always changing faces.'

'Daniel says you've been there every day in the courtroom, waiting for justice to be served.'

'I just want that monster to be put behind bars, Rachel. I hate thinking of what he did to you.'

'Thanks, Ruari.'

'I know it's a lot to ask but is there any chance you would consider giving me another chance. Any chance we could start again?'

Rachel nodded. 'I'd like that.'

Chapter Fifty-Two

He brought flowers. Her hands clutched the stems tightly on her lap as they drove. She looked at him, a faint smile curling her lips, his hand brushing her thigh as he changed gears. They were alone, they were together, unmasked.

He'd picked her up from the office for their first official date. She never thought she'd be so nervous seeing Ruari. Everything had changed. Everything was new.

He reached over and squeezed her hand before changing gears again. His touch like a fire bolt in her core. The sun hovered over his face making patterns of the passing trees. He was handsome, he was here, taking her on their first picnic.

'So, where are you taking me?' she asked, almost afraid to break the magic of the silence they'd eased into.

'It's a surprise,' he said playfully.

She shook her head unimpressed, but inside she was exploding. Her heart felt free, and nothing mattered but being here with him.

The car pulled into the long driveway flanked on either side by orange trees. The smell of jasmine wafted in the air, as they made their way towards the sixteen-hectare country estate ahead.

'We're here,' he announced, parking in front of the cape Dutch-style manor house. The walls stark white with blackened thatch covering the roof. He came around to open the door for her, his hand gently taking hers. She could sense his nerves as much as her own.

They walked into the reception area, hand in hand, the breeze blowing her skirt as it swirled around her bare legs.

'You look beautiful, Rachel,' he said, reaching to touch her cheek. She blushed, loving the caress of his skin against hers.

'Dr Harris.' A short elderly woman met them at the reception desk. 'Good to see you again. Everything is set just as you requested.'

'Thanks, Mrs Moore.' Ruari bent to kiss the woman on her cheek not letting go of Rachel's hand. 'I'd like you to meet Rachel. Rachel, this is Mrs Moore, this place has been in her family for generations.'

Rachel smiled tenderly as she greeted the woman, following her to lush lawns at the back of the manor house.

'You're all set up underneath that tree,' Mrs Moore said, pointing to the right.

Rachel followed where she pointed, while Ruari nodded his thanks and led her towards the tree. He held her steady as she removed her shoes and knelt to sit on one of the oversized linen cushions. He sat beside her.

'You've set the bar high, not sure I can beat this picnic.' Rachel smiled, seeing the champagne, fresh fruit, and canapes laid out on the blanket.

'I cheated for this one and got some help because today's special… going forward it'll be much simpler, promise, especially if I have to prepare the food myself.'

'Not much of a cook?' she asked.

'I can handle my own in the kitchen, but I think my nerves couldn't handle having you judge my food and me all in one go.'

'Trust me, I'm done judging you, I completely got it wrong the first time. I won't make that mistake twice. I do need to confess though, that I'm so nervous. I feel as if I'm seeing you for the first time.'

'I feel nervous too, not because I'm seeing you for the first time, but because I've finally allowed you to see *me* for the first time.' He reached over and touched the necklace on her neck. 'I'm glad you never took this off, even when you were confused about me.'

'I couldn't bring myself to do it. I clung to your words that somehow we could find our way to each other.'

His hand moved to the scar on her neck, his fingers gently tracing the line the stitches had left. 'I'm sorry I wasn't there to save you the second time, Rachel, I would have done anything to take your place.'

'I know,' she whispered, bringing her hand to cover his. 'I'm just glad you're here now.'

His eyes searched hers and she felt his breath against her skin. Her pulse quickened as he leaned towards her. She leaned forward, anticipation on her lips. He dropped his head before looking back into her eyes. She frowned, he seemed afraid, cautious.

'I don't want to ever hurt you, Rachel. I need you to feel safe with me.'

She nodded, sensing he wanted to take things slow. His tender consideration made her want him more.

'Ready to eat?' he asked breaking the magic.

'Absolutely, I'm starving.'

They settled into comfortable conversation while tackling the food on display.

'Want to go for a walk?' he asked, after they'd devoured the chocolate orange torte.

She nodded, he lifted her to her feet.

'So, do you still find it weird thinking of me as Will's brother?' he asked, addressing the elephant in the room.

'Not anymore. Especially since the guy I knew as Will's brother is nothing like the man I know now.'

'Sorry I was such a jerk, I didn't know how else to keep you at bay,' he said, intertwining his fingers in hers as they walked through the rose garden.

'I understand now why you did it, but at the time, it didn't make sense. I remembered you from high school, when you were the head prefect, and you always seemed so kind back then. I thought maybe you didn't think I was good enough for your brother or something, because it seemed I was the only person you were aloof with.'

'I'm glad I can be myself around you now.'

'Me too.'

They fell into a comfortable silence before going back to the picnic spot.

'I've planned a massage for us at the spa later. In the meantime, would you like to just lay here with me?'

He lay down on his back staring at the blue sky. Rachel's heart skipped a beat, the sight of him caught her breath. Moving in next to him, she lay on her back, her head nestled on his shoulder. She'd never felt happier.

Chapter Fifty-Three

⸻ ◦ ⸻

'You have got to tell me everything! You hear me? Everything. Don't leave anything out.' Chloe screamed excitedly the next day as she entered the office.

'Shhh, Chloe, I don't want the hospital staff hearing.'

'Trust me, they'll find out soon enough. That man can't look at you without love being written all over his face! They're going to be so jealous!'

'You're so dramatic, Chloe. We just went on a picnic. I seriously regret asking him to fetch me from the office yesterday, now I have to face an inquisition from you.'

'Listen, Rach, if you didn't tell me yourself, Daniel would spill the beans, so spit it out, I need all the details.'

'Okay, okay, but you can't be telling Daniel all my business if I tell you.'

'Scouts honour,' Chloe said, plonking herself on the couch in Rachel's office.

'He was amazing, Chloe. A complete gentleman. I felt like a princess, like a fairy tale kinda thing. I never felt this way, it's insane, I'm falling hard for him, like crazy hard.'

Chloe clapped her hands excitedly. 'That guy already fell for you eons ago, you're in safe hands. Trust me, you have nothing to worry about. Now spit out the juicy details.'

'There aren't any juicy details. We just had a good time together.'

'No kiss?' Chloe asked shocked.

'No,' Rachel said, remembering how they came so close, but something stopped him. 'I think he just wants to take it slow, perhaps?'

'Okay, makes sense. When's the next date?'

'Tonight.' Rachel giggled. She'd offered to cook him dinner at her place since Daniel was going out with Chloe. She needed to make it up to him for treating him so badly when he had come to visit her, and she never invited him back.

'Well, one date straight after another doesn't sound like taking it slow,' Chloe said. 'I think he's waiting for you to let him know that you're okay with this relationship.'

'I wouldn't call it a relationship just yet,' Rachel protested. 'It's only the second date.'

'Rachel, now don't make me give you another pep-talk! This man has been waiting for you for decades. Cut the man some slack and let him know you're ready to commit to him. Got it?'

Rachel laughed, if it wasn't for her first pep-talk while covered in mud, she doubted they would even be sitting here talking about her dating Ruari. 'Yes, ma'am, I got it,' she said.

'So, how's things going with you and Dan?'

'We're taking it slow. I think he's still kinda sussing me out, but after what he went through with Claire, I don't blame him. I'm looking forward to going to Rio with him this weekend, pity you and Ruari can't join us, that would have been a blast.'

'No thanks, that would just be creepy. Going on a holiday with my ex's brother.'

'Yeah, you're right,' Chloe relented. 'I think we need to plan a trip for all of us next year.'

'I'd love that!'

'Yeah, I'm sure Ruari would too,' Chloe teased.

Rachel was so happy she could share this with Chloe. She hadn't been able to stop thinking about Ruari since she left him yesterday. Her time with him was so different to anything she'd ever experienced with a guy before. She felt as if she were his world. Everything he did was with her in mind. What she had with him, was the kind of love she'd dreamed of.

The Skype tone rung on her laptop.

'Must be Sandy,' Chloe said, moving towards the door. 'Let me leave you to it.'

Rachel sat at her desk as Sandy came into view.

'Hi, mate, how ya doin'? Had a good ol' date with that hunk of a chap?'

'Oh no, not you too, Sandy! Please tell me Chloe didn't tell you.'

'Ya bet she did. Now tell me everything…'

Rachel laughed, she had two insane friends, but she wouldn't trade them for the world. She just wished Sandy wasn't back in Australia, she would have loved to have seen more of her instead of running out on her that day. She was just glad everything worked out for Travis and Mr Lemon and they got the healing they needed. She too had found her healing, and the freedom that came with it was unmatched.

Chapter Fifty-Four

Rachel was the most nervous she'd ever been. Having Ruari in her home this time felt completely different. She didn't know how to stop the nervous flutter as she walked from room to room making sure the house looked its most pristine.

She didn't know why she bothered. This was the same guy who had barged in here, bags in hand, and cleaned her entire house. She wondered what he must have thought that day, seeing the state she was in. She knew it wasn't disgust, but she could imagine how he must have longed for her to allow him in behind the walls she'd built up.

The doorbell rang. It was him. She smoothed her hands over her jeans. She'd chosen her favourite Freddy dark blue jeans, with a white button down, collared, short sleeve blouse. The front lightly tucked into the front of her jeans revealing a gold belt. She had on matching gold pumps, trying not to look like she'd tried too hard.

'Hey,' she said, reaching up as he bent to kiss her cheek. He looked ravishing in a grey, body-hugging T-shirt and faded blue jeans.

'Hi, beautiful,' he said, his eyes washing over her. She ushered him into the house. 'It looks and smells amazing in here.'

'Thanks,' she mumbled, thinking maybe the dim lights and candles were a little much for a second date. 'I thought we could stick with the picnic theme and have a picnic in my lounge,' she said motioning towards the blanket laid out on the floor. She'd pushed all the couches to the far corners of the walls.

'Where's Max and Snuggles?' he asked taking a seat on the floor. 'I don't want to sit on their spot again.'

'They're outside for now. We can bring them in later.'

Ruari nodded, pulling Rachel to sit beside him. 'Thanks for all this, but you didn't need to go to all this trouble.'

'It's no trouble, I wanted to make it special.'

'Just having you next to me is special enough.' His fingers found hers. 'After coming here the last time and giving you back your key, I never thought I'd see the day where I would be sitting here like this with you.'

'I know,' Rachel said, feeling his pulse quicken as his fingers ran through her hair. 'Tonight, I need you to understand that I've chosen to let you back in. Just like you asked me to. I want you in my life, Ruari, I'm choosing this, I'm choosing you.'

'I have one more thing to tell you then, before we can take this any further.' Rachel felt her throat constrict; she didn't think she could handle anymore secrets. 'Remember I told you the story of the girl I was in love with in high school?'

'The one who never noticed you, and you never had the guts to tell her how you felt?'

'Yes,' he said his eyes finding hers. 'That girl was you, Rachel. I loved you from the moment I laid eyes on you.'

'Me? Are you serious?'

'Yes. I couldn't tell you because of the age gap. How could a guy in grade twelve explain to a girl in grade eight that he had fallen in love with her?'

'Oh, my word, Ruari, I never knew.'

'When I chaperoned the matric dance, I thought it would be my chance to get to know you, but that never happened. After Jack attacked you, I knew there was no way I could tell you how I felt. That's the other reason I kept my identity secret in the letters. I wanted you to get to know me away from what happened with Jack, and I didn't want you to think I was taking advantage of you in a vulnerable moment.'

'So that day I came to your parents' house…?' Rachel began, trailing off.

'My dreams were totally shattered.'

'I wish I'd known.'

'It doesn't matter. All that matters is that I get to be here with you now.'

'You waited all these years?'

'My heart belongs to no one else, Rachel, it only ever knew you, it wouldn't let me know anyone but you.'

Ruari ran his fingers through her hair again before settling on her face.

'Is that why you were always so aloof with me, never wanting to touch me and keeping me at arm's length?'

'Yes, I was afraid that if I allowed myself the privilege of being too close to you, I would have betrayed myself; I would have betrayed Will. I couldn't risk it.'

Rachel reached up and touched his face, her eyes locking with his.

'Can I see it?' she asked, her hand trailing over his back. Silently, he lifted his shirt and turned his shoulder to face her. Her hands traced the familiar symbol, the familiar words, their secret for so long. It was as if she'd been connected to him all along, her heart knew it, but her mind was unaware.

He turned to face her, his hand caressing her face. 'I love you, Rachel. I've only ever loved you.'

Her breath quickened as he leaned in towards her, his lips finding hers after decades of waiting, decades of longing. She'd never felt something so beautiful, so pure, her heart beating so hard in response to his touch.

After what felt like a lifetime, he moved back from her, only long enough for her to tell him she loved him too. Slowly he lowered her to the ground, his body intertwined forever with her. He was her forever love.

About this book

The idea for this story, came about one afternoon, when Alshandra Visagie visited our home and shared her harrowing account of being attacked in her home by a stranger.

The way she told that story shook me to the core. Having known of her story my entire life, it was completely different sitting in the room and having a first-hand account of it. Her bravery and courage together with her story of survival was hair raising to say the least, but completely inspirational.

I knew then, that I needed to somehow share her story with the world.

Being a fiction author, I contemplated for months how to tell that story. Whether to tell it like she had, or whether to completely fictionalise it. Eventually, I came to the realisation that I would use this book as an avenue to present the topic of a woman overcoming this horrendous attack, through a work of fiction, and then have her share it with my readers in her own words in live chats. So if you have read this book, look out for those chats on social media, and if you are wondering which part is applicable to her story, it's found in my own fictitious account in Chapter Fifteen.

Acknowledgements

For this book, I have so many people to thank, that I truly hope I don't leave anyone out.

Firstly, this story is one of survival, and I have had to endure my own survival story. For that I want to thank God for his grace in seeing me through.

To my Husband who sits through hours of hearing me ramble on about my books, go through titles, and covers and beg and plead him to read my unedited work, I'm so grateful to you! Thank for you affording me the quiet time to write. Every book I write, has a little bit of you lining the pages, because you give me good stories to tell.

To my son Luke, your own ability to tell stories, inspires my own. You are my absolute joy and delight. Every second with you I treasure more than words could ever describe! I love you forever, you are my favourite (don't tell Daddy lol)!

To Alshandra, thank you for allowing me to write this story, and wait years to even find out what it says. More importantly, thank you for the part you played in the restoration of part of my own story. You will never know how much pain you took away in one day, and restored relationships that seemed impossible to restore.

To S. Ibrahim, I probably wouldn't have written my first book or my second if it hadn't been for you encouraging me to start writing. That encouragement, was one of the best gifts I've ever received in my life. My first book and this book are written with parts to remember that role you played in my journey to become an Author.

To Aunty P, thank you for being the first person to read this book, and for telling me its story was worth telling to the world. I don't have enough words to explain my gratitude to you, not just for that, but for decades of grace, unconditional love and strength.

To P. Laban, S. Ibrahim, F. Tarajia and R Dangor, never doubt the impact you make in people's lives daily. I'm living proof of that story.

To D. Momple, the prologue is dedicated to you. It tells the story of how one act of kindness saved someone's life. Thank you for allowing God to use you in my own life.

To Lucinda, thank you for our weekly calls, and listening to my plot breakdowns. I wouldn't have finished this book if you didn't force me to take the time to organise my life and make time to write. Your calls have become such a vital part of my life and my writing process. I'm so grateful for you my friend, you are proof that true friendships defy distance, space and time.

To my beloved friend Wanda, who also was my proof-reader. I cherish our dates and laughs together. Thank you for taking the time to proofread this book for me, and for making Pretoria feel like home. Most importantly, thank you for always being real!

To Rose, thank you for reading both my books before they were published and polished. Thank you for celebrating my success, and encouraging me to keep writing. When you read this one, and told me you could instantly think of people you knew who needed to read it, it made me feel like I'd already achieved the purpose for writing this. I appreciate it more than you know.

To my SUPER FANS Jo Bailey and Mick Tolley, who won a competition where they tirelessly promoted my first book, and got to choose the names of two characters in this book, Joanne and Vinita-Jax. I'm absolutely overwhelmed by your support and loyalty and I hope you enjoyed reading about your characters, as much as I enjoyed writing about them.

To The Fiction Café, Wendy, the Admin and Members. Thank you for all your support throughout the years. I could have never sold nearly as many books if it wasn't for you promoting it, and sharing it with the world. The response and love I have received from you encouraged me to keep writing this book, when I felt like giving up. Words aren't enough to express my gratitude!! Wendy you really are amazing, never doubt the impact you have made in our lives.

To all my author friends I've met along the way, (special mention to Isabella May and Vanessa Streete) who give me support, promote my work, give me insider tips and tricks. You truly are a brand new family, and I'm so grateful for you.

To the Blogging community, thank you so much for your support in reviewing my books and writing blogs and reviews that sometimes feel like love letters from people who truly understand my heart when writing! Your support is immeasurable! I so appreciate you.

To my family and friends who have supported me, thank you so much, it means more than you know! A special mention to my friend of twenty-seven years, Amy Wicks, who bought more copies of my book for family and friends than anyone I know! I appreciate you my friend!

Last but definitely not least!

To my Fans, words cannot express how much your feedback and reviews mean to me. Whenever I doubt whether I should be doing this, I go back and read your messages, reviews and comments! Thank you for embracing my work with such love, and for telling everyone you know about it! You are AMAZING!!

About the Author

Taryn Leigh is a South African Author, who spent her childhood with her nose buried in books. Her love for reading transpired into her ambition to become an Author.

Taryn Leigh's first book, *Perfect Imperfections*, is available in Paperback, eBook and AudioBook. She lives in Pretoria with her husband and son.

Connect with her on social media, she loves to hear from her fans, and is known to always respond.

Website: www.tarynleighauthor.com

Instagram: @tarynleighbooks

Twitter: @tarynleighbook

Facebook: Taryn Leigh Author

You can also join her fan group on Facebook for giveaways and special news: Taryn Leigh's Official Fan Group